THE THROWAWAY QUEEN

THE THROWAWAY QUEEN

WHITNEY O MCGRUDER

THE THROWAWAY QUEEN

Cover Design: Naimly A (naimlyarts@gmail.com)
Editing: Travis McGruder (witandtravesty.com)
Map Design: Whitney McGruder
Book Design and Typesetting: Enchanted Ink Publishing

ISBN: 978-1-7355064-3-2 (E-book)
ISBN: 978-1-7355064-2-5 (Paperback)

Dedicated to the parents or aspiring parents—

you deserve all the roses and sticky kisses.

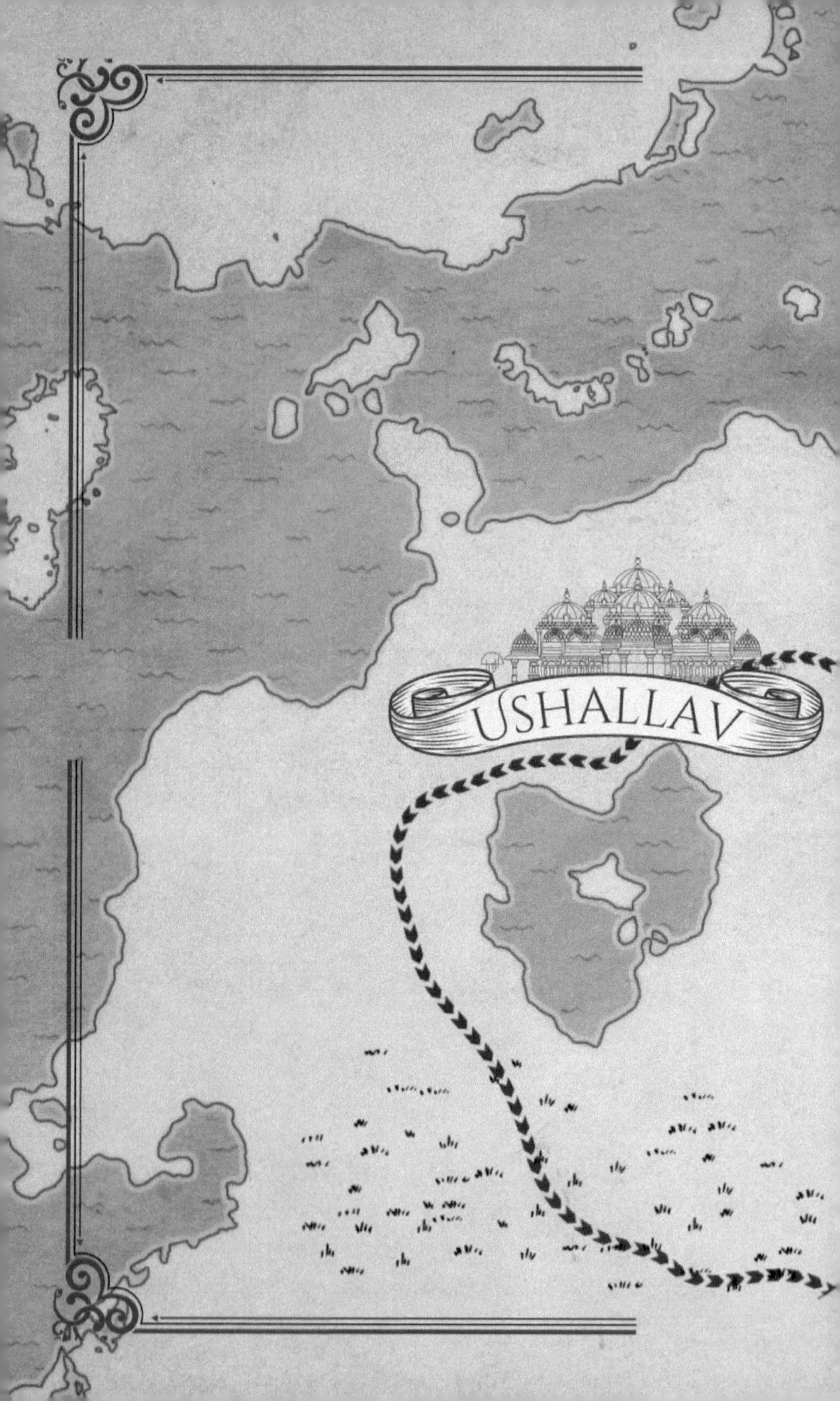

USHALLAV

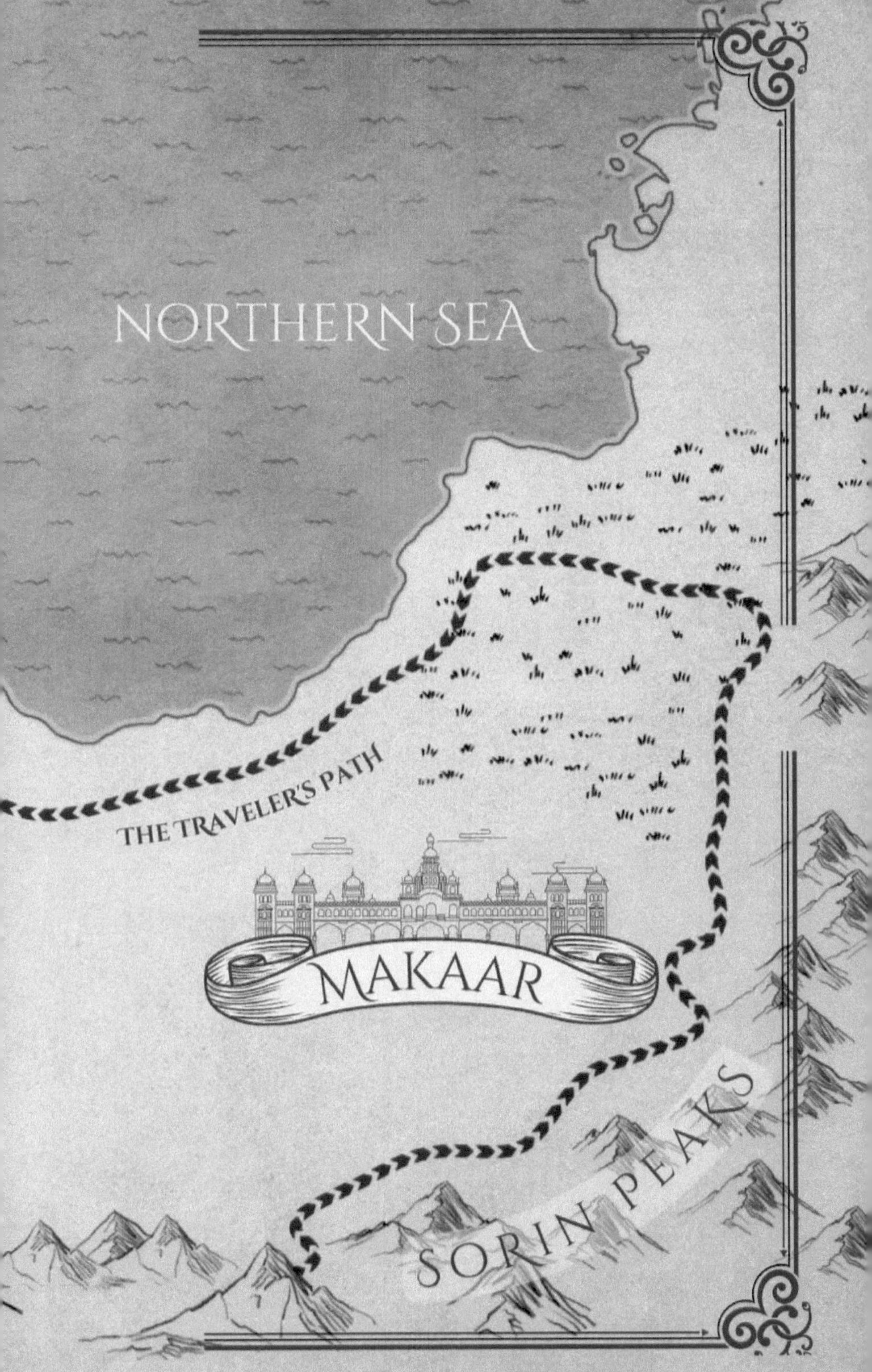

NORTHERN SEA
THE TRAVELER'S PATH
MAKAAR
SORIN PEAKS

CHAPTER ONE

As much as I have grown to love the green peaks, I was made for a more privileged world. I was made for sparkling waters and a firm sun.

I slowed my breath to practice control. The air coursed in and out of my belly as I stretched my limbs and said a prayer of gratitude. I thanked my gods for my body and my spirit. I thanked Abhijita, the goddess that Ushallavi women emulate, that I could still train my body and regain my muscle after bearing Sanjana. I thanked the Traveler for the Gavril folk who took pity on me. This was a figure new to me but without *someone's* guidance, I could've lost my baby. I usually don't pray to Bhooma, the earth goddess, but I've appreciated her comfort as I have traveled unfamiliar terrain. Above all, I thanked everyone and anyone that I have the strength to finally go home.

Before I ended my prayer, I asked for their patience, wisdom, and perspective to help me navigate the moments to come. The decisions, the confrontations, and changes to come.

After my prayer, I felt my control over my muscles again and I went to work. I ran my usual trail that slithered up the mountainside and raced back down. I approached a straw-stuffed dummy and began my routine of punches and kicks to practice my speed and balance. As my body fell into memorized movements, my heart leaped with joy at the thought of holding both of my babies again. Devraj must be getting so big now.

Last night, I had a dream about him. It might've been a memory, but it felt so real. In the dream, he was trying to scramble into my lap even though my pregnant belly took up a lot of room. He still giggled and used a chair next to me to try and wrap his arms around me. A faceless maiden reached out to help him.

Back in my reality, I wiped my forehead with my hand wrapped in frayed cotton and looked down at my belly. I lightly traced my hands over my scars and marks with care. We've been through a lot together, and this act of love was an excuse to catch my breath and stretch. My strength still had its limits.

I couldn't wait to see my son's little face. When I come home, I will never leave.

My eyes started to prick with tears; if I think about the past two years, I might lose my endurance and energy. I went back to my mountain training and left my would-be tears and poorly constructed dummies behind.

It was another run or walk up the mountain to a little lake and then back down for me.

The slope was a bit steep today, but something guided me down the mountain like a powerful waterfall. We were days away from my kingdom; soon, the Gavril people would see me off and I could put this whole nightmare behind me. It felt like the sooner I got back down to the wagons and goats, the sooner I would be able to flop back in my comfortable bed or bathtub. I could almost smell my favorite perfumes.

Claudiu stood waiting for me next to my dummies. He was a head taller than my straw victims and looked down at the lop-sided heads with pity.

I laughed and waved at him, and his demeanor softened. He carried Sanjana all the way here on his shoulders and merely looked thoughtful as he clung to her ankles to support her.

"Word came in the village today. More news."

"What happened? It doesn't sound good," I answered, wiping sweat from my face. Claudiu spoke plainly and straightforwardly with me, as Makaarian was his third language.

"King Damir has married another. He married a Makaarian woman. I don't know why we didn't hear of it sooner. But it is old news. I'm very sorry."

His words tumbled out of his mouth. My mind felt like mush. I wanted to hold Sanjana, my 2-year-old baby born in this wilderness, but I wasn't sure my arms could carry her. I could barely stand.

Damir remarried. My hope started to fray.

"It's…it's not your fault. You were just passing on information—"

"We've been away for so long and worried about the killers—"

"Claudiu, I…I can take it. Thank you for telling me," I gritted my teeth. Surely, I've been in worse pain than this. No, I'd take a hundred births over the thought. I was only gone for two years. I already felt so much shame that I left my dearest Devraj behind, but that decision probably saved his life.

Should I go home? Is there a home for me in Makaar? Of course, I was going home. Was my son okay? He needed me.

"The new queen is likely expecting an heir."

For Claudiu's sake, I just nodded my head and looked at the earth. Claudiu and I knew different kinds of pain; he was still grieving the passing of his wife. I was processing a marriage I didn't know I had lost.

"Your Highness," Claudiu insisted. "I know that look. What are you going to do now? Will you change your plans?"

I wiped my face, not sure if I was smearing away tears or sweat.

"I will still go back. My son is still there. If Damir remarried—"

"Surely Makaarians aren't as bad as you say. Their customs are strange, but we can still get you to the city in a few days."

"Devraj needs me now more than ever," I said, determined. "I must protect him. I'm his *mother*."

4

My throat throbbed a bit as I spoke those last words. We stared at the trees and the mountain's incline. I clenched my fists, not knowing what to do next.

"Will you need more time?"

"Waiting won't serve me now. I must think of something along the way that will ensure Devraj's and Sanjana's safety—"

Claudiu gave me a pointed look.

"—and get some answers for me. Maybe things will change once I return."

Claudiu just grunted. He put a hand on my shoulder.

"Tread carefully. This could start a war. Another one."

The Gavril man referred to the peace held between Makaar and Ushallav—ensured only five years ago. My marriage to Damir was meant to celebrate the end of wars and conflict. We were supposed to introduce a better world for everyone. Everyone, except me, I suppose. It's possible that if I come home and demand answers, I could upset my parents and Damir's court. It could be the last bit of kindling that ignites another petty feud. My stomach churned.

I already knew there were bitter feelings between the kingdom surrounded by mountains and the kingdom surrounded by seas. Someone tried to have me killed two years ago and almost succeeded.

I sniffed and raised my chin as if entertaining court. "My family still rules in Ushallav. I won't let things get out of hand. If someone wants to start a war, it won't be because of me."

"I know to the rest of these people, you're just a

mother," he began, gesturing to the rest of his traveling party, "but to the world, you're the queen. May the Traveler determine your path and lead you to peace. Peace for everyone."

"Thank you," I choked. "We're just about ready to go. I don't need much time." I straightened my back as though to strengthen my resolve.

"Your Highness?" Claudiu said, turning to leave. "You must grieve. Grieve until there are no more tears in your eyes. It will prepare you for what's to come."

I knew where that advice came from. Claudiu was always very stoic around me, but I imagined there was a time his cries shook the stars.

"Your advice is impeccable. Uh, I mean very helpful."

Claudiu nodded and turned to walk back to camp. Sanjana joyously giggled and swayed with his movements. She grasped his hair like reigns.

When I was sure that I was alone again, I turned to my training dummy. The urge to punch and kick was overwhelming, and I obeyed. After ten minutes, the dummy was ripped, frayed, and destroyed. My chest heaved in anger and passion as I wiped dust and sweat from my eyes. The tears stung the rims of my eyes and I yelled,

"Two years, dammit! Why didn't you wait for me, Damir?"

Later that evening, I approached the communal fire where the musicians tuned their instruments and played a few idle notes. I needed something joyous. I needed to think about something besides my pain. Sanjana sat on my lap,

6

and she went to her usual game of touching my hands, tracing the lines, and anticipating my hands becoming "jaws" and "swallowing" her tiny little hands.

"Guess who we'll get to see soon?" I breathed in her little ear. I had to smooth back her dark brown curls so she could hear me.

"Who?" she chirped happily. The Gavril folk heard her speak Ushallavi, and a few caught my eye and smiled warmly. They didn't understand but loved little Sanjana.

"We will see the king—your papa," I answered for her.

"Will he play?" Sanjana asked. I laughed at her innocent question.

"Maybe. But I know someone who *loves* to play. His name is Devraj. He is your older brother, and he loves you very much."

"Brother?"

"Yes. He's your brother. He's waiting for us to come home so he can meet you."

"I like to play," Sanjana smiled, covering her grinning lips with her little hands. She's already two years old, which means I've been away—recovering from my pregnancy, avoiding assassins, and traveling with the Gavril people across mountains and plains—for roughly that amount of time. I've been building my strength over the years so I could do whatever is necessary to ensure Sanjana's safety and future.

"You must collect your things and we will go straight to the king first thing in the morning. Do you understand?"

"Will we come back?" Sanjana asked. She repeated her question absentmindedly. I was at a loss for words.

"Do you want to come back?" I tentatively asked. *My baby, you were meant for so much more.*

"We can come back after we see the king," Sanjana said decidedly. She nodded as if approving of her own decision. *Well, with that resolve, she'll fit in quite nicely as a princess—no doubt about it.*

"We'll see," I answered. I hope we never come back, and I hope we never have a reason to leave the palace again. Despite being strong, my mind was still unkind. I still see images of trees, shrubbery, and broken branches. My hiding place while I waited for my assassins to pass over me. The trail of blood that began between my legs.

Sanjana soon forgot our little exchange and she quickly hopped up to join the rest of the children who were already dancing to the lilting music.

The musicians played a little game where they changed their pace from slow to suddenly fast, then back to slow. It meant the children had to anticipate their sudden changes so they could match their dancing with the beat. It elicited laughs from around the fire from their parents. Sanjana—still young and still learning about music—was always a beat too late compared to the other children.

As the flames and the children danced, I couldn't help but recognize a bit of myself in Sanjana. As I watch Sanjana dance despite the game she doesn't understand, I realize that I have to dance—be happy—despite the problems before me.

When I first arrived at Makaar, I already knew their ways were different from ours but my love for Damir clouded my eyes. I resolved to adjust however necessary,

assuming his traditions wouldn't ask too much of me. Once the queen's crown was on my head, everything changed. Just like the music of the game, I couldn't get anything right. I was determined to make Makaar a better place through my love for Damir—I firmly believed that we could show our countries that we weren't too different, and we could smooth over the tensions.

But how can I do that now? Damir's remarriage feels like a closed door that I can't reopen. Maybe he didn't believe in unity as much as I did. Maybe my missteps were trying to tell me something—that there was no way to win a game with changing rules.

Claudiu plopped down next to me and stared into the fire. I blinked away the thoughts and looked at him.

"We've got a long day ahead of us."

"Thank you again for accompanying us," I answered. "May the Traveler grant you success in the markets."

I nodded knowingly. I picked up on what little religion the Gavril people follow. He smiled appreciatively. The Traveler is a genderless figure that legends say was one of Father Soren and Mother Vera's children. They roam the earth and the Gavril people emulated Them in this way. They even call their route the Traveler's Path.

"May the Traveler guide your steps—again and always," Claudiu said with a sigh. "I also want to give you this."

He gestured to a small knife with a painted handle. It was simple—like something I could use to peel a potato, but I could tell it meant something more.

"My wife used to keep this close for her own protection. I know that you already know how to fight with your hands but may this simple reminder of Sariah give you her strength as you navigate Makaar."

My fingers curled around the blade's handle as I nodded.

"This means a lot. Thank you."

"Of course, Queen Anjali. It is an honor."

CHAPTER TWO

Sanjana and I rose with the sun. We didn't carry much, as we expected to show up in Makaar within days. We packed up a trip's worth of food for the three of us. I handed things to Claudiu, and he secured them to his horse's saddle.

One of the Gavril women brought a shawl for me. She gestured that I could wear it around my face and over my hair. I tied it securely at the base of my chin and smiled at her. I bade her goodbye in broken Gabrilan, and she nodded encouragingly.

She told me, "May the forest hide your footprints." She hugged me and kissed both of Sanjana's cheeks.

I handed Claudiu our last bundle. He gave me somewhat of a knowing look. I preserved the traveling clothes that I wore that day of the ambush. It was the only physical reminder I had of my status. For our journey, I wore clothes that the Gavril women taught me to make: soft trousers that reminded me of home, sturdy boots, and a long-sleeved tunic. I once practiced my embroidery on the neckline and hemline.

I looked at my complexion in a square piece of mirror. I definitely didn't look as regal without my painted eyelids or lips, but Damir would recognize me. We've trained together and bedded each other. I had nothing to prove or explain. But it felt comforting to have the old traveling clothes with us.

Once we were ready, I coaxed a sleepy Sanjana onto my back. I used a long linen cloth to wrap and hold her in place on my back. Our Gavril friends showed me how to wrap the cloth across my shoulders, chest, and waist so I could walk while Sanjana rested her head on my shoulder. My little princess was getting a bit heavy for this practice, but I predicted that she wouldn't sleep well on the horse, and she wouldn't waste any time begging me to carry her.

Claudiu approached some of the men and talked in hushed tones for a bit. I could tell the other men were describing where he could find them next. By the time Claudiu guided us to Makaar and returned, the Gavril people will have already moved on. It was another reason why I didn't expect to come here near the base of the mountains ever again. I wouldn't see old friends. The only thing remaining would be memories of difficult times.

The men embraced and clapped each other on their backs before going their separate ways. A few sleepy people waved goodbye to our little trio as they began packing up their things.

I looked up at the mountains one last time, controlled my breath, and faced toward Makaar and our future.

***

Claudiu tried and failed to encourage me to eat. I rationed my water while I carried Sanjana but the thought of eating anything made me feel worse. The Gavril man was also not much of a talker, so I was left with my own thoughts and memories.

As I followed his steps and we navigated towards common traveling routes, I thought about my carriage and my maidens. I thought about how Claudiu saved me. I was strong but I sometimes wondered how much of that strength came from me or the warrior maidens who protected me while I was a wife and mother. It didn't feel right to tease the two apart. I only felt sick.

Would Damir believe my story? That I was ambushed on my way to visit my parents in Ushallav? So many things created this two-year separation from my husband and son. There were the assassins who shook me to the core—I had Sanjana earlier than expected due to the pain, fear, and stress. Without expert nurses and maidens at my side, the pain lingered, and it cost me dearly. So much blood and tears smeared the ground and my clothes as I crawled my way through Sanjana's first year. The ability to run up and down mountains was hard-earned.

Breastfeeding was hard. Keeping my head up was hard. In my darkest days, I wondered if it was better if someone else took care of Sanjana. Her brilliance and warmth and happiness didn't feel like traits that came from me, but my dreams of Devraj and Sanjana's wet kisses got me to this moment in time. That, and the women could detect my pain and stayed with me and ensured I swallowed my food.

I wanted the women to know that I've done this before; Sanjana was my second. I knew how this worked! I barely had the language to explain myself. But this time, I didn't have my servants, my husband holding my hand, the maidens letting me sleep, or the financial security to know that my babies would never want for anything. I was just as helpless as my baby. I was damn lucky that these people looked after me when I hardly felt like I deserved it. This is the life they knew, and I would've turned up my nose at this years ago.

The second year away from home was arguably just as difficult. By the time I could start functioning like a human being, we ventured months away from home— from either Makaar or Ushallav. Oh, that was painful. We essentially got back here as soon as we could and as safely as possible.

I wasn't in the right place to think about the assassins coming to finish the job while my body was healing. But that second year? I was training so I wouldn't feel that desperate and close to death ever again. If I had to kill someone to get home to my baby, I wouldn't hesitate. They would be the ones running for their lives.

Would Damir believe me when I tell him that it killed me to be so far away for two years? Would he stand in the way of my true calling and purpose?

14

This thought put extra energy into each step. As we got closer to the outskirts of Makaar, things started to look familiar. We might've already passed by the place where my carriage was ambushed, and I missed it. We were better for it.

As I saw the entry gates, I finally put a piece of jerky in my mouth. I needed to be strong. Damir needed to hear my story. I didn't dare let myself wonder if Damir would keep his new wife or let me regain my position. All I knew was that I would be undeniable once I returned. I already died in that forest and yet here I still stand as a queen. I was back and afraid of nothing.

CHAPTER
THREE

I thought my little princess would enjoy riding the horse with Claudiu, but she would not have it. So, on my back she stayed for much of the journey. I daydreamed about my mother's healing crystals that I kept in my old rooms. I was a tough queen, but I missed a good rejuvenation practice.

Once we entered the city gates, I took in the sights. It reminded me of the first time I visited my fiancé six years ago. At the time, I did my best to take in Makaar's version of beauty. Here, the colors were darker and jewel-toned—they matched the nearby mountains. Ushallav—where I was born and raised—used warm and bright colors to welcome the sun and add sparkle to our rivers and lakes.

My sore feet felt every groove and crack of the cobblestone streets. A burgeoning migraine competed for my attention. I didn't know whether to laugh or cry once our castle came into view. My son was in there. So was Damir and my replacement.

Claudiu handed me my personal things and nodded as I headed with Sanjana to the castle. Claudiu branched off in a different direction to find a place to rest his horse and a place to stay. He agreed that perhaps the easiest way to confront Damir was to wait in the petition line with the other Makaarians. I didn't want to argue with the guards, and I did like the idea of a dramatic entrance.

Claudiu stood with me in line for most of the day and we didn't say much. Sanjana was fussy, so Claudiu took her into the market to release energy and eat food. They periodically brought me local food and I nibbled on it cautiously. I wasn't very hungry as I imagined a thousand scenarios running through my mind. It didn't help that the other folks in line kept giving me curious stares.

One of the most obvious differences between Makaarians and the Ushallav was our skin tones. I calmly returned the stares. I wasn't the only Ushallavi-born person in this city or even in this market today. Since my marriage, our people have crossed borders. Still, my skin tone is a rarity. I half wondered if anyone would recognize my face. I certainly met their gaze and continued to watch my subjects. I admit I didn't think about them as much as I should since I disappeared. I wondered if by observing, I could tell how they were faring.

Strangers would periodically give Sanjana a polite smile when she joined me in line, and they passed on. They gave Claudiu a wary glance as well. He and the Gavril were tan but not as dark as me and Sanjana. But his clothes and curled hair let the rest of the line know that he was not local.

Still, the polite, clipped stares were something that I didn't miss while I was away. I sighed. There would be more of that soon enough.

As I entertained my daughter in line, I started day-dreaming about my earliest, most cherished memories I had with Damir.

Clad in a simple blouse and pair of trousers, I approached the clean and bare room. I headed straight towards the opposing wall where all my combat gear waited for me. I strapped on my boots, attached my leather armor, and fastened the helmet over my head. Fighters don't need to train with gear against Ushallavi-constructed holograms, but it always felt familiar and right. The added weight seemed to help my balance.

I knew an hour or so of combat would keep my mind and racing heart off Damir's pending arrival in Ushallav. I wasn't expecting an intimate chat with him while he was here, but with all this energy, it only felt right to put it to good use.

I wanted to practice my hand-to-hand combat, so I wrapped my hands and put on a pair of fingerless gloves. I looked to my right and another woman dressed similarly nodded.

"How long would you like the hologram to perform?"

"Sixty minutes. The usual," I smiled. The attendant nodded and opened a panel in the wall and pressed a few buttons. The torches soon dimmed and for a moment, I

stood in near blackness. The lights shifted and created images off the walls. I could still see the armory, but the images off the wall recreated the main marketplace in our capital city—right down to the shopkeepers and their wares. Air wafted from the corners, and I suddenly smelled spices and sweat.

The people milled around for a few moments, reciting plain jabber that I'd already memorized. Then, they suddenly fled the scene—off the walls of the training room and out of sight. Three thugs approached me, dressed as local gang members. They came straight for me, but then parted to flank me on three sides

I ducked and hooked my elbow into the thug coming straight at me. I hit his nose and evaded his swipe with a bow staff. I had to quickly roll forward and get back on my feet as the other one tried to swipe at my back. Once on my feet, I delivered jabs at those coming toward me and turned to jab at the one behind me.

As much as the technology was revolutionary and I was very fortunate to have my own private training arena, it wasn't advanced enough to create fighters with unique fighting styles. It was like performing in the same play, over and over—waiting for the other player to say his lines so I could say mine. I fell into a familiar routine and danced around the thugs until they staggered and passed out.

I heard angry voices behind me and recognized this as the second phase of hologram fighters. I held up my hands and gripped both fists. It may be predictable, but the training did wonders for my health and self-esteem.

My fists and feet hit all their predictable weak points

and I felt slight pings and jabs on my body. Holograms are just figments, but they've created some that can provide slight impact to make the fight feel more realistic.

I saw a figure evading me, keeping to my peripherals the entire time. Was I miscounting those I had already beaten or was there an extra fighter?

I turned and caught sight of the fighter, and I marveled at his armor. Well, his armor was fairly similar to mine, but I mentally complimented the engineer that created the stunning visuals. He looked so lifelike. I couldn't see his face, but I could tell by his skin that he was meant to be a Makaarian fighter. Fair enough. Perhaps they finally added something fresh to my training routine.

Gleefully, I let out a fighter's cry and ran towards him head-on, prepared to make a show and kick his helmet right off his head. I made the attempt and felt strong hands grab my ankle and throw me back to the ground. I looked up in shock; this was advanced imagery—even for Ushallavi wizards.

I hoisted my legs behind me and over my head so I could right myself and stand on my feet. I held up my fists and barely dodged a fist meant for my abdomen. We spent a few minutes exchanging blows and blocking them. My brain and body worked overtime to anticipate his every move. It was difficult to balance both offense and defense, but I was definitely enjoying the exchange.

Once I find out the name of the brilliant engineer, I should brag about his work to my father and ensure my other siblings get to try this training sequence.

I finally got my chance to jump, spin, and strike my foe in the jaw with my heel. It connected and I finally saw

the hologram stagger and drop to one knee. For the first time, I stood and breathed heavily. I flexed my muscles and prepared for him to get up, but the third set of thugs approached me, and I was prepared to deflect them too.

Before I got my chance, the hologram raised his hands and pleaded, "I yield! I yield!"

It came out more as a chuckle than a true cry for mercy. I froze in place as the thugs rushed past and through me as the lights on the wall fizzled out and the lamps roared to life. The fighter was still there and didn't disappear with the rest of the facade.

"Who are you?" I suddenly snapped. "Tell me right now." My eyes flicked around for any sign of the attendant, but he wasn't there.

"Your betrothed," the fighter groaned, taking off his helmet. There Damir was, his brown hair flattened to his face and a smile plastered on his face.

I took a few steps back, taking my helmet off. My heart raced as I considered what I was wearing and how indecent I must look. Well, according to his customs.

"Who let you in here?" I said, this time much softer and with my formal princess voice.

"I wanted to see you. It seemed like you were ignoring me, so I did what I could to get your attention."

"I didn't even know you arrived. I-I could've injured you!" I protested. "You—"

"That much is clear!" Damir laughed. He groaned a bit as he let himself fall to the floor to sit. "I was told about your progressive training methods, and I had to experience it for myself. We just barely arrived. My entourage thinks I'm taking a nap."

"Either you're good at sneaking or you should fire your staff. My lord, you put yourself in danger. I'm sure it is against your custom for your bride-to-be to give you a black eye. At least, aren't we not supposed to see each other before the wedding?"

Damir's face fell when he understood my seriousness. I crossed my legs and joined him on the floor but from a polite distance. I drank in the visage of my betrothed—a young man I knew through letters up until this moment.

"I know our customs are different and may seem overly formal, but there's no rule that we can't court each other and converse. Is this why you're surprised to see me?"

"Yes. I was explicitly told by your adviser that it was imperative," I said, my cheeks brimmed with sweat and heat. "I was just trying to respect your customs."

Damir gestured for me to come closer to him and I got on my knees to meet him. Once I was close enough, he quickly pulled me close, and we embraced. I collapsed onto him, and he groaned as I put my weight on him. I had to laugh as our armor clanged against each other.

I felt confused but relieved. Had I misheard Benedikt, the adviser? He made a point of giving me this "advice" in a brief letter addressed to my father, so I wondered whether his motives were genuine. I just remembered that he said that Makaar needs a noble, honest king. I could do my part by helping Prince Damir remain focused and "pure" as he takes on this mantle.

At the time, I didn't care; all I could think about was showing Damir my favorite parts of my home—finding quiet moments to hold his hand and stare at his gentle,

handsome face. I also wanted to learn more about Damir before I joined his household in Makaar.

Regardless of what Benedikt may have told me, I knew I could follow Damir's lead.

"My adviser may have been misguided, but we are most certainly allowed to see each other and touch each other."

"Good. It's very hard to stay away."

"I like your thinking."

"Come," I said, rising to my feet and pulling him up with me. "Let's clean ourselves up and have a proper conversation—with less kicking and shoving."

"Are you trying to put naughty thoughts in my mind?" Damir said, smiling and arching his brow. I chuckled, remembering the words "honest" and "pure." No matter. We hastily took off our armor and Damir took my hand before we left the training room.

CHAPTER
FOUR

Suddenly, my thoughts returned to the present as the two double doors opened and the guard regarded me.

"You're permitted to enter. Keep your petition short and simple." I blinked a bit, realizing it was finally my turn.

My petition would be anything but simple, but I nodded. I hoisted Sanjana onto my hip and nodded to Claudiu as I crossed the threshold alone. It was time to introduce Sanjana to her father.

The guard gave me another long look before looking away and gently but firmly closing the doors behind me.

I recognized the room and felt overwhelmed. Nothing much had changed since I left. It felt insurmountably strange to be back inside—the familiar smell of the stone and woodwork, the layout of the room…it felt stranger to be in this room dressed as an outsider. Well, more of an outsider than usual.

The room was silent as I lifted my head and looked Damir straight in the eyes, letting him see for himself the woman I had become. The romantic in me almost started tearing up at the sight of my king. As far as I could tell, Damir had aged a few years and shaved his beard. Gods, *he looks so strange without it.* He regarded me curiously but not too closely—just enough to regard the tears glossing my expression.

"Welcome madam," Damir said. "Please state your petition."

I coughed and laughed at "madam," but I tucked my smile away and pulled the scarf from the crown of my head to let it rest around my neck. I gripped Sanjana for courage.

"I've come to see my husband. I am Anjali of Ushallav, and this is my daughter, Sanjana," I began. I couldn't bear to wait for a response and so the words gurgled out. "You were told that I was killed two years ago but I'm alive and—"

Damir suddenly rose from his chair. It shifted slightly, creating a startling, scraping sound. All murmuring or soft sounds stopped.

"Anjali?" He dared to come down a couple of steps. The rest of my story stayed choked in my throat. His guards tensed at our exchange. Damir's assistants and a few servants stopped their activity. It didn't prevent Damir from standing a foot away from me. I held my mouth in a firm line, not wishing to betray my emotions in front of *all* these people. Gods, how I wished he would take me in his arms and make everything better.

"But they said you were ambushed—n-no one survived—"

"We were ambushed. And I survived with Sanjana still in my belly. The Gavril people took care of us until we were strong enough to come home."

"But it's been—" Damir began.

"Two years, I know." I nodded, tears streaming down my face. I could tell he wanted to take me into an embrace and take his child in his arms, but he held his professional ground. His scribe was furiously writing everything down. The court will set itself on fire over this.

"You're here," Damir breathed. "I…I tried. I did everything I could to find you. I want you to know that."

He cupped my face with his hand. His thumb wiped away a tear just for him to see. I kept my breathing steady and let myself truly study his face as I tilted my head into his palm.

"You must come with me," he said hurriedly. "You've come a long way, waited all day, and I must learn more about what happened. Why did you wait in the line?"

"Your majesty—" I began. He looked at me, pained. I lowered my head and finished. "You're already married. What more can I hope from this?"

He held his jaw firm and his eyes glistened. "Everything I can possibly give. We'll sort this out, Anjali, my love."

"Please," I said, blinking as if coming out of a daze, "I must see Devraj."

He nodded enthusiastically. "Yes, of course."

Sanjana held her arms out with pure trust and love toward Damir.

"This is your father, princess." I could barely get the words out. Damir's eyes clouded with tears as he took our baby in his arms and hugged her tight.

"King Papa?" Sanjana ventured. Damir's charming laugh filled my ears.

"Just call me Papa," he said. "I'm so happy you're here, Sanjana."

He looked into my eyes and then back at Sanjana. It hurt so much—all the things we couldn't say—but it meant the world to me that I could introduce the two for the first time.

"Your majesty?" one of the assistants piped up. The man didn't even finish, like he had already asked a complete sentence. The assistant avoided making contact. My king nodded and sighed.

"Yes, inform my council and Queen Einora—Makaar has just earned her queen and princess back from the dead. I need the rest of the day to myself. If you must... notify me of any dissatisfaction in the morning."

Damir gripped our daughter fiercely, took my right hand with his left, and ushered us on.

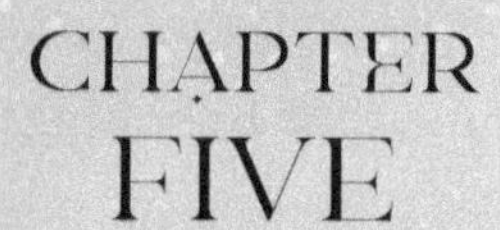

CHAPTER
FIVE

From that moment on, there was a flurry of activity. Damir was flanked by three maids who bowed quickly, then ushered me through the castle as quickly as possible. I hardly saw anyone in the halls as they rushed me by, and I kept my gaze forward to avoid further eye contact. As we progressed, Damir placed Sanjana in my arms.

"These three will help you get situated. I'll be back soon."

"Where are we going?"

Damir and I looked at each other and then at the maids who didn't dare look us in the eye. I could tell they were stunned and timid.

"We could freshen up the guest quarters," one of them suggested.

"That is a fine suggestion," I said before Damir could speak. I didn't want the maids to feel even worse about being thrust into this situation. I just wanted to see my boy and rest. I looked up at Damir. "Where's Devraj? Can I go to his room?"

Damir put his hands on my shoulders as if to stop me from whirring. One of the maids gasped quietly in shock.

"I'm going to fetch him now. You've been traveling and need time to slow down. There's just…quite a bit to think about right now. I want to just talk to you, but I must clear up some things first. Then we can catch up together. Promise."

I gave him a skeptical look. I thought someone else would "clear things up" so he could be with me and our children. I wanted to be with him now and let him catch up on his duties later. But the queen in me knew that other people needed to know about my arrival. I felt elated and bursting with joy just a few minutes ago; the weight of the king's crown swiftly deflated those feelings.

"You know where to find me."

I gave a bow to my husband and held Sanjana close. She thought she was being passed back and reached out to her father and king. I murmured in her ear,

"Let's walk around and explore. Papa will come to play soon."

Damir gave Sanjana a lingering, proud look before taking his leave.

The maids offered a deeper bow and began silently leading me in a somewhat familiar direction. Whenever my family came to visit, we would spend time in these rooms. Often, my entourage would bring their families and partners here to visit us while they served me. Echoes of their laughter and socializing floated around my mind. Meanwhile, other workers turned from their tasks to watch us proceed through the hallways. I had to wonder whether the whole staff or good old Benedikt would hear of my return first.

We eventually stopped at the main doors of the guest bedroom.

"His Majesty will return shortly. We've been asked to take you here to wash up and relax," one of the maids explained. I kept Sanjana close as they threw open the doors and began drawing warm water for us. Sanjana looked up at the ceiling and the large mirrors adorning the walls and spun around to take in the whole room multiple times over. I winced as her tiny feet left smudges on the carpets.

"Mama," Sanjana giggled in Ushallavi, "this is *really* pretty."

If the servant girls heard her, they didn't show it. For the first time in a while, I stood in the center of the room and watched the maids do their work for me. It felt odd falling back into old patterns. They were doing their jobs and for once, I felt like I should pitch in and help. But they were performing their duties; I needed to do mine.

Being back in the castle has already brought back memories of how my entourage helped me feel safe and comfortable in Damir's home. Their killer was still out there, I remembered. I nodded to no one in particular—but I hoped the spirits of my closest companions could see my determination. I was weak before but now I was poised to deliver justice.

"Miss—erm—Your Majesty?" a maid faltered. She shook her head and continued. "We aren't sure what to provide for your young daughter."

She was asking for directions. She didn't want to lose her job over clothing. Luckily, the wheels in my head were already turning.

"If you still have my things, there should be some clothing for her there. I kept all her gifts and there's likely something there for her. If you can't find anything, we can just wash what she's wearing."

She bowed and nodded in understanding. "We'll do our best."

"We'll be waiting just outside," another maid added. "Take your time and let us know if you need anything."

I nodded and thanked them for their preparation. I saw they left out a gown for me. It wasn't one of my embroidered lehenga cholis, flowy Anarkali suits, or colorful kameez churidar but it was finer than what I traveled in. Sanjana enjoyed her moment of freedom as I took off her dusty clothes and let her run around. She toddled gleefully toward the tub.

Just as Sanjana got in, I heard a knock at the door.

"Your Majesty?" one of the maids called and I answered. She stepped inside, clearly aware she was the bearer of some kind of news.

"The king wishes to invite you to a meeting with him and the Makaarian council in a couple of hours. What shall I tell him?"

I pursed my lips. This wasn't my ideal way to come home but I was willing to say yes if it meant I could finally have some alone time.

"We'll be ready. Thank you."

As I finished braiding my long hair and drying Sanjana's curls, I heard a knock at the door.

"Your Majesty, I couldn't stop him—" I heard on the other side but was cut off by the door swinging open. There stood Devraj with his hand still on the door, taking in the sight of me and his sister. He was dressed in his study clothes and panted heavily. He looked well taken care of and fed…

"Mama!" he cried as he ran straight into my arms and practically knocked us all over. He kissed my face and I tried to get a better look at him as he cried out for me and hiccupped.

"Deep breaths, Devraj," I murmured. "It's me. I'm right here. I know it's a lot to take in."

"They said you were killed in the woods," he said. "Now you're back forever!"

"We're back, Dev. I've missed you every day. I love you, baby. I love you. I won't leave you. I'm here."

I smiled and held him close, even though he was hotter than a kiln the way he fussed and worried. I whispered those words over and over again, *I love you*, until my son calmed down.

"Dev, look who also came to see you," I said, as I peeled his sweaty face off my chest. "This is your sister, Sanjana."

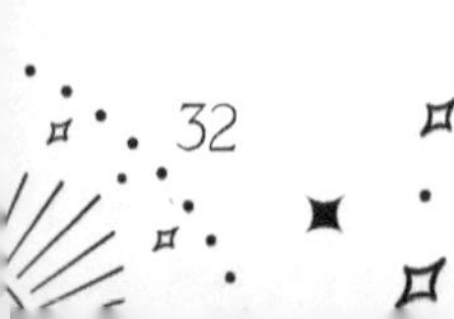

He looked delighted but confused. Very much like his father at this very moment.

"When we went to visit Grandma and Grandpa, I was pregnant. You remember?"

I gestured to my belly, and he placed a hand over mine.

"Someone tried to stop us, but we survived. And Sanjana is here. She's so happy to meet her big brother."

"I'm this old," Sanjana proclaimed, holding up two fingers.

"Yes, almost three years old," I smiled.

"I'm five!" he proclaimed as he hugged his sister. I could see little tears running down his cheeks. I knew he would understand the situation. "You can play in my room, Sanjana."

I wiped my eyes as I collected myself; the corseted part of the dress made it difficult to breathe deeply. I looked up and the servant girls stood meekly at the doorway, not looking at us. They smiled a little at Devraj's sweetness.

"What did you do while I was away?" I began. "I want to hear all about your adventures."

"I just played and played," Devraj said. "Papa was really sad, and he played a lot with me and my toys."

"And what did Papa and Marita say when I was gone?" I asked. I hoped I'd see Marita, their nanny, soon. Surely, she would tell me what a mother needs to know.

"He said," Devraj attempted, but soon switched to Makaarian, "he said someone bad took you away. Grandma and Grandpa said you were late, and they came here. They brought lots of toys! But you were gone."

I tried not to look disappointed that he spoke better Makaarian. It's not like he had anyone besides Marita to practice Ushallavi with.

"Yes, someone very bad tried to hurt me," I said in Makaarian. "But some very kind people who lived in the mountains were there to help me. They helped me and Sanjana when she was born. I hope you get to meet them."

"In the mountains?" Devraj asked.

"No, silly," I chuckled, "Maybe they'll come here and have a huge party here. Grandma and Grandpa will come and see you again, but this time, no one will be sad. We'll all be here together." I took him in my arms, and he didn't squirm away. "I am happy to see you. I love you so much."

He wriggled to be even closer to me than he already was. "I have you and Papa and baby Sanjana. And Einora. I'll never be sad."

My breath caught in my throat. Einora. His step-mother. My replacement.

"But why didn't you come back sooner? You were gone for so long!" Devraj remembered.

"It wasn't safe, Dev," I sighed. "Having a brand-new baby is very hard. I needed to wait for Sanjana to be big and strong. But I was also scared. The bad people could still be looking. I didn't want them to find me."

"Are they gone now?" Devraj said. He twisted himself so he could look up into my eyes. He looked worried but determined.

"I don't know," I replied. "That's why I'm both happy and sad. I'm sad because they could still be hurting other people out there. I hope to find them and—"

"And be only happy?" Devraj finished, trying to be helpful.

"Yes," I said, shaking my head with a smile.

"Madam," someone in the doorway said. I could tell she wanted my attention but had no idea how to address me. I smiled politely and rose to my feet. Sanjana and Devraj also stood up and reached for my hands.

"Yes? Are they ready for me?" I answered.

"Yes. Please follow me," the young attendant replied. I met her in the doorway where she gestured to the hallway. There, we saw a couple of guards waiting for us attentively. I squeezed my children's hands and they squeezed back as if it were a game.

We silently went down the hall. The corset made it hard to breathe and relax, but I knew it would do wonders for my poise. I tried to breathe in as deeply and calmly as I could.

"Papa?" Sanjana asked.

"Yes, hon. We're going to see your papa."

CHAPTER SIX

This war belonged to our grandfathers and our fathers inherited it. Damir and I got to grow up in a time of peace. As we say in Ushallav, the war god, Zayant, fell asleep and the peace god, Tanul, opened his eyes.

There was a time shortly after our engagement party that Damir started training with me. My mind drifted back to a moment when we stretched and relaxed under the morning sky.

"You don't seem afraid anymore," I teased. I had just earned my handmaidens and he was often visibly intimidated by them.

Damir stretched his torso and tucked his hands behind his head before laying down. That earned a blush from me.

"I still don't understand how my grandfather had the audacity to raise arms against your people. Sure, we are proud of our scholars but there's no arguing out of a spear in your gut," he mused. "But I'm not afraid. I admire them. I admire you."

"Go on," I smiled.

"You just…really know what you believe in. You and the other girls—uh, women—follow Abhijita so faithfully. Sorry if I said that wrong—"

"You're fine."

He said her name slowly and carefully. I was patient and so in love. He could've said a completely different name and I wouldn't care. It wasn't every day that I watched a Makaarian try to learn about our ways and our language.

"Right. But still. We have the Firsts, and we try to emulate them, but I don't know anything about them. We have tall tales about what they might've done when the world was first formed but I don't feel all that connected to them. You talk about Abhijita like she's real. Uh, no offense."

"I think you are still a bit afraid," I laughed. "It's our strong beliefs and creations that got us in this mess, isn't it?"

I sat up and crossed my legs and looked down at Damir still on his back as I continued.

"Our kingdoms are very strong but couldn't be more different. You are blessed by the earth and the mountains, and we have our shores. If you ask me, we're just not very good at sharing."

"'Not very good at sharing'?" Damir laughed. "That's an interesting way to describe two decades of war."

He was referencing the fact that as our countries grew and flourished, fear and jealousy took root on either side. I wanted Damir to get used to my training and my hand-maidens because Makaarians never felt comfortable about our traditions surrounding Abhijita. Makaarian women dance, create, read, and raise children. They did not train for war.

Meanwhile, Ushallavi didn't exactly feel comfortable with how Makaar kept growing. Soon, they would take over the mountains and what lay beyond the snowy peaks. Perhaps they weren't strong fighters, but they could prevent us from trading and interacting with other kingdoms.

Those are just a few things that I could glean from my tutors and my parents.

"Well, now, we're going to show the people that we can share. We can keep what makes us special without having to resent each other," I smiled. Sure, I sounded optimistic, but this was long before I experienced Makaarian court life for myself.

"Even if Makaar got you and you alone, I think we'd be better for it." Damir's dreamy smile drew me in. I flattened myself onto my stomach and kissed him. He cupped my face and we kissed for a long time. Not long enough according to my young heart.

"I hope they are ready for me," I said, coming up for air. "I know things aren't going to be easy, but I hope to one day see our countries as true allies."

Damir smiled. "You seem a lot more passionate about politics than I was told. I could use your help convincing my father's councilors to relax a bit."

"You mean *your* councilors."

"Yeah. One of the many things I earned after his death."

"Your father would be proud. I wish I got to know him a bit better."

Damir's mouth set into a firm line. He lost his father and some of his siblings in the war. Someone from my side likely took them from him.

"He taught me to be respectful but wary of Ushallavi people like you. Maybe that was right to do in his time but that's not what I want to do. I will ensure that no matter what people think, they'll still respect you—respect us. My father's council will have to catch up with me."

I smiled. To be honest, I was worried I wouldn't fit in. I already felt homesick just thinking about it. To know that Damir noticed and cared was enough. We could face anything together. We promised that much.

CHAPTER
SEVEN

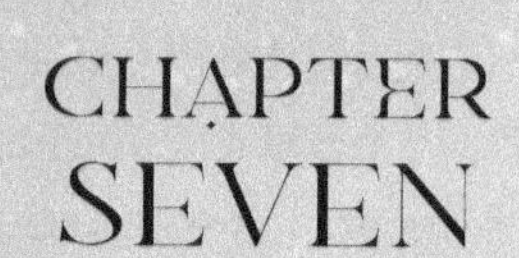

The atmosphere felt charged as soon as I stepped into the room with Devraj at my side and Sanjana on my hip. Anyone with eyes could see that I was the mother of these two children, and I was very much alive.

The room itself held a very ornate table with weary Makaarians sitting in just about every chair. Damir looked haggard but clearly emotional to see the three of us enter this space. Servants dotted the room as they lit candles and replaced empty plates and goblets with more refreshments. Sanjana squealed with excitement and her shrill cry bounced off the high ceilings. She repeated herself, delighted with the results until I shushed her. She certainly commanded everyone's attention—as a princess should.

Damir rose from his chair and let Devraj come to him. He nodded patiently as Devraj recounted what we did while we waited for this moment.

"Let Mama sit here, and you can sit in your chair."

As if on cue, a manservant appeared with a narrow, raised chair that copied the other chairs except there was an extra rung between the legs so my prince could sit on his own. He proudly sat between his parents and Damir let Sanjana sit on his lap.

The rest of the council watched our little family as we situated ourselves. Meanwhile, I took a quick scan of the room. No women were present. I didn't know how I felt that Einora, Queen Einora I should say, was not present. Where was she? Did I care?

As a servant brought my children some dates and milk, I locked eyes with Benedikt. I gave him a curt nod as I helped Sanjana. If I could make her cooperate with me during this meeting, I'd let her eat as many dates as she could stomach. Devraj was explaining all the food on the table as though Sanjana had never eaten before. Damir gave me a small smile before motioning to Benedikt.

Oh, Benedikt. I've never met someone quite like him—the kind of person with the pleasure of being paid handsomely to be right while being an asshole about it. Benedikt was the keeper of all things culture, order, and tradition. He was roughly ten years older than me but acted like he had already lived multiple lifetimes. He looked every bit the Makaarian champion: his pale-yet-tan skin and perfectly straight hair could tell you that he benefited from the beloved traditions he swore to protect.

I wondered what his traditions would advise us to do—after all, the kingdom now has one king and two queens.

When I was engaged to Damir, I learned to be wary of Benedikt. I was raised to trust my counsel, so I decided not to fall for this trick a second time.

It was a shame that Damir really looks up to him. He told me many times that Benedikt was helping him reshape the future of Makaar in a way to be more open-minded to cultures like mine. I've yet to see such evidence. Even as the queen, it took far too much poking, prodding, and measured explaining to make those changes. It took months to get his support to allow me to attend previous meetings such as these.

The counsel seemed doubly put out by the presence of their first queen and children. This was new and unexpected for them. And Makaarians hate spontaneity.

My attention returned to Benedikt's words as he began the meeting.

"We are astonished at the miracle we see before us: the return of Queen Anjali and Princess Sanjana. King Damir called this meeting to order to discuss their sudden and joyful return. We hope to learn what happened and what caused the disappearance of part of the royal family. Perhaps we can piece together how the kingdom must move forward once we know the full story. Queen Anjali, please begin when you're ready. Our historian is ready to record."

I looked around the room of men with jackets decorated with their achievements and love for their country. The historian looks up at me, his quill poised. I gave Damir a quick look. I wanted to unfold and unpack my difficult years with him, not in front of his coworkers.

"My name is Anjali, princess of Ushallav. I was crowned as queen of Makaar once I married Damir almost six years ago. I am the mother of Devraj, the heir to the Makaarian throne, and he was born within a year of our wedding date—"

"I hate to interrupt you, Your Majesty, but we want to hear about your last moments before you disappeared and what happened during the past three years."

I looked over at Benedikt and tried to not roll my eyes.

"I hate being interrupted but if you insist." Oooh, I've never said something like that before in this room and it felt like I regained a year of my youth. "Well, as many of you remember, we had a huge feast to celebrate the forthcoming birth of our princess, Sanjana. Damir and I had already chosen that name at that point. I had news that my brothers would be back from their military training and my whole family would be reunited at the palace, so I made plans to visit them during the summer months and celebrate with them. Damir and Devraj planned on joining us soon after, especially if Sanjana was born during that time. Then—"

In my mind's eye, a few images flew across my vision. I remembered the arrows burrowing into my carriage and suddenly seeing the sides burst into flames. There was shrieking and calls to arms as my soldiers and my handmaidens rallied to fight off our attackers. I stumbled out, feeling nauseous and clutching my belly. I pulled my cloak closer around my person and used a fighting staff I secured under the carriage. I thwacked any attackers who came close to our travel party and ducked behind cover.

I remember seeing the gilded carriage roaring in flames and bodies littering the forest floor. My soldiers were all dead or dying, and my handmaidens were also slain. The sight made me grieve so deeply that I thought I would lose the baby I carried. I suddenly felt that weight push down on my shoulders and hips. I struggled to stand.

I cleared my throat. No tears yet.

"We were ambushed. Our attackers did not wear any symbols, so I don't know who sent them or why. But our carriages were set on fire, and I was the only one who escaped. My soldiers and handmaidens fought bravely but they were lost. I fled with nothing but what I had on my person and a fighting staff."

"My queen, how did you manage that? Didn't they look for you?"

"My maidens and I planned on having a decoy. I swapped clothing with one of my maidens for further protection," I said. I remembered Gamani sprawled on the ground with three arrows stuck in her neck and stomach. She wore one of my expensive Anarkali pantsuits and her expertly braided hair lay limp over her face as if hiding her face in shame. The circular pillow meant to look like a pregnant stomach was coated in someone's blood. Shame still haunted me.

I continued. "They thought they killed me with arrows, but I was able to conceal myself in the woods until I felt sure the assassins were satisfied and left. I did what I could to pretend I was dead."

I made sure to look each council member in the eye and wondered if they would dare question this tale—this trauma. As far as I could tell, they gave no indication of emotion. They weren't moved to any kind of surprise or remorse at my story. I narrowed my eyes in suspicion. I long wondered if they were behind this attack. Was I right or wrong?

"How did you survive for two years? While taking care of our baby?" Damir asked. He seemed genuinely concerned. He knew I was strong and capable, but he didn't know the half of it. His hand flinched like he itched to hold mine. He gripped the armrests of his chair instead.

"Some very kind traveling folk found me and kept me safe. The women helped me bear Sanjana and the men protected me."

"Gypsies," a council member added with a slight sneer.

"The Gavril people, you mean," I curtly returned. "They deserve our gratitude. They saved my life and protected Sanjana."

"That's me," Sanjana said happily. She had juice all over her cheeks. I quickly dabbed her face with a napkin. I heard scoffs at the gesture and snorted. These counselors probably did whatever they could to avoid nurturing their children in any capacity.

"We will be sure to send a reward to the Gavril people when we can. But why wasn't it safe enough to come sooner? Did you know we were looking for you?" Damir asked.

"It wasn't safe Your Highness," I said, trying not to lose my temper. I lowered my voice a touch and gestured to my stomach to say, "I nearly…the worst almost happened. The kind women who watched over me helped me heal physically and mentally from…everything. This wise council is likely aware that the Gavril people travel with the seasons. We traveled for months to return. And, unless you know who was responsible for sabotaging my carriage, they are still at large. Gentlemen of this council, I want to make it clear that I chose to protect my life, my daughter's life, and the lives of those who rescued us."

I paused and my chin finally trembled.

"The question is, how long did *you* wait until you were sure I was dead, and the kingdom needed a new queen?"

I blinked and looked up at the high ceilings before looking at Damir and the other Makaarian nobles. Oh, have I waited for this moment.

"Once we had confirmation from your family that you and your party didn't arrive and our guards confirmed that they did not find you along your route, we deemed you officially lost to us," Benedikt said. "We mourned your loss for a month. Your family attended the funeral services. How relieved they will be to know you are alive. Or have you already told them?"

I did whatever I could to not choke on my emotions. My parents. My siblings. I need them. Their guidance.

"I have not reached out to them. I felt it my duty to come here first," I said. The way he so formally recounted my own funeral and their procedures felt insulting. They buried my birthright and memory in an empty casket. They made my son watch.

"We're glad that you came," Damir said softly. This time, he did take my hand and I let him.

"Your Majesty, it must've been painful to recount your darkest days. But we'll need to inquire further. Both kingdoms have their share of gangs and miscreants, but this is the first time since our alliance that anyone would be so bold as to attack someone of your stature. We'll need further information—anything to identify them. We are all robbed of justice."

"Soon, everyone will know I'm alive. What if they attempt to return to Makaar and harm the children?" I directed my question to Damir.

The rest of the room tensed with that notion. I likely doubled the number of meetings with that one question.

I looked around. "While I am grateful to be home, I owe it to my handmaidens and my children to get to the bottom of this. I must know who tried to murder me and why. It could be personal—it could be political. I must do what I can to protect my family and Makaar. And I won't ask for permission."

Benedikt let my words soak up the air and the historian's parchment before breaking the silence.

"There is much to discuss. We, too, care for the sanctity and security of the royal family and their subjects."

"Papa, can Sanjana play with me in my playroom?" Devraj asked. Count on a toddler to interject during a tense discussion. I smiled wearily.

"Perhaps that is a good idea if Queen Anjali finds that agreeable," Benedikt said, looking at my husband.

"What happens now?" I asked. My muscles tensed at the idea of letting my children out of my sight. But I couldn't bear to go another day without knowing what happens next—to me, my children, and this other queen.

"We will adjourn at the moment, as the sun is finally setting. His Majesty will discuss matters further as he has requested to converse privately."

Enough with the stuffy words.

"If Marita is still here, she can watch over the children."

"Yes. She will be there and will love to reunite with you soon," Damir said, smiling.

"As will I," I said, rising to my feet. I wasn't sure whether the nobles truly believed my words or cared that I was alive. I wasn't sure I cared what they thought even though Damir cared very much. "Come, Devraj and Sanjana. Let's go play."

They bubbled at my side as we left the room with barely a curtsy or nod of acknowledgment.

CHAPTER
EIGHT

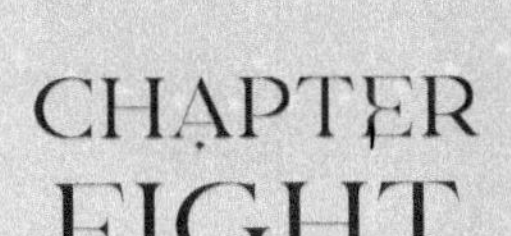

I dreamed and fantasized about this reunion a thousand times. I envisioned sweeping in and kissing Damir and wrapping my arms around him like I'd never kissed him before. I could practically feel the warm sheets over me and the words he would whisper in my ear. Words just for me.

And then I found out he remarried. Those fantasies soured and curdled. Then I started plotting and crafting arguments. I was imprisoned by my own worst fears.

A stifled meeting with the council? Well, I wasn't really expecting that.

"Anjali, keep it together," I murmured to myself.

"Playtime, Mama?" Devraj asked. He tugged on my hand excitedly. He repeats himself in Ushallavi so Sanjana could hear. She immediately tried to wiggle out of my arms. The Gavril children play by running and that's all she knows. I couldn't get there fast enough.

I took my children hastily down the corridor and up the familiar stairs. The only changes to Devraj's room were fewer infant toys and smells, and slightly more mature interests. His larger toys looked like recent birthday gifts from my parents and our best carpenter. Toy swords and gilded horses. A bow and arrows with dull tips.

It was a joy to return but I felt heavy memories. It was only a few years ago that I kissed him goodbye in his bed as I left for my journey. I held his little hand and promised that I would see him soon. At the time, I looked forward to the break from the stifling Makaarian culture. Had I known…

Would I still be Damir's first and only queen if I hadn't left? Or would the danger eventually have found me inside the castle walls? I have my suspicions that my nationality was a huge factor in the assassination attempt. If some extremist didn't like that I was their ruler, what does that mean for Devraj?

Perhaps Devraj needs handmaiden-level training, too.

I squeezed my eyes shut as I tried to encourage myself to come back to the present.

As I set Sanjana on the floor, she all but flew out of my grasp. I heard clamoring coming up the stairs and into the doorway. Sanjana barely touched a nearby toy before I picked her back up again. A very disheveled Marita stood in the doorway with a hand to her heart. If I wasn't holding my daughter, I would've done the same. I haven't had a moment to truly relax since we arrived at this castle.

I slowly let Sanjana play with her brother. She didn't know which toy to stick in her mouth first.

"My queen! You are alive!" Marita gasped. She aged only slightly since I left—her hair was still woven in her usual crown braid, and she earned a few more gray hairs. "I heard you were in the castle and many of the folks working here thought they were seeing a ghost. Oh! Is this your daughter? Our baby Sanjana?"

I felt slightly relieved to hear her usual banter as she took Sanjana into her arms and spun in a circle.

"I remember when you were still in your mum. You made her very sick," Marita teased Sanjana in modest Ushallavi.

"Sanjana, this is Marita, Devraj's governess," I explained with a slight chuckle.

"What's a guh-ness?"

"She plays with me whenever I want!" Devraj said proudly. "She sometimes teaches me things."

"I tend to the queen and her children," Marita said, rubbing her nose against Sanjana's. "I'm like an auntie only I'm paid for it."

"Ah-tee!" Sanjana proclaimed.

I laughed at Marita's honesty—something I treasured immensely when I was pregnant and otherwise felt alone. We hired her because she's also bilingual; I kept her because she understood many things about me just by speaking my language. I didn't have to over-explain certain things to Marita and Damir. Everyone else was still catching on to this new way of life Damir and I created.

"You're back after all these years. Oh, you poor thing." She eagerly held out her free arm and she held me close with Sanjana still on her left hip. Devraj joined us, not wanting to be left out. I cried softly at the sudden gesture and burst of smell: Marita smelled of soap and breastmilk. A flood of memories gurgled to the surface as I remembered my loneliness, my apparent inadequacies, and Marita's gentle guidance.

"What happened, my queen?" Marita said. She rubbed my back and made shushing sounds. "Where have you been?"

"I'll try to be brief—I've had to explain myself so many times already. But we were ambushed," I said into her shoulder, then raised my face. "I survived in the woods and the Gavril people kept me safe until I could bare Sanjana. I came home once I knew we could make the trip."

"Oh, my days, you poor thing. But you're so strong. Only you as a queen could have overcome such trials." She held her palm to my cheek, catching my stray tears. "His Majesty will sort things out, of course, won't he? I can assure you that he was very sad to be apart from you all this time. You have seen him already, correct?"

"Oh yes," I said, wiping my eyes. "Well, I met him very formally and cordially with his advisers. I'm about to speak with him in private. I could use your help—please watch the littles? I'm...I'm worried that Damir and his council will decide that I can't stay here. Perhaps they've already picked Einora over me and Damir will just go along with it. I'm here to protect the children."

"Surely, he won't abandon you. But of course, I will watch over the kids. You deserve some rest!" Marita was a woman who not only respected Damir as a king but as my husband. I knew she was trying to comfort me, but I've only been dwelling on the worst-case scenarios over the past few days. I knew there would be some kind of fight but not *what* kind of fight.

"I…I don't know anything about the new queen. How long have they been together?"

We hardly talked about her during the meeting. I'm eager and loathe to meet her.

"Ah yes, Queen Einora is a vision. She is sweet to everyone. She's the daughter of a local nobleman, so many people knew of her before she was crowned. I believe they have been together for a year."

"Does…Damir love her?" I asked in a small voice. The least I can be is happy for him. But I secretly wondered if it was easier to love her than me.

"From what I've seen, yes. She was the only one who could help him out of a very dark and gloomy space. Things definitely cheered up around here once she bore him a son."

Of course. I was warned about her child. Of course, he has moved on. It just felt that much more real now that she has also given him a child.

I must've worried Marita because she quickly pulled up a chair for me and I sat down, grateful. My senses weren't registering. It was like I couldn't hear or see. My stomach twisted at the thought. I was not raised to share.

"This must be difficult to bear," Marita said calmly.

"I'm quite shocked myself that I'm the one to tell you more about Queen Einora. But you're here. You're alive. You've done nothing wrong, my dear. I know you're a strong woman. You'll advocate for the right thing."

"I certainly hope so. I just have so many questions. Who wants to hurt me? Who would hire assassins to attack me? They didn't even want to keep me ransom." I lowered my voice so my kids couldn't hear, "They were sent to kill. And the council didn't seem aware of such hatred toward me. Or maybe they are aware—I have a hard time reading them at times. All I know is that I can count on one hand how many people knew my travel plans. Nothing feels right."

"You think a Makaarian would actually do this?" Marita said. "The staff found you very exotic and refreshing, the way you befriended them and respected them. I can vouch for their innocence."

My eye twitched at the use of the word *exotic*. "Will you help me?"

"I will do anything I can for you," Marita smiled, taking my hands. I wasn't sure if she really knew what I was asking. I wasn't sure what she could do. I just needed someone here that I could depend on. Someone to take care of my children as I dug deeper.

"I know. Thank you so much, Marita. And thank you so much for being in Devraj's life. He looks so healthy...I can't describe how grateful I am—"

"I've missed you, too."

I sneak a peek at Devraj. He let Sanjana chase him—their cheeks were bright. He giggled wildly as he rushed toward me and grabbed my clothes. I hugged him at my side. I still can't believe he's here and he's okay.

"The children will be safe here with me," Marita said. "This is their domain and I protect it. You've been stalling for long enough. It's time to sort some things out with your husband."

CHAPTER
NINE

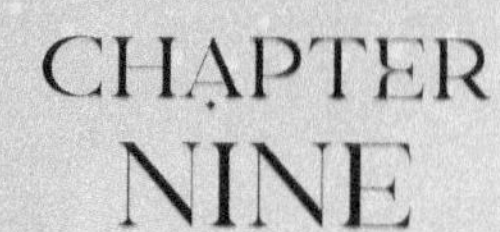

I kissed the children before going to the guest wing. If Marita worked her charm, the littles would be asleep by the time I finished speaking to Damir. After I washed and dried my face, I straightened myself to my most confident stature and made my way back to the council room.

Before I could over-think my entrance, I marched up to the entry and spoke to the two guards that I was here to see the king. They performed their duty as they stood to the side, opened the doors, and silently ushered me in.

Across the room, Damir sat up straight before standing up.

"You look as radiant and beautiful as ever," he said,

quickly closing the space between us. He took my hand and pressed it against his lips. "Of course, you never did like these corseted gowns."

"I'll feel more myself once I have my old wardrobe again." It felt too soon to ask what he did with my things.

"I missed you," Damir said, tears welling up in his blue eyes. "I already missed you when you went to your family, but I was crushed when I first heard that you wouldn't come back. That you were dead." His hands held mine. I could tell he craved my touch.

"I'm having a very difficult time being here knowing that you have a new wife. And a new prince. Any other details I need to know? I've had quite the day today and I'm tired."

Damir gestured to a chair, and I complied. I sank in. My hips rested on the edge of the chair, so I didn't have to sit properly in the corseted gown.

"I know it's been difficult. I know it was not fair to start your first day home with meetings. I wanted to spend time alone with you and hear your story without everyone else hearing it. I wanted to cry. But…you know how things are. I'm trying to keep things civil. I don't want anyone to feel hurt."

"Does Einora know?"

"Yes. I visited her before the meeting."

"And?"

"And what?"

"From your perspective, I just came back without any warning. Surely, she's wondering what will happen to her and her son. We're all wondering what comes next. And

I feel selfish for wanting you to just make the choice that things should go back to how they once were. I want my life back. I want you, Damir."

Damir leaned onto the armrest of his chair.

"Yes, things are difficult. I know that you're worried. I will take care of it. I will take care of us."

Damir's soft voice offered meager comfort. He tentatively raised a hand to touch my face. I moved away, feeling his fingers brush against my cheek.

"You replaced me, Damir," I choked out. "I was fighting to stay alive and raise our infant daughter and you just married some other woman. How can you just say that you will take care of things?"

Damir took in a sharp breath as if he were censuring himself from yelling.

"Anjali, I didn't know what to do. I couldn't be in charge of my country and raise my son all by myself. I thought I lost you and needed someone to fill that space. I waited as long as I could before considering remarrying anyone. Devraj needed two parents."

"This reeks of Benedikt and you know it." It felt good to blame him for something even though it was immature.

"You're always critical of his counsel—"

"He has always been critical of *me*. He'll tell me one thing, I'll try to do it, and then tell me I made a mistake. Remember back when we were engaged? He seriously told me that we weren't supposed to be around each other until we wed—"

"You really remember that? It was so long ago."

"But it happened, Damir. This is just one instance of many. That's what matters here. I can't win. Not when

Benedikt is here calling the shots. You act like you're married to him instead of me or Einora—"

"Okay, just cool down, Anjali."

"I've waited years to say my piece. You don't get to tell me to cool down." I pointed a finger at him. "What am I supposed to do now, Damir? You have two wives, and your people forbid you from having us both. What a pickle, indeed. Do I fight and take you back? Do you want me to go home so I can go back to being dead? What's more convenient for you, dear?"

"Stop! Enough!" Damir roared. His order echoed and died. Tears rimmed his eyes as he knelt on the ground and grasped my hands. Stunned, I didn't move. A part of me wanted to kneel and stop the tears but another part suggested I stand my ground.

"Anjali, I truly don't know what to do. You are the mother of our children and you'll always be the queen of my heart. I also love Einora and Gregori. She was there for me and comforted me even though I was a mess and missed you. Whatever I do, it will hurt one of you. I lose no matter what I do. We are all in a tough place. Please believe me that no matter what happens, we're going to do it together. I don't want you to live on and hate me. I want to put control in your hands and Einora's hands. No one else will tell you how to feel or what to do."

I relented and tugged Damir's arms. He took the encouragement and rose to his feet. Before I could have second thoughts, I tugged him for an embrace and breathed him in. His hug tightened and we stood there—hugging, breathing, crying—until I could feel my heart relax.

"I came here to make sure our children would be safe and happy," I murmured. "But it's unfair to do so without thinking about us. I don't know how things will go but I'm committed to figuring it out with you. When I married you, I promised you that I would do that."

Damir's gaze looked broken but hopeful.

"Perhaps we'll truly come to a reasonable solution if we look at who put us in this situation. Your carriage was attacked. That's treason against me, too."

"If you value your wives and your children, then that would be a wise move. There's a very short list of people who would know my plans. It means we have a traitor in our court. It's possible they're still here and could harm me or the babies."

"Now that you're here, perhaps we have enough details to find this assassin and execute them," Damir suggested. "For a time, we conducted a private investigation, but we also never knew what happened to you."

"I'm sure your advisers told you to move on. I wouldn't put it past them." I put a hand on my husband's cheek. Our eyes connected and my fury fizzled.

"Anjali, if only you knew how much I want you right now. I've missed you more than I can say and now you're here…"

All my favorite places lit up at the notion. My husband was already in my arms. For years, my body focused on staying alive and nourishing my baby. Now, the younger warrior stirred within me. I gripped Damir's upper arms. We had a shared desire and I'd be damned if traditions stood between us.

"Do we have to tell anyone? I mean, if I go with you."

Damir took my hand, the one still on his cheek, and kissed it deeply. He moved and breathed like he was ready to love my body but held himself back. I thought of Einora sleeping somewhere in her quarters, unaware that we were even together and left alone.

"We deserve this," Damir groaned.

"We'll worry about tomorrow when it arrives." I gasped before pulling Damir's face close and kissing him deeply. Damir's hands immediately grasped at my butt—searching for it under layers of skirts. His hands then traveled up and down my back and waist.

Moments later, he led me to the bed we once shared. No one stepped in and reminded us of reality. Instead, we left our worries, anxieties, and protocols in piles of discarded clothing.

CHAPTER TEN

I am trying to open my eyes a bit more, but my vision will not clear. I know that there was something I need to sign—if only I could read the scroll. Someone presses me for a signature, but I hesitate. I cannot see and it feels like I am deliberating on the matter for hours—days. Everyone is counting on me. Everyone is waiting.

"Please just sign the scroll, Your Majesty," I hear. It sounds like Benedikt's impatient-yet-quiet tone.

"I cannot read it. I cannot open my eyes," I protest. I want to cry but I do not know why. I am feeling all this pressure and I want to escape.

Suddenly, I can focus on the signature line. It looks huge. The quill I hold is comically tiny. It is like using a nib of chalk to write out a speech. I still cannot see but my blurred vision makes out a scribbled line that hardly looks like a signature.

The scroll snaps up like a lion's jaw. I do not see Benedikt at all. Instead, I see Damir towering over me. I think I am sitting or kneeling on the ground—he is so tall.

"How could you?" he wails. "Don't you love me?"

"I love you, Damir! Please believe me!" I cry. I can hardly hear my words, but I feel heavy and disheartened.

"You just signed away the children. You just divorced me. You are unfit to be a mother. Unfit. Unfit…"

I want to scream but a choked sound is all I can muster. Why can't I speak? I want him to hear my pain.

"This is not fair! Please!" I muster. It comes out as a murmur, and I am so angry that my voice will not carry.

"I hope the children forget you."

I watch in horror as my children take their father's hands and the sweet brown of their skin fades. Their features shift and they no longer look Ushallav like me. They cry like it is my fault. Their skin is not white like Makaarians but instead a tinge of gray. I need to hold my babies—they are dying!

Once I blink away tears, I discover that I am in a carriage. *The* carriage. I try to scream as I am in my hellish cage again. The wild carriage is moving faster than I imagine is possible. I already strain to see but colors blur past me.

At this point, I think I am dreaming, so I will the carriage to stop. I believe wholeheartedly that I can still control the situation.

The carriage stops. I am still standing in the carriage and the abrupt change does not knock me down. The doors spring open on their own. It is dark outside, but I have a funny feeling that I know exactly where I am. If I just crouch down, I will be safe.

One arrow. Two. Like a flock of birds, the inside of the carriage is punctured by arrows. I try to scream once more but I cannot find my voice. I want to get out. I want to live! The arrows bend in unnatural ways, so they hit me while I am hiding in a pocket of the carriage.

I try to scream and scream until someone shakes me awake.

"Hey, honey." Damir held my shoulder as he spoke comfortingly. I looked around and realized that I was only having a nightmare. I was still in Damir's bed. Our bed.

"Oh gods, it wasn't real," I exhaled. I felt hot and sticky. I also felt hot with shame. Patches of my dream become forgotten, but I still remember the accusation.

You are unfit to be a mother.

As if to make things worse, I started to cry. I should have felt relief. I was a survivor. I lived in the woods and gave birth—I took care of Sanjana without any queenly privileges. I earned my strength and reclaimed my title. So why do I feel like a fraud for lying next to Damir? I already earned him fair and square.

"It's okay," Damir cooed. He wrapped a bare arm around me, and I sank into his embrace. We just cuddled there until everything felt better.

"I feel awful," I finally croaked. I sat up in bed. I rubbed my eyes, grateful that I could see clearly. "What will your other wife think of us?"

I glanced over my shoulder. Damir propped himself up with one elbow and revealed his shoulders and chest. He sighed and rubbed his eyes, too.

"We said we'd think about it in the morning. And it is already here."

"Do you regret last night?"

"No. I've been waiting to feel that way for too long." He reached out and took my hand. He then gently rubbed the pad of his thumb on my palm.

"I ought to meet her. Einora."

Damir looked like he wanted to hide under his blanket and disappear.

"Everything is so complicated," he murmured. "But you're right. Whatever happens next should be up to you and Einora."

"Not that I know how I feel about it, but your country is against polyamory, isn't it?"

Damir chuckled. "The people have advocated for it. The royal family still hearkens to tradition. That's the same for your family, right?"

"It's not all that glamorous—being the king of Makaar. People tell you what you can or can't do because they assume it's what your dead great-great-grandfather would've wanted. We're the ones living and breathing. You ought to have a choice, too." I caught Damir's eyes. I didn't expect his eyes would rim with tears.

"Maybe Devraj will have more flexibility when it's his turn."

"I hope so. I hope he doesn't have to go through anything like what we've overcome."

As soon as Damir brought up our son, I couldn't help

but gasp. I promised Marita that I would pick up the children last night so we could stay together. I obviously forgot. My clothes were still on the floor. It truly felt like I was caught cheating on my husband—*with* my actual husband.

No wonder I felt so different—this was the first night in literal years that I didn't need to wake up to nurse Sanjana. For a moment, I think to myself, *Maybe I am unfit to be a mother* before I snapped out of it. Marita was on my side. She would understand. And it was just one night with my actual husband. I refused to feel guilty. I had to shed the part of me that cared what other people thought about me.

I still needed to see the kids, so I brushed the blanket away and got off the bed. Damir rose from his side of the bed and came over to meet me. I laughed. He and I still weren't wearing anything. He pulled me close, and I let him.

"You're so beautiful," he murmured in my ear.

"I know," I smiled. "You're beautiful, too. I miss the beard, though." I kissed him and he drank it in. It was unclear who was trying harder to delay the inevitable.

"Marita will wonder where I am," I said. Damir nodded and brushed a stray curl of hair from my forehead.

"And I must ensure that Einora is not kept in the dark about the situation."

I nodded. It dawned on me that he had a third child to see, too. The idea felt too foreign and separate from me. We quietly washed up a bit and dressed ourselves. Damir asked his servants to leave us be so we could savor these moments before facing the reality the day would bring.

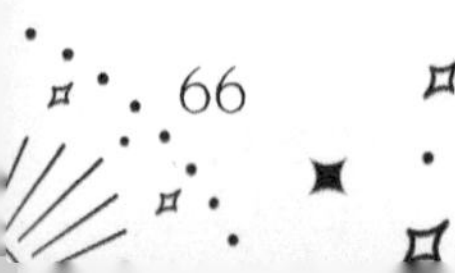

CHAPTER ELEVEN

As much as I needed to concentrate on this letter, I didn't want to let my children out of sight. So here I sat near the window in the playroom. The desk was low—just inches above my thighs as I sat cross-legged. It wasn't my original personal desk, but it did the job. I studied the quill in my hand, wondering how I could possibly explain to my parents and siblings that their princess is now alive. And she's using her free time on vengeance and determining if she wants to fight another woman for the throne.

The words weren't coming—both because I wanted to explain things in the best way possible and because it had been years since I'd written anything in my own language. The things time does to the brain.

As I was struggling with my pride and itching for a dictionary, a knock came at the door. I looked up from my desk, not wanting to shove it away. I stood up since my kids eagerly toddled toward the knocking sound.

A man in a simple messenger uniform stood at my door with a folded piece of embellished parchment.

"His Majesty has granted me the right to deliver you this invitation and hopes it finds you in good health," came the message. He held out the invite, and I rolled my eyes and rose to receive it. It didn't take long for me to feel impatient over formalities.

"What's the celebration?" I asked. I briefly skimmed over the calligraphy. I found my answer on the page as soon as the messenger said,

"It is to celebrate your return to the courts of Makaar and to introduce the kingdom to our new princess."

"What?" I asked sharply. The feast was meant to celebrate us in two weeks' time—which was not enough time to order a traditional Anarkali suit. I knew it was a petty reason to be upset but it was the first thing to come to my mind. I missed my clothing and jewelry. I wanted to wear my dress that opened and showed my trousers and midriff—I wanted to show my pride in my body and my culture. And I wanted Sanjana to really dress like a princess with Ushallav heritage.

"How is this even enough time for us to prepare? Whose idea was this?"

"Qu-queen Einora requested as such," the messenger said, not confident in his impromptu response. "Her Majesty would like to address rumors already all over the kingdom and court—"

"Do I look like someone who cares about rumors?" I asked, then abruptly shut my mouth. "I apologize. You are simply doing your job. I will discuss this with the right people and let you go about your business. Thank you for…the message."

"You are too kind." the man bowed quickly and disappeared.

I put a hand to my brow and slumped my shoulders. Two weeks? Would that be enough time to show my face to every creature in Makaar? Would that be enough time for my parents to arrive?

For a celebration meant for me, it didn't feel like anyone chose to consult me. I looked back at my desk and the pages with crossed-out sentences.

"Dev? Sanjana? Mama needs to go speak with Papa for a moment." Marita was sitting on the floor and catching Sanjana if she toppled over. They all looked up at me. The kids were unbothered, but Marita gave me an encouraging nod.

"Go. We'll be fine."

I soon stormed past the guards and flung open the door.

A guard tried to warn the king.

"Your Majesty, she—"

"You know I hate surprises," I said over the protesting guard. I looked to Damir at his desk—I could hardly see him with the stacks of books and papers across his workspace and Benedikt standing a pace away with his arms folded. I swallowed a grimace as I realized Damir wasn't alone.

"Ah, Queen Anjali," Benedikt said. "What can we help you with?"

I glared at the Makaarian.

"Is everything all right, dear?" Damir said. His question was tinted as if he knew he would be apologizing soon enough. I raised up the written invitation.

"Can anyone explain to me why I was the last one invited to a party for me and my daughter?" I said, sticking with my first plan: come with fire and indignation. "Will my parents and siblings be in attendance? What is the meaning of this?"

Damir ran a hand through his hair and scratched under his crown.

"The council felt it was imperative to show transparency on the matter," Damir explained, removing his hand from his head, resting his elbow on his desk, and gesturing to me. "The people have heard of your return, and they wonder who their true queen is. We feel the feast will show them there are good feelings between you and Queen Einora. The people deserve to celebrate your return and settle back into their lives."

"So, this was not Einora's—Her Majesty's—idea?" I asked.

"We discussed things with her, and she agreed to fulfill her duties to oversee the menu, the music, and the decorations," Benedikt added. "It shows good feelings between the two of you."

"Yes, you've said that already. I would normally agree except I haven't even met her," I didn't know whether to glare at Benedikt or Damir. "How is this transparency if it's built on a lie?"

Benedikt just smirked.

"So, will I meet Einora today or what?" This was starting to sound like an idea that was put on Damir, Einora, and me. Benedikt was the only one all smiles.

"She can meet with you sometime today," Damir said, giving me a look. It was our unspoken language that we used around Benedikt: *We'll speak of this later, my dear.*

My lips formed a thin line. I thought I was frustrated but now I was livid.

"Does this further calm your mind on the matter?" Benedikt said. Damir rubbed his eyes with his left thumb and pointer finger. I doubted there was more I could do or say. Damir was almost a totally different man when Benedikt was at his elbow.

"What about my family?" I asked. "It takes a week to even arrive here. It seems entirely unnecessary to give us two weeks to prepare. Damir?"

"They were the first to be notified of the feast. We should hear from them in a few days," Benedikt answered.

"I would like to be notified as soon as possible when we hear from them." I looked at Damir. I've barely had a moment to put quill to paper about my return and now they're going to hear about some party? Why does this feel so wrong?

I didn't address Benedikt, but he answered.

"Of course."

Damir looked at me with pain behind his eyes. He's not the man who touched me with such fire and gentleness the night before. I apparently needed to leave him to his work. He already gave me a lot to think about.

I curtsied and said, "Well, I have some letters to write and some preparations to make."

Benedikt bowed to me, and Damir rose to do the same. I held back a frustrated groan as I left the room. I avoided eye contact with the guards I wrestled with moments before.

I clenched my fists. I come home and it's right back to this. Right back to the games and the deceit. It's like I'm home but my husband is not. There's something about the smirk and the look that Benedikt gave me. I didn't like him before but now I hardly trust him.

As I walked toward Devraj's playroom, something caught my attention.

"Who tampered with the Watchful Eyes?" I asked aloud. The painted, gilded "eyes" that once adorned the forgotten nooks and crannies of the castle had thick cream-colored drapes over them or the Eyes were otherwise gone. The one looming above me was half painted over as if the painter was rushed.

At first, nearby servants didn't answer. I was about to restate the question when a small reply came. "They were removed or covered when you were declared dead, my lady."

I considered the response and the politeness of the reply. "Well, now that I'm back, will they be restored?"

"That is a matter for the king and queen to settle," came another polite answer. I nodded silently and went along my way.

The Watchful Eyes are considered a necessity and an art form in Ushallav. They symbolize the might and wisdom of our chief god, Ishka. His followers—magicians, and scientists—found a way to capture images of movement and sound to replay over and over again. It's our prime specialty and pride: it symbolizes that our gods truly see and hear all, and they share that with mortal rulers to fairly judge their people.

But in all honesty, the Eyes helped ensure the king and queen were the first to know anything and never be left fooled or surprised. Seeing the defaced Eyes truly mocked my situation; I hadn't known that I was replaced with a Makaarian woman, and she was now tasked with planning a party in record time—a party I didn't consent to.

When I came to Makaar, the Watchful Eyes were meant to be a wedding gift for Damir and me. It was meant to be a part of home and an upgrade of security to ensure peace and prosperity. It was a sign of good faith, too—Ushallav was giving Makaar their technology—and me.

At the time, Damir didn't understand the importance but welcomed it since it made me happy. There were other aspects of Ushallavi culture that he understood and embraced.

I'll have to ask him about the lack of upkeep. Maybe he didn't really understand their importance or maybe they reminded him too much of me.

I looked up at the ceiling and remembered the room where I could see all the captured images. Maybe one of the Eyes saw those responsible for killing my entourage and ruining my marriage.

The room itself isn't that far from Devraj's nursery. In fact, the room is concealed in my old rooms. The chief sorcerer saw to it.

It dawned on me that I had a huge problem. There was a huge probability that Einora moved into my rooms. She stood between me and the key to my justice. I knew the gods had to be on my side after all this time. I desperately needed to see what they saw. But it also felt like they had a cruel sense of humor.

CHAPTER
TWELVE

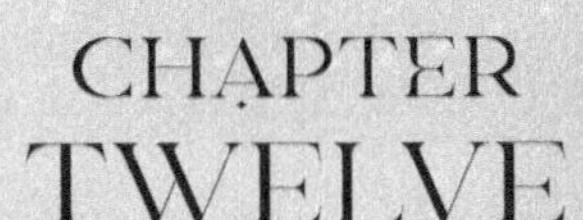

I checked on Marita and the children during lunchtime and helped Marita put them down for their naps. All the while, I pondered my next move. My answers—my closure—lay in a secret place and I had a right to see what the Eyes could see. No one—not Benedikt, or Einora, or even Damir will stop me.

I couldn't stop thinking about the Eyes, even as I played with the children and coaxed them into their beds. Once I felt that they were safe with Marita, I changed into a slightly more regal Makaarian gown and walked towards my old rooms before anything or anyone could stop me.

I knew my way to the queen's quarters easily enough, so it didn't take me long to reach the wing. I wasn't privy to the queen's schedule, so I was operating on instinct and adrenaline.

When I didn't see any guards posted in the wing, I took my chance. Sure, that wasn't necessarily a good sign, but it made my next few steps much easier. I flung open the door and held up my fists defensively. I took a quick look around the room, my brain and eyes competing to act first.

I was suddenly struck by the colors and mood of the room. Soft blues and purples accented the bed, drapes, and carpets. It seemed purposefully fashioned to look and feel like a lovely field of flowers—complete with fresh air from all the windows and some incense.

I was not alone.

A golden-haired young woman was breastfeeding a young infant. The baby fussed and snuffled at my sudden intrusion, but the young lady quickly smiled and encouraged the baby to keep sucking. I could tell she was alarmed but her expression quickly ebbed away.

Her hair curled sweetly around her collar bones. She wore a nightgown and had her blankets pulled up to her elbows. A woman—likely an attendant—rose from her seat and greeted me with a concerned and stern look.

"Can we help you? Where are the guards?" the older woman said, her tone as tight as her braided bun. I suddenly blanked and had to breathe for a moment to collect my thoughts.

"My name is Anjali—princess of Ushallav—"

"Yes, I recognize your name and features. From the

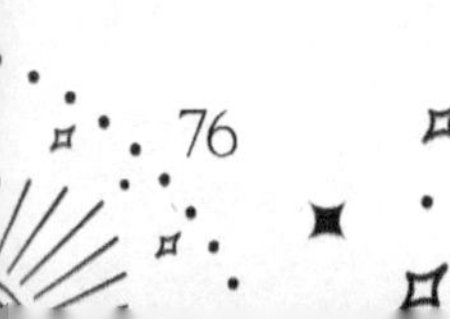

formal paintings," the breastfeeding mother said. "I'm Queen Einora and this is my midwife, Wendi. And this little man is Gregori."

She looked down adoringly at the baby.

"Oh, you're the queen," I said dumbly. She was breastfeeding in the queen's quarters and was the most beautiful Makaarian I'd ever met. She looked so serene and perfect. Perfect for this world created for her and Damir.

I forgot myself. My feet did the thinking for me, and I immediately left the room.

I could feel heat rising up my neck in embarrassment and the feeling didn't subside until I was out of my old wing. I felt resolved to try again later but at that moment, I felt so fl ustered.

I am a trained warrior. I am a princess with the fi nest training Ushallav had to off er. So why did this picturesque moment throw me off ? I'm better than this. Am I losing my touch? I knew that if my head was clearer, things would've still been awkward, but I would've done something worthy of a good fi rst impression—not stammer my own name.

"Woah, are you all right?" Damir gripped my shoulders to steady me, and I fl inched and looked up at him, unsure if I should be honest or cold with him.

He came out of nowhere and continued talking as though he didn't notice my discomfort.

"Well, I was going to let you know that the messenger is en route with your letters. If you're lucky, they'll catch up with the formal invitation. Your parents will hear from you within a few days."

"That's…very kind of you," I nodded formally as I tried to sidestep him and move on. He stepped with me and blocked the way.

"There's no one around. Can you tell me what's troubling you? I didn't think I'd expect to see you around here." Near Queen Einora's wing, which was the one detail he wasn't saying.

"Sometimes I forget that these rooms aren't mine anymore," I murmured. He bowed his head at my somewhat stinging remark.

He patted my arm affectionately but smiled slightly.

"We've kept your possessions—I made sure of it. We can move everything to your new rooms, so it feels more comfortable. I'll have my staff take care of it at once. I know you've been there for a day or so, but we're trying to take care of things as quickly as possible."

"What exactly is the plan?" I asked, wavering. "Einora and I plan a party and then decide who is getting a divorce? No tutor can teach you how to handle these sorts of things. Not even Benedikt."

Damir shook his head, smiling.

"You can stay as long as you'd like, Anjali," Damir said softly. "Even after you figure out who sabotaged your travel party. I forbid anyone from turning you or our children away. And the same goes for Einora and Gregori. You are not just a guest and you're not a problem."

I bit my lip and nodded.

"The Watchful Eyes," I began.

"What do you mean? Oh, the Eyes." Damir nodded. We walked and talked so we could talk in a more private area—his wing.

"I noticed they were covered up. Can you order them to be restored? Have a Ushallav sorcerer come fix them?" I asked before folding my arms. My stomach churned at the inflection in Damir's voice. This meant a lot to me.

"I'm sorry, my love." He looked up at a nearby scarred Eye. "When you were, uh, considered truly gone, it didn't feel right to keep them. I know they're for both of us, but they really belonged to you. At the time, it felt right."

"But I'm back now. You already said you could help me find my killers. If I can access the room and the Eyes, I can potentially use them to see what happened a few years ago. I could get clues about who is responsible for this."

"I see," Damir replied. He relaxed a few degrees. "You're right. I must still bring this to the council. You must know that this might raise some concerns—"

"Yes, I do know that the staff did not understand them and why we had them. But someone here had to know about our outing, and they might still be in this castle—in this household. You can't seriously think I want that person or group of people around our children. Or Einora and her new baby."

I did my best to keep my annoyance to a minimum. I knew I wasn't asking for much, but it certainly still felt like it. I didn't want to wait much longer to learn the truth.

Damir stroked his chin where his beard used to be.

"I'm sure we could work something out. If we don't tell anyone besides the royal family or the counsel, they won't notice the difference, will they?"

"During the party, a reliable sorcerer can restore the Eyes while ensuring they blend in with the walls. I just need them to find the information I need." Perhaps this was something I should just take on myself—I didn't need Damir and his council for this project, right?

The Eyes are a gift and very religious. It felt wrong to see them so neglected and marred. I silently prayed that Ishka would have patience with us while I fix this problem. I hoped He would still provide his sight so I could find closure.

Damir knew this already. Didn't he? Even if they made him sad, the Eyes and their wisdom would be passed on to Devraj.

"I ought to remind you that they are mine to use. And I'll need access to my old wing to use them. You can restore my furnishings and my old clothes but…"

Damir looked around and for a moment, I worried someone was listening. But he just gave me a mischievous smirk.

"You tried to sneak in."

I gaped at his very-accurate accusation.

"Don't try to pretend like this is a game. I walked in on your wife breastfeeding. Thank you for not mentioning how positively perfect she is." I couldn't bear saying much more. I folded my arms and looked away.

Damir was visibly embarrassed; his neck turned scarlet.

"I've been handling this terribly, Anjali. I'm so sorry. It is as you said—there's no formal training for such a situation."

Regardless of whether we were alone, Damir wrapped his arms around me. I let my head rest on his chest, and he rested his chin on the top of my head.

"I'm really sorry. I love you. I also love Einora. I love Devraj, Sanjana, and Gregori. And I don't know what to do because letting anyone go will just gut me."

What he wasn't saying was that the crown and castle were still dripping with old traditions. For every kingdom, there could only be one king and one queen. I knew this growing up: I would have privilege and power but everyone else would have a say in how I used such power and privilege.

When I married Damir, our love came with duty. It was our duty to soften the bigotry and mistrust between our countries. Would I fail that task if I let Einora take my spot?

"I know we need to reach a decision. But we all need time. Please don't make me and Einora plan a celebration and expect to announce anything. Honestly, my focus is on the Eyes and learning what happened. They won't lie. It'll be much easier to make this decision with you once we know who forced us into this corner in the first place."

Damir shifted. "Can I...participate? Will you show me the Eyes? I just want to help—promise."

"You didn't...sneak in there when you thought I was missing?"

Damir paused.

"I've never felt comfortable going in there without you. Do you remember we went in there a few times before the kids?"

His question tickled my memories, but I wasn't ready or willing. My arms were still folded as he tried to nudge me playfully.

"But to be serious, I didn't bring up the Eyes with my counsel. If I did, I'm sure your spirit would haunt me. We did our own investigation which involved lots of interviews and interrogations. When we didn't get any results or leads, we just ramped up our security."

"And Ray cooperated?" I asked, eyebrow quirked.

"Of course. I'm sure your brother and the rest of your family are delighted to see you soon at the party."

"We got married to show good favor after the war. I'm relieved nothing bad happened because of my absence."

"Things were…tense for a time. But nothing we couldn't talk through."

"How did they feel when you married Einora? Did you ever, uh, consider marrying an Ushallavi?"

Damir smirked slightly and looked down.

"If you'll believe it, I could not woo any Ushallavi nobility. I could barely protect you—there weren't any available prospects who wanted to fill your shoes."

"So, you're saying that Einora or her family members took pity on you."

Damir nodded. "I wasn't really my charming self when I was seeking…y'know. She was really the only one who genuinely reached out. Devraj liked her, too. I trusted his judgment."

I sighed. I wasn't enjoying this. Devraj was *my* baby.

"I worry that once my return is fully public, my assassin will return to finish the job. I just want to find out who they are before they attack again."

"Nothing will happen to the children. Marita is highly trusted and has even trained herself in medicines should the worst happen."

"What will we do if we discover the killer and they're Makaarian? Or Ushallavi?"

We winced.

"You and your handmaidens were attacked. The killers took out my soldiers, but this seems very targeted."

"What do you think I've been piecing together for two years? Someone was clearly not starry-eyed about our union. Or didn't like me. Maybe they hoped you would marry a Makaarian. Ever think of that?"

"I try not to dwell on that. Even if you never returned, my resolve never wavered. I didn't want to let that person win. If they have a problem with our alliance, they'll need to face me directly."

Damir's arms loosened so I could step away. I smoothed my hair and wiped a tear from my eye. He continued, "I look forward to hearing what you learn. It's possible that whoever tried to kill you was trying to send a message. And I want to serve justice to anyone who tries to strike you down."

"Thank you, dear." I was stunned. Damir looked tired and distant this morning. Now? This—Damir without the Benedikt—was the man I married.

"I'll talk to Einora and Benedikt. You'll have your Eyes. I'll see you at dinner?"

I nodded. I needed time with my kids after my embarrassing encounter with Einora.

Damir bowed. "And for the record, I look forward to seeing your parents and siblings soon."

"Depending on what we sort out," I said with a slightly devious smile, "my mother might not be so pleased to see you."

CHAPTER
THIRTEEN

If I waited another day to meet Damir's second wife, I would probably lose my mind. After a few hours of letting my kids nap and practice their Ushallav, I straightened the three of us up and told Sanjana we'd meet some new friends. I gave Marita a tight smile and she put a hand on my shoulder.

"Come back and chat when you're done. I'll have your favorites prepared."

Gods bless the Maritas of the world.

I held hands with both Sanjana and Devraj. Together, we walk to my old wing. I asked Devraj to knock on the door for me and he gladly did so. His knock was almost swallowed by the thick, imposing door so I knocked with him. The guards outside the room stood there; what were they supposed to do when a queen wanted to meet another queen?

Wendi, the midwife, answered the door and glanced up and down at me and my children before letting me in.

"The king and queen are expecting you," she said softly. I couldn't tell if she was just technically saying the right thing or if she was trying to rub something in. The king and queen? She knows who I am—she's seen the portraits and my son, her future king.

She opened the door enough that we could squeeze through. The children immediately darted for Damir to greet him. I merely stood there with my hands clasped behind my back. I glanced at Einora and smiled politely at her, bowing my head slightly. She returned the gesture.

I could tell immediately that we both wore outfits that suited us and could communicate to the other something that only women could communicate: *I am a queen, and you can't shake me.* My gaze pierced her form, trying to discern what her corseted dress and makeup were trying to conceal. She must've recovered quickly from her post-pregnancy pains because she looked as though she was glowing and fashionably plump in all the right areas.

I remember the days of putting on my makeup and jewelry like armor to appear like my body wasn't healing or falling apart underneath. I think back to the bandages and healer's herbs that held me in one piece after I had Sanjana. I wonder whether Einora was okay. I wonder if Wendi is her Marita. I closed my eyes briefly to focus.

I wore a dress of mine that still fit me—one of my favorites. The staff found it the day before, to my delight. The cream and gold Anarkali gown opened from the waist

to reveal matching trousers and heels. This look always makes my skin shine beautifully; I felt more like a traditional Ushallavi woman, and I couldn't help but feel proud. Marita helped me braid my long hair. Everything I wore glittered just the way I liked it.

I wanted her to know that her days in this room—in my space—were numbered.

I could tell that Einora looked at me, too. She still smiled politely but her eyes flickered at the jewelry at my wrists and neck then to my midriff.

After sizing each other up, I looked at Damir and sat down on the proffered cushion.

"I trust you both are enjoying the day thus far?" I asked. Marita always warned with a wink that my Makaarian always sounded blunt, direct, and slightly judgmental. I didn't really care in this moment.

"Yes," Damir sighed happily, taking his own seat with equal distance between me and Einora. "I hoped we could better get to know each other."

I gave him a polite, forced smile. We sat in a calculated, even triangle. The symbolism was not lost on me.

"I wanted to officially meet you sooner," Einora said, smiling, "But things with Gregori were complicated. He had to come sooner than expected. But he and I are better now."

I knew that look. There was a lot of pain behind that smile. She almost certainly fought for her life but tried to smile through the pain. Royal coffers can't take any of that agony away.

"That must've been difficult," I said in honesty. "You don't need to apologize to me for such a thing."

"Well, better now than later as they say, right?" Einora said cheerily. I couldn't imagine she was *that* happy to meet me.

"I've got you now!" Devraj bellowed.

"No, no, no!" Sanjana cried with glee. They tumbled together next to our triangle of cushions and laughed.

"What are you playing?" Damir asked with a grin.

"Sanjana taught me a game! I'm the hunter and she's the elk—I have to catch her to win," Devraj said, breathing hard from exhaustion.

"The Gavril children taught Sanjana that game," I explained. "It's similar to what Makaar children call 'soldier and robber.'"

"Ah, I see," Damir said. "She seems well-adjusted after such a long time in the mountains and away from civilization—"

I glared at him until he stopped talking. Damir tends to fill the air with babbling when he's nervous or in deep shit. I didn't need to hear any direct or indirect commentary on my solo-parenting abilities.

"Right," Damir sighed, running a hand through his hair. "Yes, well, this is a good time for you two to get to know each other."

As he said so, he stood up and smoothed his trousers.

"You're leaving?" I asked, almost panicking. *Is he serious?*

"I thought you two would be better at this without me here. Besides, I'm requested for a suit fitting for the upcoming celebration—"

"Damir," I said tersely.

88

Einora didn't say anything, but she looked apprehensive and upset, too. Wendi stood like a stoic bodyguard.

"I'll come back once I'm done," Damir said, bowing to both of us. Einora, by rote habit, inclined her head. I didn't move. He was leaving me here with *her*. Damir smiled, which looked devious from my perspective, said goodbye to the children, walked out of the room, and shut the door behind him with a soft click.

I looked down at my lap, not sure how to respond next. I wanted to be respectful and mature, but at this point, I was so angry with Damir that I could spit.

Einora laughed nervously, rocking her baby.

"I've...never been to Ushallav," Einora began. "And I bet you know so much about Makaar. Would you tell me about your home? Oh, would you like to hold Gregori?"

She quickly placed her only child in my arms before waiting for my answer. I instinctively said something in Ushallavi as it all happened. I cursed Damir's name.

After I shifted the baby into a more comfortable hold, I sighed and bounced him gently.

"Okay, you'd like to hear about Ushallav," I said, twisting my lips to the side in thought. "Well, it's definitely warmer there. We get plenty of sunshine. May I have a blanket for Gregori? I'm worried the beading and embroidery I'm wearing will—"

"Oh yes, thank you for thinking of that," Einora said. She gestured to Wendi to bring one of his blankets and the midwife brought it immediately. She looked like she really wanted to be anywhere but here.

"Wendi, I can look after my own children," I said, giving her an out. "If Einora doesn't need you, it's perfectly fine to have a moment to yourself."

The woman, just a few years older than me, looked to Einora for her input. I honestly wasn't looking forward to hearing her potentially scold my kids. They weren't well-behaved—they're still children—but there are certain types of people who sounded extra annoying when they watch *your* children.

"I'm perfectly fine, Wendi dear," Einora said. "Anjali is so thoughtful. You deserve some rest and relaxation after all your help today."

"If it pleases you, Your Highness," Wendi said. She bowed her head and didn't look at either of us. I looked down at Gregori's baby face and waited to hear the door click shut again. Einora turned to me, practically beaming.

"You must be so kind to your servants back in Ushallavi. You're so attentive."

"Yes, I do my best," I said tightly. It didn't seem like Einora mixed up *Ushallav* and *Ushallavi* on purpose, but I still bristled. "Gregori looks like a healthy young chap." I looked down at his pearly pink skin and how starkly it contrasted with my brown forearms. He looked so much like Damir. He was so tiny and adorable. I wanted to frown.

"You look well, too." I meant it.

"Oh, coming from a mother of two beautiful children, I'll take that as a high compliment," Einora blushed.

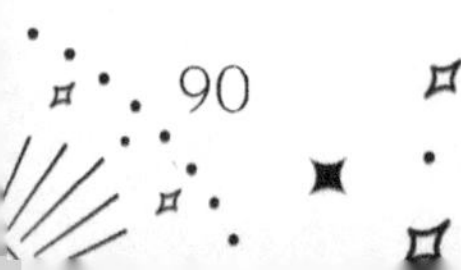

"Your arms look so strong. Are all Ushallavi women built so strong?" Would her face break with all that smiling?

"Nearly all of our women train their bodies," I answered. "All women in the royal household are specially trained for hand-to-hand combat. My maidens—attendants—train with me. It's a tradition and a safeguard against any potential threats. For me, it boosts my spirits. We build community through our strength."

"Oh my, a warrior mother. That's what you are," Einora nodded. "It must help with chasing after your little ones. Gregori just eats and sleeps like an angel which is all I can handle right now."

"He'll be a strong young man eventually," I said. "And you're a strong mother. You don't need strong arms for that."

Through my peripherals, I could see that Einora blinked her glassy eyes and dabbed the corner of her eyes quickly with her finger. I didn't say it to butter her up—it just looked like she needed to hear it. Sorely. I needed to hear that when I once lay helpless next to Sanjana in a moving wagon.

"It's so hard to feel strong when I haven't been able to walk for so long. Besides Wendi and Damir, you've been my only other visitor."

"What a shame. And here I thought the women of the court didn't visit me after having Devraj because they weren't fond of me," I rolled my eyes.

"You mean—?"

"I invited people to visit but it's common for visitors, at least according to Makaarians, to wait until the mother is strong enough. My mother and sisters-in-law didn't like being alone. I got to visit them whenever as long as I brought their favorite treats."

"How remarkable! I'll have to think of that when I'm pregnant again," Einora said, excitedly. "But I understand what you mean. Makaarian and Ushallavi women endure the same things differently, it seems."

My heart twinged twofold. It was already difficult enough to remember that this was Damir's son I was holding. Einora's experience also concerned me. Benedikt's little trick on me came to mind.

"Did someone tell you to seclude yourself or did you not ask—?" I raised a skeptical brow. I pivoted after I heard a scuffle and a cry. "Devraj, be careful with Sanjana's arms. She doesn't like that. Thank you, Devvy."

Their game and giggles resumed quickly.

"Well, I asked Wendi once, but she said I wasn't presentable. I probably wasn't. I don't think noblewomen—or at least the ones I know here in Makaar—talk about such intimate things," Einora said sadly. "You're so open about it. I could blab to you all day about Gregori and anything else that comes to my head. I'm positive I would be loony if Wendi weren't here."

Before I could consider my words, they came out, "Well, now you have me, so you don't have to feel that way."

"Do you truly mean that?" Einora said, her eyes shining. "But...? By the Firsts, you're so hard to hate."

"Pardon?" I laughed, despite myself. My ears heated up so by what I said that I barely heard her response. I was still reeling. Why did I care about her feelings and her life before meeting me?

"Oh, look at us. Sitting here cross-legged like sisters. Really, us?" Einora said. She pulled a handkerchief from her sleeve and dabbed her eyes. "For the past few days, I've just been sitting here helpless and wondering how long it would take for you or Damir to just…ship me out of here."

"You don't really mean that, do you?" As if I didn't have the same worst-case scenario looping in my mind.

"Look at you! I bet you could hold ten children in those arms! You're the most beautiful woman I've ever seen. I can totally see why Damir would fall in love with you. He only married me so Devraj could have a mother and Damir could—"

Her voice cracked when I reached out with my left hand and took hers. Gregori was still nestled in my right arm.

"*No* one is taking you or Gregori anywhere. This is a very sensitive situation but…but we don't have all the answers yet. Someone tried to kill me. *That* person should be punished."

Einora looked as white as a sheet, and her cheeks were crimson.

"You must hate me," Einora whispered, putting her other hand to her mouth.

"I don't hate you—"

"Surely, you're upset to learn that Damir already re-married," Einora said.

"Did you attack my carriage? Did you try to kill me?"

The interrogation stunned the both of us, but I kept my stare steady.

"No," came the soft reply. "I could…I would *never*." I took in a deep breath.

She looked like she needed something to hold to replace her darkest thoughts. I instinctively handed Gregori back to her. She accepted him readily and her hand immediately went to brush his thin, soft hair.

Sanjana saw her opportunity and plopped in my lap, exhausted. I didn't realize how active the two were during our chat—Sanjana was hot to the touch. I heard Devraj collapse theatrically to the ground behind me.

"Being the hunter is *hard*, Mama."

"Hunters must rest, Devvy. Come here." He scooted gleefully to my side. I see him give a soft smile to his stepmother. He didn't seem afraid or wary of her. He still clung to me, and it anchored me. Sanjana wandered off to play with one of the baby toys.

"Look," I sighed, looking for words. "We're both taking a lot in. I didn't know Damir remarried until a few days ago. You just found out that I'm alive."

Her eyes widened.

"You didn't know for so long," she breathed. "You're so brave for coming back."

Devraj nestled into my side. I didn't know how much he was paying attention.

"I missed Devraj. He's my baby."

"I'm not a baby! Greggy is a baby!" my son insisted.

"That's right. You're my big strong boy. I still wanted to give you hugs and kisses. Do you still like hugs?"

He squealed as he hugged me as tightly as possible. He squeezed a smile out of me.

Einora didn't blink at first, but then she shut her eyes and started crying.

"I'm sorry if I upset you," I murmured. This was honestly not the first time a Makaarian woman has cried because of me but *I* wanted to cry.

I turned to Sanjana and motioned for her to get up and come to me. "We can leave and give you a moment of peace—"

"No! Please don't leave!" Einora interjected feebly. She leaned forward to put a hand on my shoulder. I looked at her, bewildered, and didn't move. "Your honesty is so refreshing. And I don't deserve your kindness towards me and my son. It would be my pleasure if you all stayed. If you want to, I mean."

I looked at my exhausted children and saw a window of opportunity open to me. I'll be able to have a mature conversation *and* get my kids tucked in for naps. It takes Damir's council days to accomplish what I can do in hours.

"Your Majesty—"

"I beg you to call me Einora."

"Einora, yes. All right," I said, flustered. "There's something important I'd like to talk to you about. I'd like to talk to you about why I came back to this castle and why I was gone in the first place. I just want you to hear me speak for myself. But my children are tired. I just need to take them to their room so they can nap comfortably and under the watch of their governess."

Einora sat with bated breath.

"I promise I will leave for a moment and then come straight back," I said. "Is that okay with you?"

"Certainly," Einora breathed. "You won't be long?"

"Not at all. I promise."

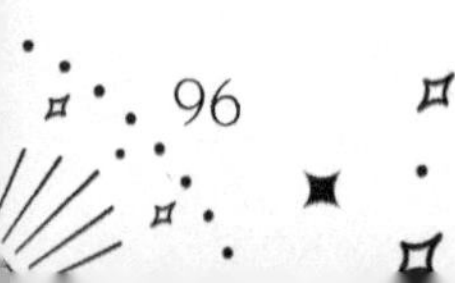

CHAPTER
FOURTEEN

Soon enough, I was right back at Gregori's nursery and knocking on the door. It took hardly a moment before Einora opened the door.

"I half expected Wendi to get the door, but then I remembered she's on break," Einora said nervously as she ushered me in. I could tell she had since recovered and refreshed herself from her crying. Gods, I'd hate to imagine if Wendi found her with tear-stained cheeks after meeting me. "You certainly kept your word."

What she didn't know was that regardless of how she felt about me, I needed access to her room. My answers were just beyond a false wall.

"So, I was hoping to ask you something. Are all Ushallavi women—or people—so frank with one another?"

I thought a bit before answering. "We believe that speaking freely means our friends are truly friends. We don't want to watch each other make unnecessary mistakes or assumptions. I'm also speaking in Makaarian—I'm told that I sound sharp in your language. There's not a lot of room for vague language."

"My, the gossip must be quite a bore," Einora giggled. "I don't think you sound sharp. You sound powerful."

"Exactly," I chuckled. "My voice is my power. Or it's considered my power where I come from. What is your power here?"

Einora paused and pondered.

"Perhaps, that power is my feelings. I just feel things and see things. I see you and what you've been through. You didn't deserve any of it."

We stood next to our cushions for a moment of silence. I blinked and smiled. Perhaps our countries needed more Einoras. The queen exhaled and gestured for me to sit.

She began, "So, you said you had something important to tell me?"

"Yes," I said, taking my seat again. She quickly checked inside the crib and smiled down at her son before joining me. "There is a secret chamber that was installed in my rooms as a wedding gift from my parents. Well, the chamber is now in your rooms."

Einora waited, her eyes bright.

"You see, the room is rightfully mine and I'd like to access it once more."

"Oh," Einora said, looking a touch disappointed. "Is that why you came to my rooms that other time?"

"Yes, embarrassingly so," I answered. Einora gave me a look like she couldn't imagine me being embarrassed about a single thing.

"What do you keep in there?" Einora said. "Is it an extra wardrobe?"

"I keep…information," I said. "Have you heard of the Watchful Eyes? Do you see them in the hallways?"

Einora shook her head no but looked keen on learning more. I had a feeling that she doesn't tilt her head to look up very often.

"They represent the eyes of the Ushallavi god, Ishka—He is all-seeing and all-knowing. It was a gift from my parents as part of tradition."

"So, these eyes are like spies? It sounds like a bizarre present if you ask me."

I chuckled. "I'm not trying to convince you otherwise. But they may explain what happened to me two years ago. I can see into the past. Did Damir explain what happened to me?"

"Damir told me what he knew at the time," Einora replied solemnly. "To think someone would attempt to murder a pregnant woman, let alone the queen—"

"We never caught those responsible," I said, bravely taking her hand. "Because we don't know who nearly killed me, I went into hiding. I was protected by the Gavril people. These attackers tried to take Sanjana from me before she could even arrive, Einora. I cannot rest peacefully until I discover who the killer is—or who hired them. The Eyes could tell me if someone in the castle is responsible."

"You think someone in the castle did this?" Einora gasped. She glanced over to the crib warily.

"You more than anyone understand why we need answers. Even if the proof shows that everyone here is innocent, I just need to know."

"I need to see this for myself," Einora said.

"You mean—?"

"I can't forbid you from something rightfully yours," Einora said, placing her free hand over mine. "But I want you to show me. Please."

I stood up from my seat. I wasn't sure if I was willing to negotiate that. I wasn't sure if my heart could open up for her. For Gregori. For anyone else. It felt like giving and surviving and sacrificing. But the way I saw her walk to the crib, grasp the edge, and clench her other fist…

I took a beat to breathe.

"Sure. I'll show you. We'll have to use your private chambers. Will you take Gregori, or will Wendi come back?"

Einora picked up her son with speed and care. He sniffled as she gave me a determined look.

"Wendi doesn't need to come back."

Einora lead the way to her private room, which was just a door or so down the hallway. I knew the way, but they were her rooms right now. No one was around to witness the two queens walking shoulder to shoulder.

She opened the doors, and I was barraged by natural perfumes, light silks decorating the windows and furniture, and flowers. Again, it was the room that looked like a field of blue flowers.

100

"All right," Einora said. "I am very much excited to see this room." She stood in the middle of the room as if anticipating it to appear anywhere. I sighed and went to the top right corner to the left of Einora's bed. There was a small table there, so I gently moved it to the side so I could pass by.

"You must understand that I would like privacy opening the door," I said. "Besides Damir, you're the only one who knows that it exists. Please don't tell anyone, okay?"

"I promise," Einora smiled. She gently shifted Gregori in her arms, so his little face scrunched into her right shoulder before turning her back to me. I had to smile.

My body shielded the quick movement that clicked the door open. There's a slight catch that springs a segment of the wall up and away from the rest of the wall.

"Most peculiar," Einora breathed.

I looked at her, then her bed, then back to her. Einora seemed really impressed.

"Ushallavi architects aren't the only ones who know how to create false walls and secret passageways. This castle has a few secrets of its own."

Einora looked eager to learn more but didn't move from her spot.

"Would you…like to come inside?"

Einora nodded nobly, almost relieved, and joined me. I pushed the door and it slid to the right and gave us enough room to pass.

"I won't shut the door," I offered. Einora didn't respond but looked around instead. It was pretty dark and musty. The room is small enough that it felt dangerous to allow fire to light the room, so I felt around in the dark for the heavy curtains and pulled them to the side. Long slits in the castle walls allowed discreet light to pierce the room. The afternoon light greeted us and illuminated the dust.

"How do you see the information? Or make sense of it?"

I hesitated briefly and resolved to turn on the mechanics that opened the Eyes. Well, I never turned them off, per se, but I do have to get the mechanics up and working to reveal what I wanted to see.

I coughed slightly. Everything was covered in a thin layer of dust. It felt like uncovering an artifact even though this was only abandoned for a couple of years.

To answer Einora's question, I approached a panel and rotated a knob. It went in a huge circle like I was charting a circle on a map. After a few rotations, I turned to her and said,

"I'll show you. But I'll have to close the curtains again. Do you want to stand or sit?" I closed the curtains and again she looked around, her eyes hungry to drink everything in.

Images suddenly flickered across the ceiling, and I craned my neck to see them.

"I normally lounge on the cushions on the ground and stare up at the images like they're stars in the sky," I found myself saying. "I used to watch the images and breastfeed Devraj before he would fall asleep."

"How remarkable."

The images were pretty normal. They depicted people walking through the hallways. Based on what I saw, I could

see that they found half of the eyes and had them covered up. There were spots in the ceiling that were blacked out, so I could tell which Eyes were opened and which ones were covered or gone.

"So, this is what Ushallavi queens do with their time? Spy on their staff?"

"Oh yes, and we spy on our people, too," I said, wryly. She turned to me in shock, and I laughed. "It's not what you think. The Eyes are seen as a spiritual thing—it reminds us that the gods see our actions and our hearts. If there is an injustice, we can settle issues with or without the Eyes. It's not perfect but it's tradition. Maybe the Eyes will show me who is responsible for all this."

I sighed and paused. The images I saw were relatively the same as they always looked. It would take some time to notice anything suspicious that would aid my cause.

"I didn't really use this room very much," I said softly. "Just on the days that I felt lonely."

"Lonely? You?" Einora piped up. "I would imagine that I would have a hard time leaving you alone if I had the choice."

I paused for a moment. I had no idea where Einora was from—what her family's social situation once was. Perhaps she didn't know what life was like here for someone like me.

"You were a part of the court, were you not?"

"Oh, yes," Einora said. She was looking up at the images and not at me. "I'm embarrassed to say but there was a rumor that you didn't accept visitors to your chambers and that you hardly spoke a word of Makaarian. I could be misremembering—I do that sometimes."

I chuckled and shook my head.

"I thought you were comfortable with how things were, and we were just in the way," Einora mused. "It looks like my assumptions led me astray. And now I wonder if people feel the same about me. Either way, I certainly hope the Eyes tell you what you need to know. There *is* an injustice that They must sort out."

She repositioned Gregori and smiled at me. I found myself smiling back.

"I'll be honest, I'm really upset at Damir for leaving us alone today. But look at us. We could find the assassin together before the rest of his council put their trousers on."

Einora laughed like I was a jester. I couldn't help but smile. I hated to admit it, but I can see why Damir found solace and love in Einora. Besides Marita and Damir, she's the only one that helped me feel like I could actually right these wrongs.

"My queen, Anjali—"

"Please, just call me Anjali."

Einora blushed in the dark. "Anjali, what will we do when we catch them?"

"I've been thinking about it for a *long* time. I've trained for it. They'll be alive just long enough to confess."

I don't know if this answer satisfied Einora; she didn't say anything.

I rotated the knob in the opposite direction and the images faded from the ceiling. The projector petered out, but I could hear the hum of the system still working and subtly recording.

Pleased, I sighed. It felt good to see something so Ushallavi again. Soon enough, we were out of the room and the door clicked back into place.

CHAPTER
FIFTEEN

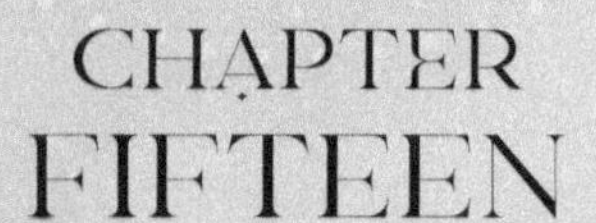

I discretely closed the door and it melted seamlessly into the rest of the wall. I turned around to see Einora with her back to me, giving me similar privacy as if I were changing my clothes. I smirked.

"Oh, it sounds like you're finished," Einora said, before turning around. "It's just so important to you—I didn't want to ruin anything."

"Don't worry about ruining anything," I said, then smiled. "I would've come in here regardless—even if I had to break in."

Einora frowned. "Well, I don't like that alternative at all."

She twisted her face in such a way that I could tell she was being comical, and it worked. I laughed and shook my head until she broke character and giggled with me.

"Anjali," Einora said, returning to seriousness. "I don't deserve any of your kindness. I must be fair and honest with you. It's been quite difficult to know you're here and wondering what you think of me. I feel like a mistress or a whore rather than a queen or a wife. I've told myself many times that I should just make Damir take you back. I could be happy with just Gregori, right?"

I stood, stunned. This felt like too much to handle at the moment. I was stunned. She just kept talking.

"I don't think I would be this kind if the roles were reversed," Einora whispered. She bowed her head. "You're so brave."

I cringed at the word *brave*. Brave? That word didn't feel right to me. I coughed and shook my head.

"There's something more to this, isn't there?" I held up a finger and she stopped talking. I continued, "Who would ever make you feel this way? Does Damir tell you these things?"

"Oh, no," Einora sputtered. "He has never been cruel to me."

"Then who is it? Benedikt? Your parents? Wendi?"

Einora shook her head as though in a nightmare.

"I-I don't think anyone would say it to my face but isn't it obvious? I was your replacement. You're the sun and I'm but a distant star."

"Einora, please. This…this doesn't help you, me, or Gregori—no, no, no."

She was already crying as she heard her self-deprecating talk escape its prison. Without thinking, I pulled her in for a hug. My left arm draped over her right shoulder and my other hand wrapped gently around Gregori's wrapped form. We shared a moment where I wrapped my arms around her, and her forehead sunk into my shoulder and neck area.

"I think you, Damir, and I are under a lot of stress. But we're going to figure this out. We need to find this assassin, right? We're going to do whatever is best for this moment and for our kids. Your son is just as much of a prince as mine. I'll be damned if anyone says anything different."

I felt Einora nod and then pull herself away. She pulled a dainty handkerchief and dabbed the inner corners of her eyes.

"My mind—sometimes I can't really think straight. You know what I mean—I don't have to explain it. Thank you for trusting me and Gregori. I think your children are charming and smart. And the room with the Eyes is wonderful."

I nodded. I absolutely understood what she meant. It's not easy being a mother *and* a queen. And yet here we are.

"Well, I know that I might be the last person you want to spend time with, but I could use a friend. Wendi is nice but I like you a lot. And more importantly, I want to help however I can. It just seems like so much to take on yourself—maybe I presume too much. Shouldn't Damir take care of this? I don't doubt your strength, but the emotional labor of it all…I know couldn't do it all alone."

My chin trembled but I otherwise held firm. "I've got you, so I don't have to do anything alone."

"Someone tried to hurt you. I don't like it. I…won't stand for that. Mother to mother, that's not right."

Einora shifted her stance a bit. She stood a bit taller. The tears in her eyes made her glow a bit. I wanted to say something, but I pressed my lips into a line. Something planted deep in my heart, and I almost started to cry.

"I hope you know how much I appreciate that." I cleared my throat. "I just want to say one more thing. I'm still concerned with the way you talk about yourself. For what it's worth, you're still married to Damir. Shouldn't you share these feelings with him?"

I could tell that she was not prepared for that. Her cheeks pinked at the suggestion as she answered,

"I feel it will only make it worse. Seeing me would only remind him of what he's losing because I'm here."

As much as I wanted Damir to choose me without question or committee, I knew that was self-doubt talking.

"You love him," I replied firmly. "Right?"

"Yes," came the soft, urgent reply. "But maybe not enough. I feel like a fraud. I don't deserve these gowns, these stone walls, or Damir's heart. You do."

I looked at Einora and for a moment, none of us could find more to say. Well, I knew exactly what to say. I could break this girl's resolve in half. But I wasn't mad at her. I just couldn't get myself to hate her. I'm not sure about Damir, but I just couldn't wish her ill will.

"Look, I know what you're going through. More than anyone else here. You've joined Damir's world. And he doesn't exactly know the sacrifices you've made. You're tired all the time and questioning yourself. It's normal. It's only fair to yourself and your son if you advocate for yourself."

"Your words are like spun gold," Einora said. She giggled a bit as Gregori stretched and started to cry. She addressed him and then me, "I'm here, I'm here. Yes, if I want to know what the king thinks of me, I shall ask him myself."

Why was I being so *nice*? I felt caught between appreciating Einora's budding friendship with me and recognizing that she was the reason why my return was so fraught.

"Spoken well, Your Majesty," I nodded. All this calculating and questioning took a lot out of me. Despite herself, Einora threw her left arm around me, and we both giggled. I giggled and sniffed back tears and emotion.

We remained there in silence. I wasn't sure what to do or think first.

"Well, I'm rather hungry," Einora chimed in wearily. "Do you suppose it's time for a snack or two?"

"Perhaps," I answered. "But I'll order some for my children in their room."

"We could all eat together," Einora offered.

"Oh," came my forced reply. "I just need some rest. But I will join you, Damir, and the rest at dinner this evening, and I'd love to share food with you another time."

"Oh! Of course. Well, now that I've formally met you, I really do hope to see you more often. I hope we can become friends."

At this point, I was heading for the door and my hand hovered over the door handle. At that moment, I felt a lot of things at once. She was right—it was difficult to hate her and see her as my enemy. Here I am considering her an ally.

As I looked up, she was still standing in the middle of the room. She positioned Gregori so he was on her chest, and he rested his chin on her shoulder. He snuffled and cried as though he was ready to eat. Einora stood with gleaming eyes as if she wasn't ready to be left alone.

"We're going to find this assassin. Together." I grasped the door handle. "Just like everyone else in this castle, you won't be rid of me so easily."

Sanjana, still sound asleep, lay in her bed with her bottom in the air and drool trickling against her cheek. Despite my motherly stealth, my son stirred. His sweaty hair was stuck to his forehead and neck.

"Mama," he whispered for me. I scooped him in my arms and held him close. Oh, I was never leaving him again. Sight and sound until he gets married and even then, I wonder if I'll ever recover from the two years robbed from me.

I stroked his hair and watched him fall asleep once more. I gingerly slipped a blanket between his face and my embroidered dress and trousers. I probably should have just changed into a lighter gown, but I wasn't about to trade this moment of solitude for the world. My son still needed me and that's all that mattered.

I eventually laid myself down on the rug and encouraged my son to lay on the blanket near me. I closed my eyes and thought about what happened. Einora not only seemed like a great stepmother to Devraj while I was away, but she wants to help me catch my assassin.

Interesting.

As Einora plans the party and I pick up the pieces, I can let the court do its scheming. Let people talk. Let gossip reign. Meanwhile, I will be able to take note of who seems to disapprove of our unlikely friendship. Perhaps my win is their loss; I could potentially lure the guilty party out from the shadows.

My main concern was the children—all three of them. This killer—whoever they are—was not above harming any of us. Einora might think that being my friend is helping but I doubted she was in a place where she could defend herself should the worst happen. I still held my suspicions that my enemy knew exactly where and when to find me. I likely knew their name. I tried to put that thought away for now. Instead, I thought about whether Einora had time from now until the party to do some training with me.

I grinned. Okay, so Makaarians aren't all so bad. Except for Damir. He better look damn fine in that suit at the party.

CHAPTER SIXTEEN

I didn't have a moment's rest between my first conversation with Einora to the festival she was asked to prepare for me. My brain buzzed with a lot of conflicting feelings.

Anjali, you want to be queen…right? What are you doing?

Before I found out the truth about Einora, I planned to return, ensure Devraj was well, find my killer, and make a lot of changes in the castle. I admit, I once focused a lot on motherhood—it took a lot out of me—and let Damir take on more of the politics. I could see that for our united dream to come true, Makaar and Ushallav needed me. They needed me and my maidens in those council meetings. They needed to see that a world where everyone got along was a world worth protecting. I didn't want Devraj or Sanjana to feel like guests in their own home.

As much as I saw the potential for a friendship with Einora, I needed to act for myself and my children. I can't be the handmaiden for Einora. If I respected her as Damir's partner, I would trust that she can handle her problems on her own. I just won't add to them.

Satisfied with my ponderings, I wrote them down. I kept a secret bound journal to write down things like funny things the kids say but also these important ideas about my almost-murder. Unless I wrote them down, they would linger in my mind until they soured.

I put down my quill and spend some time soaking up Devraj's sunshine. Marita and I helped my children practice their Ushallavi. We wanted them to feel comfortable once reunited with their extended family members.

During the party planning days, Damir and I tried to keep things strictly business to the public eye. Sometimes, I gave in to sleeping in his bed and reminiscing on our early married years, but I couldn't get Einora out of my mind the next morning. We didn't tell her about our shared nights, and I felt bad about it. Again, Damir was still legally my husband, but the feelings still lingered. So, it was mostly party planning by day and reuniting by night.

Einora peppered me with questions as she put together our celebration-turned-festival. I started to look forward to smelling all the familiar smells from home. She also told Wendi that she wanted to go on daily walks to get out of her rooms or consult the chefs or decor experts.

This gave me ample time to visit the room of Watchful Eyes. Well, the ones that still worked.

So thus, we three adults focused on taking each day at a time—none of us wanted to look the future in the eye.

I normally enjoy parties—especially ones celebrating me. But I don't enjoy political parties done to appease a handful of nobodies. I could tell the other noble families wanted to get an up-close look at me, my children, and how we were faring.

Seeing my parents was the only part of the festivities that I was looking forward to. I wanted to speak my native language and hug them. It's been so long.

The perfume on my mother's neck brought tears to my eyes. She brought the smell of home with her. She took me into her arms, and one of her hands held the back of my head. After she whispered some words of comfort in my ear, I hugged my father. He kissed my forehead like I was still his young princess.

My mother swore not to cut her hair ever again due to my passing—her dramatic flair, and nothing concerning actual tradition—so she had her massively long hair braided for me to see and admire. Father had a bit of gray and white hair peppering his black hair and whiskers. I wasn't sure if it was my sudden "passing" or current trade disputes with neighboring countries that made him look wizened and tired.

"Mother, father," I began. Devraj interrupted me and squealed with delight. He called out for his grandparents in Ushallavi. He practiced all morning. My parents, Jagdish and Indali, knelt to meet Devraj and they kissed his face and hands. I picked up my shy and smiling Sanjana. My parents looked up; their eyes moist.

"Princess Sanjana, we're so happy to meet you," my father said in Ushallavi. Sanjana nodded in understanding. She reached out a hand and let them hold her together. I drank in the scene as the king and queen of Ushallav doted on their grandchildren proudly and joyfully.

"Sanjana is perfect. How I wish we could've seen her when she was born. But no matter, she is wonderful. You look well, too."

"Mama, we'll have plenty of time to catch up. I promise."

"It's good to see you, sister," came another familiar voice.

I didn't think I'd be so happy to see my family, but there stood my oldest brother and the sitting king of Ushallav. King Ray and his wife Tejal sauntered into the throne room. Their children squealed and hugged me before approaching my kids—their cousins. I gave them each a hearty hug.

"I hope you're doing well during this time," my sister-in-law whispered in my ear. "If you need anything, Ray wants to help however he can."

"I know. It's good to see you, my queen."

I turned a bit and noticed that Damir was standing behind me with his hands behind his back. He looked dashing in that suit that he fitted for during my meeting with Einora. Next to him stood a very nervous and sweet

Einora. She held Gregori close. She looked beautiful in a lilac gown and her hair braided under her crown. Einora curtsied as well as she could while holding Gregori.

My parents, Ray, and Tejal smiled politely as I introduced everyone.

With a slight accent, my mother returned the bow and said in Makaarian, "It is nice to meet you, Queen Einora."

I could tell my parents were being polite. We all knew what it looked like—what it felt like. They were being polite for my sake but also to play nice politically. Ray and Tejal bowed to Damir and Einora—royalty acknowledging royalty.

"We are all happy that you all made it safely. We'll show you to your rooms and we hope you join us for dinner."

In no time, we collected in the guest wings. Their traveling party practically brought the moon as a gift. My children and I received mounds of new and lovely clothing. It was as if my mother thought I was still wearing my traveling rags. The children each received way more toys than I could imagine possible, and I received new and updated training gear—mama loves her gear. They brought plenty of materials for me to teach my children Ushallavi and other cultural matters. My parents didn't skimp at all—and they certainly packed like they didn't expect anything but my return to the throne.

They noticed my hesitancy in my letters and in my demeanor—so unbecoming of me.

"Anjali, if you're not trying to take this man back, then what's keeping you here under his roof?" Mama asked. Father was in full play mode with my children and the other grandchildren on the floor. It was something I could only imagine my male relatives or Damir doing.

I sighed. "I must get justice and find the person or group that tried to murder me—and successfully murdered everyone traveling with me. Mama, I was pregnant with Sanjana. I must do what I can to see that person hanged for trying to take Sanjana away from us."

"And your marriage," Mama nodded with a frown. "Are you the queen of this country or not? Damir has a good heart. But you need to take care of yourself. There are plenty of good men—and women—with good hearts out there."

"Thanks, Mama," I said, nodding at her. I know she was only trying to help—but this was beyond all of us. "I am focused on trying to figure out what I'll do once I find my assassin. I can't say for sure who's responsible. It could rip apart all the work you and father have put into establishing peace."

My mother's eyes gleamed. The warrior in her energized.

"I need time to work with the Eyes. I...it hurts too much to think about anything else right now."

"You love him." She cupped my cheek with her hand and my eyes welled with tears. "You are a good queen. A good mother. A good woman. Just please tell us what you want to do. You have our support. The Eyes will guide you where we cannot."

"Mama—"

"You would've been the best thing to happen to Makaar," Mama said, pulling me close. "But it looks like fate can't stop that. Your legacy can be raising a fine prince and princess—the finest Makaar has ever seen."

I knew that was a possibility. The throne was still mine for the taking. No one could fault me for it—not even Damir's cold adviser, Benedikt. But something gripped me and asked me to reconsider. It was not kindness for Einora. It was some kind of kindness for myself. Something I hadn't thought of since I was engaged to Damir.

"I've truly missed you," I murmured with a smile. I leaned over and nestled between her cheek and shoulder like I did as a younger girl. She kept me there with a hand over my head and ear. "I needed you out there in the woods."

"You can stay with us after all of this is over. As long as you need," she said. "As long as you have the cute children with you, I won't let you go very far."

"Oh good," I chuckled. "I'm glad I have the proper bargaining chips."

"But they're treating you well here? Until you make your final decision?"

The adults present craned their necks to listen, even though they were busy interacting with the children or with those bringing in luggage and packages.

"They're helping me and the children as best as they can. Damir and Einora are being very gracious. Say, when is everyone else coming in?"

"Harshad and his wife will get in soon," Father said from the floor. "You know how newlyweds can be. Although they are very happy to see you and the children."

"They'll be here later tonight when most of us are asleep," Ray added. "I'm staying up to welcome them properly."

"So dutiful to your siblings," I said with a sly grin. "You haven't been so nice to us since you realized how heavy the crown is."

"It keeps my head warm at night," Ray smirked. His children were old enough to read and they were playing with the younger children or reading. Sanjana and Devraj took a liking to their cousins immediately.

"Just promise you won't embarrass me too much at the celebration tomorrow evening," I said, giving a glare to everyone in the room.

"What? You don't want people to notice you're there? Even though the celebration is for you?" Father said, rolling over and positioning himself so he could look back at me.

"We even heard that we would meet the Gavril people," Mama smiled. "It will be good to meet them. Especially this Claudiu fellow. Where is he?"

My brother gave me a look as though he suspected Claudiu was more than a friend.

"He traveled back to his camp to bring them back into the kingdom," I explained to my mother, then I turned to Ray. "And he's still mourning the loss of his wife. You'd do well not to insinuate anything more about him."

His eyebrow cocked.

"I'm not his type," I said dryly. "I swear, you're worse than a gossipy auntie."

"Anyway, we'll get settled in. Know that I expect to hear more about your plans before we leave. As your brother and as your king." Ray has never been this stern or mature in all my days.

My brother rose to his full stature with his hands behind his back. His days of shirking his duties and pranking his brother and sister were over. Now, he wanted to bring closure to the mystery behind the assassination of his sister and unborn niece.

I owed my family an explanation, but I didn't know how many times I could repeat myself.

"I'm handling each day at a time." I looked my brother in the eye, wishing he would not look down on me and my situation. "I will use the Eyes to uncover the truth. And the next step will come down to who plotted all of this. I will need your support regardless of whether the villain is Ushallavi or Makaarian."

He looked upset that I would dare accuse one of his subjects of this deed. I cut him off.

"Things were fragile when I married Damir and it's clear that there's still something driving a wedge between our kingdoms. You and I both know that my travel plans were very private—and yet disaster struck us en route at a *very* convenient location. Someone with power is responsible and I will consider everyone suspect until the Eyes prove otherwise."

I looked around; some of the adults were distracting the children on my behalf. Sanjana looked up at me; her eyes round and trusting. As if she knew my thoughts, she toddled over to me and raised her arms until I picked her up. She was with me and still trusted me.

Ray gave me a crooked smile that calmed me down. He looked at us and nodded.

"We're here to celebrate you today. Soon, we'll get to work."

SEVENTEEN

Everyone entered ceremoniously to take their seats. Gods, I don't miss planning these stuffy parties. Per Einora's arrangements, we followed the order of the royal procession: my parents, Ray and his family, Damir and Einora—holding a jovial Gregori, then me with the children.

By the time I came in, everyone was standing and waiting to see me. I didn't try to upstage Einora at all, so we were equally matched in the current fashions of our homelands. I wore a lehenga choli—a top and a long silk skirt that flared out enough to sit comfortably and still fill my belly with food. My mother brought an outfit in my favorite colors: deep crimson and white. The dress itself didn't have sleeves and had a modest neckline, but the beading and jewelry work that decorated the bodice and cape that trailed behind me was no modest matter.

Mama's entourage braided my hair nicely and added fresh jasmine to create a natural crown to enhance the small circlet on my head. The one I wore as Makaar's queen. It matched the armbands on my biceps—as both were decorated with the same sapphires and diamonds.

Einora looked absolutely radiant and happy as I approached her and Damir standing together. We formally bowed to each other, but I made a mental note to speak with Einora to compliment her on her gown. I know she was happy to truly wear something extravagant as the white and gold gown she wore, but I think she was more delighted to celebrate with us and show off her son. This was her realm and she governed it well. The way she let her hair hang around her like ribbons of sunshine really added to her merry look. When I smiled at her, it was genuine.

"I hope this will be a good evening for you," Einora murmured. "This is all for you."

I nodded and gave Damir a polite look before taking my seat at his other side. He does, in fact, look damn fine in his suit and crown. The suit in question was a curious mix of Makaarian and Ushallavi influence: his trousers and tunic were tailored to look much like what his forefathers wear in their portraits, but the embroidery and colors were noticeably a nod to Ushallavi shores. I admired his ability to seamlessly marry—pun intended—the two together for a brilliant look.

My family sat together at the next table over. We wouldn't be separated for long; Einora arranged that everyone would have a seat, but everyone could mingle and try foods at other tables as the event went forward. The room held low, long tables laden with foods of every color and flavor. I and my children lingered by the bowls heaped with jasmine rice, curry, and dates, among other delicacies. There were cushions to eat either at the tables themselves or the guests could grab their food and lounge elsewhere in the room on other soft cushions.

As I sat down, my children clamored on my lap. They wore matching outfits that Mama delighted in designing and commissioning. They didn't wear jewels, but the embroidery was magnificent. They matched my lehenga choli in fabrics and style so there was no questioning which children belonged to me. I looked to the table that Damir and Einora occupied. Devraj and Sanjana deserved to sit there—as rightful prince and princess. There were technically vacant seats for me and my children but the image of Damir sitting by all his wives and children felt…like something I still wasn't ready to face. I still leaned over to my children and told them,

"If you would like to sit and eat with Papa, you can. You can move around and sit anywhere you like." Sanjana snuggled close to me and stuffed a date in her mouth, but Devraj looked excited.

"Maybe after I sit by Grandpa," he said with a huge grin on his face.

"That's my little prince!" Father bellowed merrily. He mussed Devraj's hair and my son buried his face in my father's tunic for a hug. My father laughed and pulled my son close.

As if Papa's joy were a cue, the music began and signaled the start of the feasting.

We tried our best to mingle with the other partygoers, but there were still some uncomfortable glances across the room. We had a celebration like this for my wedding, but it was clear that people on either side weren't quite warming up to the idea yet. The brave ones who wanted to look good in Damir's eyes ventured over to our party to greet my family and say something remotely intelligent to my parents and eldest brother.

Ray excused himself from his seat and went to Damir to talk and exchange pleasantries. I remember how Ray was the first to accept Damir as my love. He didn't tease me for fancying a Makaarian, even though our marriage was largely arranged by our parents. I was surprisingly touched that my brother and spouse shook hands briefly before embracing. Sure, politics was the undertone of everything that happened this weekend, but they honestly acted like close friends reuniting once more. Damir gestured to Einora and Ray kissed her hand politely.

Damir caught me watching them and I quickly looked away. It was like meeting and courting him all over again—staring and then looking away. Not wanting to openly admit my admiration and interest in him while wanting to be closer to him. I shook my head. My younger self died in the woods on that fateful day. She was gone.

"Your Majesty, you look wonderful," a Gavril woman

smiled at me. The Gavril people were given fresh clothes and spa-like treatment for the special occasion. It was my honor to see them sharing the table with my parents.

"Thank you, dear," I answered with a smile. Another one kept profusely thanking us for the invitation and special treatment. She earned a massive eye roll from Claudiu. It was fun to see him dressed up so nicely. He didn't let anyone cut his beard and hair, but someone managed to wash it and style it similar to Makaarian fashion. Smooth and wavy. I'm sure his mind was elsewhere. Out of respect, he approached me and greeted me, but I could tell that this was not his preferred way to celebrate. Too many people.

He bowed and spoke in simple Makaarian, "Did you get everything you wanted?" He turned and looked at Einora before turning to me.

"Things are complicated. I haven't given up hope," I answered. He looked around the room once more.

"It isn't safe for you or Sanjana until you find the killer."

"If you see anything amiss, I would appreciate any information. This is not just a party. This is a hunt."

"If I didn't see your morning training routine, I would think that you were crazy." He nodded, impressed and wary.

"This room has two royal families. Everyone's on high alert or on their best behavior." I patted his arm.

"Attention guests and family," my brother bellowed. "Thank you for your gracious hospitality. Today, we honor the return of my sister and my niece."

The room politely clapped and waited for Ray to continue.

"As many of you know, a Ushallav queen owes her serenity to her maidens." He gestured to the group of wizened women who surrounded my mother and the younger generation of women around his wife. Those grannies could easily wrestle Damir and win. I would pay good coin to watch them dogpile on Benedikt.

"A queen surrounds herself with quick, strong, and compassionate warriors. Anjali's maidens fought bravely and were lost to an unknown enemy."

I gasped at the memory. Swaran, Gamani, Leela, Maliha, and Neha. We trained together as young women, and they accepted the call to protect me once I became queen. They traveled to Makaar to guide me and help me feel connected to my culture and my roots. They took turns watching Devraj so I could feed him and sleep. They helped me recover body and spirit from pregnancy. They were my sisters. I could still see their faces smeared with blood and dirt. I thought I mourned them, but their sacrifice still gutted me. Why was my brother bringing up such a personal and deep wound?

"As we honor these warriors for their sacrifice, I would like to announce a surprise for my queen-sister."

Ray gestured to the entryway of the room and four beautiful and strong women marched into the party room. They wore matching attire: teal vests, pearl-shimmering sleeves, and trousers in a matching teal hue. Their hair hung long and straight and their chins pointed out and proudly.

The Makaarians seemed wary of the new arrivals. This party couldn't mend old wounds just like that. Benedikt in particular took a sip from his cup and tried not to give away his emotions.

The women walked quietly towards where I stood in the room—Claudiu at my side. They looked at me—I could tell they hoped I was surprised in a good way.

"Maiden trains maiden as a queen trains the next queen. Today, I present Queen Anjali's new maidens."

My family was clearly delighted by the surprise, and they applauded. The Makaarian nobles painted themselves to look impressed and unaffected. I stole a quick glance around the room. Einora looked happy for me but slightly nervous. Damir gave me an encouraging but sad smile. I hardly spoke to him since my family arrived.

I looked at the three women before me. I broke the formal air by spreading my arms wide and pulling them all in for a hug.

"We are happy to see you, Your Majesty," one of them whispered. I felt overcome as my children came to my side and looked up curiously at the women.

"These are your protectors," I told them.

"Will they play?" Sanjana asked. The women smiled and two of them picked up each of my children. One of them seemed very familiar. Sure enough, it took me a few seconds to recognize the hand tattoos. I wasn't expecting the several scars on her arms and face.

"Leela?" I said quietly, but loud enough to get her attention.

"My lady?" Leela returned.

Leela was *my* handmaiden. She was there. I saw her bleeding to death in the forest that day.

"Leela, you're alive?"

I immediately reached out and grasped her shoulder. She wrapped an arm around me and Sanjana who was still in her left arm.

"My lady, it is so good to see you," she said into my shoulder. We parted after a fierce hug and we both found tears streaming down our faces. Leela dabbed the tears away before my eye makeup could smear.

Mama looked up at the commotion and asked, "What is going on, my Anjali?"

"Everyone," I said, mostly to my family, "This is Leela. She was one of my handmaidens that accompanied me on that day I was ambushed in the woods. She survived!"

Leela put my daughter down so she could put one hand in a fist and grasp it with her other hand in a gesture of quiet strength and modesty—the way handmaidens of the royal family show their reverence.

"It is true. I almost didn't make it, but by the will of Abhijita, I stand before you today. And I can testify of our fierce Anjali's wit and strength."

Someone survived. A fellow witness. One step closer to closure.

I had to sit down, and I steadied my hand on my mother's shoulders as I returned to my cushion.

"What is wrong?"

"I'm fine," I replied, but when I looked up, it was actually Einora attentively at my side.

130

"I know that look. You're feeling lightheaded," Einora murmured. She called for a damp cloth and a servant left to fulfill her request. Claudiu and Damir stood nearby, watching over me.

"It's all coming back," was all I could say. My children grabbed my hands as though their touch alone could revive me. I smiled at them as best as I could as someone administered the cloth to my forehead, and I began my breathing practice to calm my heart.

"I'm so sorry if my appearance has upset you," Leela said, kneeling next to me.

Ray came up to me, alarmed.

"I didn't think you would faint at my grand surprise, little sister. Forgive me. She arrived a few months ago after we thought she was lost to the woods. Once we learned you were alive, she has been training to be by your side once more."

"It took me a long time to recover from my wounds," Leela said, turning her neck in a way that I could see a puckering scar trailing from her ear to her shoulder. "But I was reunited with the Ushallavi household. They offered me refuge so I could recover and mourn. It brings me great joy to see you again, my queen."

"Lords and ladies," Einora said, as she stood and straightened herself. "Leela, one of Anjali's late handmaidens has reunited with her queen. Our Anjali is overjoyed at their reunion. A toast, for two friends who were once thought dead and are now with us today."

Everyone raised their glasses in unison, my family included, and everyone drank to our reunion.

"Thank you, Einora," I said. I could tell the rest of

the room was murmuring in concern or curiosity at my sudden weakness.

"How did I do?" Einora asked me, smiling helpfully.

"Perfectly," I smiled back. I leaned up and away from my mother so I could sit by my own strength.

"Leela," I said, matching Einora's hostess voice, "Tell us your tale of what happened three years ago."

I looked to Damir, wondering if he was embarrassed for me or because of me. He stood at his spot, frozen in place. I could tell he wasn't sure what to do but held Gregori in his arms so Einora could keep things merry and peaceful. He nodded, and I realized Leela was also looking to him for permission. Everyone waited.

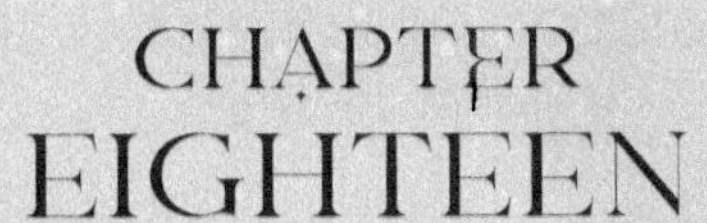

CHAPTER
EIGHTEEN

I rubbed my stomach as the carriage lurched on. My hips and backs were padded generously with pillows to accommodate for the bumpy ride.

The silence was marvelous. I didn't realize just how much I was looking forward to this trip until the last wardrobe suitcase was fastened to the carriage and the driver snapped the reins. As I closed my eyes, I appreciated the rhythmic sound of the wheels in motion.

"I'm equally sad and…excited? Sad and excited that Damir will take Devraj on their trip," I said aloud, my eyes still closed.

Neha was serving as my decoy and rode with Leela and Maliha in the carriage ahead of us. Gamani and Swaran sat across from me and giggled. Something about me wearing a matching maiden uniform, sitting on a mound of pillows, and not worrying about my toddler brought a giddy feeling.

"I haven't been home since the wedding. I wonder how much things have changed," Swaran mused. She looked out the window a took in the breeze and the lush forest rushing by.

"If I can be honest, it'll be nice to just speak Ushallavi for a month." Gamani settled in her seat and took a spare pillow and set it behind her head.

Swaran nodded. "Yeah, I could do with a break from listening in to see if the Makaarians have anything to say about us."

"Or the stares. I never thought I would appreciate blending in with the rest of the palace staff."

"I can smell the naan already," I sighed. They sighed with me. Sanjana had not made her appearance and yet I knew she craved fresh flatbread. I couldn't wait for the fiery, acidic feeling in my throat and chest to go away so I could enjoy my favorite spicy dishes again.

There was a pleasant silence as we enjoyed the ride.

I opened an eye and saw Swaran look thoughtfully—sadly?—out the side window.

"Everything all right?" I asked. She sighed as she continued to stare.

"I thought that as I followed Abhijita, I would always feel bold and strong. I didn't realize how difficult it is to be her follower when away from home. Should I increase my training?"

Frowning, I shook my head.

"I trained the best. Abhijita would be proud of you

for following her wherever she needs you. Wherever I need you," I said. "I don't understand. What's troubling you?"

Swaran and Gamani looked at each other for a moment.

"We are *heroes* in the eyes of our people. These Makaarians treat us like garbage. It's been a rough three years, my queen."

My heart sank. Swaran was right. While I've enjoyed marital bliss with Damir, it's also been the hardest years of my life. We've been nothing but eager to cooperate and coexist, but our Makaarian allies have been wary of us. The Eyes, the training center, the muscular handmaidens, and the loud-mouth queen.

Days before our trip, I unleashed my fury on Damir's council because the staff and members of the court kept using a slur while my handmaidens passed by. They didn't dare use any foul language around me or Devraj, but I still took it personally.

My handmaidens were right; the court was unrelenting with their barbs and jabs. And because they whispered and laughed behind their fans, the council couldn't (or wouldn't) understand our plight. Direct language and action were championed in my father's court—here, it was scorned. It was difficult planning our harmonious future when they couldn't even stomach our most-prized traits and values.

Damir was…Damir about it. He promised they would talk about it. We rolled our eyes as we packed our bags. I was too focused on seeing my parents and finally meeting my baby to care.

I had this feeling that if I visited home more often, I would be able to face these Makaarians and continue to build our multi-cultural future. My babies would have strong parents and anyone who treated them unfairly would face accountability.

These Makaarians will one day learn.

But first, I dreamed of having this baby and resting while the handmaidens took care of us.

Gamani took Swaran's hand. She gently ran her thumb over Swaran's knuckles, earning an appreciative glance.

"No matter what the Makaarians think, they can't wish us away. We proudly follow Abhijita's path. Her beauty and strength will help us navigate this moment, and the next, and the next. Despite the struggle, we are making history just by being true to our ways."

"Well spoken," Swaran whispered. As she gripped Gamani's fingers tighter, she looked at me. "Will things be better? Honestly?"

I was about to answer when Gamani shifted.

"What is that?" she barked.

An arrow whizzed into our carriage. Then another, then another. We started to smell smoke and I gripped the bottom of my stomach. I braced myself as the carriage lurched to my right and into the road.

I heard my maidens cry out as they leaped into action. Someone leaped out of the carriage and someone else cradled my head.

"We're under attack!"

136

As Leela spoke, my mind flashed back to that day. I braced myself to relive those horrible memories again. I could remember holding the young woman in my arms. I remember her telling me to flee, and before I could attempt to carry her away with me, she wasn't responding. I remembered shaking Swaran and urging her to wake up—realizing life left her eyes. I had to run if it meant saving my own life and bearing Sanjana.

I looked to my daughter as a testament to my efforts and sacrifice. She stared at Leela in awe.

"She's talking about you, Mami," she whispered. I nodded and looked up to hear Leela continue.

"I didn't think I would survive," Leela continued. She shared her story in Makaarian—much to the surprise of Damir's and Einora's families. "My sisters in the work were all dead around me and I was fading fast. The last thing I saw was my mistress fleeing into the woods while holding her stomach. I knew that I did my best, so my queen would live another day and bring our princess into the world."

She looked at me with tears in her eyes and bowed her head.

"By the love and mercy of the gods, my legs gained their strength and my training kicked in. I was able to use my resources to patch my wounds and travel back to Ushallav. You were gone and I could not track you. We needed help."

There was a general murmur in awe. Even walking without injuries, it would take weeks to make the trip. I glanced over at Claudiu, and I noticed he frowned the whole time. I looked at Leela to see what he saw in her.

I wasn't sure what he was thinking, but I wanted to ask him later. Damir also looked troubled. Perhaps he was not fond of this story, either.

"I admit, I felt like such a fraud and a fool to not go after my queen, but my injuries were too severe that I thought I would be of no use to her if I was maimed. I went to see the doctor in hopes of restoring my health and then finding her as soon as possible. I needed to see my family."

"Why didn't you come directly to your king and queen?" Queen Tejal questioned.

"By the time I recovered, Queen Anjali was already pronounced dead, and everyone was already traveling back to Makaar to mourn her death," came the solemn reply. "I-I thought that she was found and properly cremated to the gods. I am ashamed of my ignorance."

I saw Damir wiping his eyes from where he sat. Einora's eyes were bright with tears as well.

"It's a solemn story, but it's the reason why we are here," I said, drawing all eyes to me. "This celebration is a testament that our stories are never over. There is always a happy ending beyond the horizon. We must only search for it."

"Well said, Anjali," Damir said, rising from his spot. He held Gregori with his left arm and raised his glass with his free hand. "And now that you are restored to us, we must restore your majesty and rites that a princess of your stature deserves. You may travel and serve your people as you see fit. You are royalty in both lands and no one else will serve with the grace and wit that you will serve."

"The council supports this decision," Benedikt said, standing up and raising his glass. I wondered how much it pained him to say anything kind at this moment. But I smiled all the same. "We toast Anjali as a friend and protector to all."

Everyone in the room raised their glasses, and I raised my glass as a gesture of good faith. I really wondered what his words meant—he couldn't have picked a more neutral speech. I needed to know more. I could at least admit that he was balancing favor between me and Einora admirably.

I held Sanjana's hand and Devraj held my skirts as we all cheered and drank from our cups. Einora gave a cue and the music livened up. People from each family rose to dance. They clustered in the middle of the room meant for group dancing. The children—regardless of country of origin—squealed as they entered the fray and twirled with their siblings and cousins.

Once I felt better, I locked eyes with Damir and joined in the dancing myself.

I laughed—from dancing and drinking—before clamoring back to my spot at the table.

"I won't be able to move for days," I murmured with a giggle. "We'll all just lay on the floor like Iwin back home." I referred to the family dog. From what I was told, she was back home nursing a litter of pups herself.

"We're in no rush to leave you," Ray said, patting me on the back. I couldn't remember the last time I could truly enjoy myself with mixed company. Leela danced her way over to me and my kingly brother. We waved to acknowledge her.

"My queen. I was married within the last year or so. May I seek permission to visit my husband in Ushallav from time to time? He is tending his mother and has finally found employment that suits him."

"Yes, of course!" I replied merrily. It was always a joy to see a handmaiden find a husband. It made their task harder, but it was enjoyable to become close to her family. After all, I started this party with more handmaidens than expected. I could really use the help. "You may travel and perform tasks for me if the opportunity arises. Just let me know in advance when you need to visit home."

"This is far better than I could've imagined," Leela smiled. "I was meant to be your handmaiden, and it delights me that destiny has truly struck again. Thank our mighty Abhijita—she who was the first handmaiden."

"Well spoken," Mama nodded with a smile. She gave me a look that spoke of pride and peace.

"Come play and dance, Leela!" Devraj said, tugging at her wrist. She smiled and joined them.

As I watched them, I felt mixed emotions. With Damir, Einora, Claudiu, and Marita on my side, I wasn't sure I needed more people to help. It felt overwhelming. But it also brought me passion and determination; it was a blessing to have someone on my side that would fight for me and Ushallav. Leela was dutybound and I could trust her. She out of everyone here knew what it meant to seek justice for the other maidens.

I gasped, and the air caught in my throat. *Perhaps she saw the killer's face. What else does she know?*

CHAPTER
NINETEEN

As everyone was settling down for the night, I made sure to take a moment of Leela's time. I ensured Marita had an eye on the kids; my children and their cousins were either wildly running around way past their bedtime or they were asleep on a spread of cushions. I made eye contact with Leela, and we walked out onto the balcony to enjoy the summer air.

"I can't begin to tell you how relieved I am to see you, Leela," I began. She leaned against the balcony with a drink and looked up at the sky. "I thought I lost you all that day."

"I failed, my queen," she murmured. "You needed me most and I wasn't strong enough."

"But you can help me now. I'm looking for the person responsible for this. Help me fill the gaps and seek justice for our sisters. It's possible that you noticed something that I didn't."

Leela's eyes glistened with tears. "What happened to you all those years? Abhijita be praised for watching over you."

I felt slightly impatient. Didn't she know? "I was rescued and protected. The people attending this party helped me when I couldn't help myself."

My handmaiden—the woman who helped me clean up vomit and poop out of embroidery and rolled her eyes when Benedikt opened his mouth—cried and nodded her head.

"You always find a way to survive and rise above the rest—even when it's so hard. My queen, we are blessed that you are still standing. Perhaps I can help somehow. I will do what I can," Leela promised.

She paused as if she were reliving that moment in her mind again. Gods, I was still so grateful that she was here and alive. It felt like one less person weighed on my conscience.

"I'm not sure if I can remember much that would help, my lady. I just recounted my story during the party. I couldn't identify anyone's faces and hardly anyone spoke. It was so quiet." Leela shuddered. I nodded, trying to be understanding.

"Well," she began. Her face looked like she noticed something from far away. "I thought I heard one of them say 'spread out.' In Makaarian. Of course, my Makaarian isn't as good as yours. I could be wrong. Does that help?"

I took a sip of my last drink of the evening. I tucked my other arm over my stomach and under the opposite elbow. Makaarian. I had to admit, it made sense. I couldn't think of any reason why someone from Ushallav would do this to me. The Ushallavi people love me and were surprisingly very supportive when my engagement was announced to the people. Makaarians…if I had to put it into words, I think they collectively hoped that they could still enjoy their culture and religion unchanged. Sure, change is difficult but from what I experienced in Damir's court, Makaarians are uncomfortable with even the slightest change. And here I was—wearing my own clothes and raising my children my way.

This clue still burned and caused discomfort. I would absolutely need more evidence to prove anything.

After thinking to myself for too long, I nodded and tried to smile.

"It's a difficult memory to relive. Don't strain yourself. But things will get better once we discover the truth."

"You deserve justice, my queen." Leela bowed. "The drinks were too good. I might need to go rest for the evening. Or morning." We giggled. The Ushallavi do enjoy a party that goes on until sunrise.

"Let's sleep on it and see what a new day brings." I sighed and gestured back to the doors. I saw my sweaty son sprint through a hall—too fast for Marita. I chuckled and went after Devraj. The morning might not be kind to any of us.

CHAPTER TWENTY

Saying goodbye to my parents proved very difficult. While they were in town, I trained with my siblings, my parents, my new handmaidens, and my new extended family. My brothers teased me about how my training rooms could use a few enhancements and a mighty scrub, but I didn't care. You haven't lived until you've held your new sister-in-law in a headlock as your mother urges you to clench harder.

The children played for hours. It was so delightful to hear my children chattering in Ushallav and learning so many new words.

For those days, it felt like I never left home—that I never left Damir's side to fend for myself in the woods. It felt like everything was easy to control and easy to enjoy.

Mama held my face in her hands and gave me tender, ceremonial kisses on my forehead, chin, and cheeks.

"You were made out of tough and tender materials," she told me as she pulled my forehead to hers. "You owe it to yourself and to Abhijita to live up to your creation."

I nodded and we parted. Before leaving, my father fixed my crown proudly and held me the way he did when I was much younger—holding me close so I could smell the incense from his office on his jacket.

"That crown suits you. I better not see you let anyone take it off," he murmured. I could feel his words humming.

I replied, "Of course, Father."[1]

"You must report to us immediately if anything is amiss," he advised me. My mother nodded in agreement. "We know you can handle yourself, but we will send in the best of the best if necessary."

"No one gets a second attempt to assassinate our princess and our grandbabies," Mama asserted. I laughed as she pinched my cheek. I knew she was being lighthearted and dead serious all at once.

"I will find this assassin soon enough," I promised. "And then I can come home."

They nodded with glassy eyes. It was a painful promise, but one I needed to keep.

"I know the memories will linger," Mama said, taking my hand, "and that is normal. They may cloud your mind and make it impossible to move or breathe or act. Use those painful memories to unlock the truth behind who attacked you. Believe your memories—don't second-guess them. You must honor the memories—no matter how painful."

"How many times must I relive the past?" I whispered. A few years ago, I would've cried at the thought, but at this point there were no more tears to shed.

"At least once more," Father coaxed. "Try to remember what weapons they used, any colors you remember, or how the attack unfolded. If you study your adversary, you can have a clearer understanding of how they will strike you next. Just like your training."

"Just like my training," I breathed. The Eyes wouldn't be enough; they weren't on the travel route that day. I would have to rely on my own eyes and ears and no one else's. "May Ishka guide my mind and my heart to seek my justice."

"Well spoken," my parents said as they nodded in unison.

"Grandma, where are you going?" Sanjana asked. My mother turned and crouched down to Sanjana as though I were no longer present.

"My sweet little one," she cooed. "We are going back to Ushallav where we live. One day you will stay with us, and we will play. We'll take you to the lakes and oceans."

"I want to go now!" she beamed with excitement. Devraj heard her enthusiasm and joined in.

"Please let us come!" he added. He tugged on Father's hand, which I knew was killing him inside. It was sure hard to deny them such a request.

"We must stay for just a while longer," I reminded the children. "I already told you. It will only be for a while longer and then we will see them again. I promise."

My parents had already tried to convince me before—they were brimming with the thought of taking the children and keeping them in safe hands while I looked for the assassin. Every time I thought of one or both of them traveling that same route without me to protect them, my mind and my heart froze. No, not going to happen. Besides, I had been away from Devraj for a few years already. I wouldn't budge on the subject.

The best thing my family could do for me now is narrow down my suspects. Working alongside Ray, I'm sure we can find out if our foe is Ushallav or Makaarian.

"We can't bear to go without hugs!" my father smiled. He knew how to diffuse moments like these. The kids rushed into their grandparents' arms as I waited my turn.

It was tough, but I knew once the assassin was found and dealt with, things would be better for everyone. I could be free.

***

Once Damir and I formally bade farewell to my family, things quieted down. A few attendants, including my handmaidens, watched us. I could tell that they wondered what would happen next. Damir took my hand, and we went to his personal office. I nodded to my handmaidens, and they quietly headed towards the children's playroom.

"Did your family have a good time?" Damir asked.

"Things went better than I expected. I was not expecting the replacement handmaidens so soon. It's remarkable how a few extra people can make it easier to do my work and help the kids."

"Your brother is wise. I made sure to thank him for the built-in friends and tutors. I do miss the women who served you years ago. They were very brave."

I nodded. They were my friends before I married Damir. They were somehow no match for my assassin and that still bothered me.

"I wanted to talk about the next few steps. You said you wanted to focus on finding clues about who might've been involved with this whole plot. I support you. Einora and I worked out a time where you could use the Room of Eyes to do your research without any disturbances. I hope you'll share whatever you learn with the council. While you are undoubtedly the strongest woman I know, this isn't just your fight. It's mine, too."

As he spoke, I chewed at my bottom lip. I was torn. Sure, it would be great if someone else could tackle this problem, so I don't have a mental breakdown. But no, I don't trust anyone but myself to discover the truth. Ultimately, I had to decide whether I trusted or wanted Damir's help.

"I'm sure using the Room of Eyes already makes your council complain and squirm. I'll play nice."

Damir smiled. "That's my girl."

He reached out a hand and I let him take mine. It reminded me of the one time we danced together at my own party. I wasn't sure whether or not he was trying to show equal favoritism to his current wives. To me, it took me back to my courting days when I dreamed of ruling by his side and creating harmony between our worlds. Maybe it was the alcohol that I hadn't enjoyed in years, but I smiled and laughed with him as we danced.

"Something else is on your mind."

"Is it that obvious?" His kind smile broadened. He dismissed everyone around us so he could speak to me.

"I merely realized that beyond the party, I haven't really spent any time with you. I miss you."

Something in the way he smiled at me filled in the blanks. I had to decide whether I would give into my rightfully earned husband or whether I would remain all business.

"What am I to you?" I asked. That surprised him.

"You're my wife. The mother of royalty." He kissed the hand he held and then lightly kissed the side of my neck. He moved along my jawline until his face was right in front of mine. He switched to Ushallavi as he said, "You are my best friend."

He was earnest—I couldn't help but grin. He knew how to charm me.

"What if your council hears about all this flowery language? Just the thought must make Benedikt blush." Damir thought for a moment before looking me in the eye.

"I've struggled with this ever since you've come home. No—I don't mean it like that. It's just...how do I help you *and* Einora? How do I function as husband, father, king...?"

His hands were around mine. They squeezed earnestly. Like it was up to me to ease his burden. But I had my own worries. With each day, I wondered if he was really fighting for me or if he just wants me to back away. At that moment, it seemed like none of us wanted to do the mature or logical. We were lonely. We were human.

"I know what you mean," I finally answered. "Maybe we can put that off for just one more night."

His brow arched. I gave him a smile. I was still his and he was still mine. And with that choice, I spent more than just one night with him. I was tired of my past affecting my present.

CHAPTER
TWENTY-ONE

I had to take a break from looking over the images on the Watchful Eyes for hours. My rigorous schedule started to wear me down—I'm not the same patient warrior I was a few years ago. I still pushed myself to wake up early, train hard before the kids needed me, studied the Eyes for hours into the afternoon, then play with the kids until it was time for sleep. Leela and my other new handmaidens helped me with each aspect of my day while still giving me my space when I needed it. I occasionally chatted with Einora or spent intimate moments with Damir.

Even with my productive schedule, I couldn't dash through time fast enough. More often than not, what the Eyes show is irrelevant to my questions. The pressure was on, but I had a feeling that I was starting to arrive at pertinent moments of the timeline. The hard parts of my story.

I needed a long cleansing breath after I came across something rather painful. It pulled me out of my afternoon exhaustion and straightened my posture. I propped myself up and craned my neck.

One of the Eyes just outside the door captured the moment when wardrobes, furniture, and tokens from my home disappeared into storage.

After seeing that moment, I lowered myself back down on the pillows. It felt like I was a ghost haunting this place. I wanted to tell the staff that I was still in the woods recovering from the most stressful and harrowing moments of my life. I wanted to tell them that their queen was a survivor. I wanted them to know that I would be strong enough to take all those things back. But at that moment, I felt bitter. I've felt a loss of control many times, yet this seemed like the pinnacle of powerlessness.

I got up to turn off the projector and monitors, but I stopped myself just in time. My face is feet away from the image depicting Damir standing just outside my door with our young Devraj on his hip. They just stared into my room and stood just out of everyone's way. My baby buried his face into Damir's shoulder. Damir put a hand over the back of his son's head and neck, and gently stroked his hair.

After that painful memory, everything went dark. I turned off the images playing against the ceiling, and I couldn't have exited quicker.

Einora was on a walk with Gregori, so she was not on the other side of the door to greet me. That was lucky and ideal since I had no desire to chat or pretend that I was happy or approachable.

Just as I secured the door and it disappeared into the wall, a knock came at the door. Curious as to who it would be, I opened the door. I found Leela and the children.

"Oh, forgive me, Your Grace," Leela said with a bow and a smile. "I was just looking for you. Dinner is ready downstairs. I came to fetch you."

"Thank you very much, Leela." I didn't feel hungry at all, but after seeing my sad young boy on the screens, I was grateful for this moment to be with him again. Even though he was getting too big to carry, I still lifted him in the air and kissed his forehead.

"Do you come into this room often?" Leela said, peering slightly into the room. I could tell she was curious.

"Sometimes," was all I said. I brushed after her and went down the hallway at my normal gait. I felt guilty for not telling her about the Watchful Eyes room, but it wasn't something that any of my handmaidens knew about. They didn't ask and I didn't tell—that was tradition. Something in me noticed that I could tell Einora but not Leela. *You had to tell Einora so you could gain access—nothing more,* I reminded myself.

As I rounded the corner, my heart stopped.

At the end of the hallway, Damir was standing there with Einora. She was holding Gregori, and I couldn't tell who she was happier to see—her son or her husband. They shared a quick kiss and headed down the hallway without noticing me at all. It was clear that they didn't know I was there or that I was meant to see this tender moment. I felt like a ghost once more.

I stood there dumbfounded and numb until my children tugged on my hands and encouraged me forward.

CHAPTER
TWENTY-TWO

My vision was hazy, but I breathed in relief. I was still alive. I clutched my swollen belly, willing that baby Sanjana would stay put. She was not ready to come out. But the things I just saw jostled everything inside of me.

I lay on my back and looked up at the patches of sky that peeked through the thick trees. If I could calm down, then I knew the pain would dim and I could walk again. I knew that I could walk and find water or food. I knew everything hinged on having a calm demeanor. I grappled at the greenery around me and took in fistfuls of grass and leaves. I wanted to tip myself over but couldn't. The contractions were making it hard to move or keep quiet. I quietly moaned and whimpered.

I witnessed so much death. I held them in my arms. Neha's last wish was for me to find safety. She had a clearer head than I did at the moment. Neha—dressed as my decoy—looked small with all the heavy, illustrious fabric around her. She cried quietly and looked up at me, her breathing harsh and short.

"You are our queen. You must live to tell what happened. You must live to be a mother," she told me. I stared in horror as her head shifted to the side and her blood trickled out of her wounds and mouth. Her body shuddered and her brown skin grayed. These were words for me from the gods themselves, and I knew I had to honor their call. It didn't make it easy. I was thinking about her words while I lay defenseless in the grass.

Since I wasn't wearing my fancy travel attire, I was covered well enough to withstand a light drizzle of rain. I blinked away the rain and mist and tried to calm down.

The killer could be anywhere. They could've come to finish the job, I thought to myself. *I won't let that happen.*

I wasn't sure how far away I was from the carriage but if they were anticipating our arrival, they could be close by. I assumed that if they could count well enough, they would notice that one body was missing.

That was the main reason why I couldn't calm down. I would have to fight for my life. Again and again and again.

Suddenly, my vision zoomed as though I was traveling in the air like a bird. It was like my mind could travel back to where the carriage lay dormant and broken. The area was littered with arrows. Black arrows. I wasn't sure what that meant, but they didn't look like anything I've seen before. I'm no expert but they didn't look like something any guard—Makaarian or Ushallavi—would use. Did this help or was this a ruse? I wondered if the color signified a group or if the arrows were poisoned. One was still stuck in my leg—I gritted my teeth. I pulled it out and hid the remains. I didn't know what I was feeling beyond panic. I just didn't want to die. I needed to move and find shelter.

I suddenly heard a low voice in the brush. I couldn't understand the speech and it horrified me. *Who was it? Was it my killer?*

It came closer. It didn't sound threatening, but I was a frazzled pregnant woman, so I was preparing myself for the worst.

The voice sounded like it was inquiring about something. It finally settled on a few words, "Who's there?" I froze. I recognized that the person was speaking tentative Makaarian. I didn't dare answer.

Just as I craned my head to get a better idea of the voice's location, I felt hands graze over my face and shoulders.

"Don't touch me," I hissed in Makaarian.

"Breathe slowly, woman." The man had wavy brown and silver hair and a full beard. He was only dressed in dark leathers and cotton that made him blend in well with the rest of the foliage. He held his hands up in mild surrender before he firmly held my hand. "I need you to breathe in slowly and gather all the air you can muster, then breathe it all out. Can you do that?"

"What the hell are you talking about?" I barked. "Get away!"

"You're hurt and you need help. If you calm down your breathing, I can help you to safety."

"I was just attacked and everyone's dead—I don't want to go anywhere with a stranger," I mustered. The more I talked with him, the more I could tell that I couldn't fight him off, even if I wanted to. My mind wouldn't connect with my body.

"Call me Claudiu," he said, smoothing my hair away from my face. "Now we are not strangers. If you want to save your baby, then you'll need to save your strength. We have plenty of medicine women and midwives to help you."

"How can I trust you? You could've been the one that attacked me and my entourage."

"Entourage, huh? Are you some noblewoman or princess?"

"That doesn't concern you. I may be heavily pregnant, but I will kill you with my bare hands if it's necessary."

"My wife used to say that when we didn't have the goat cheese quick enough for her cravings," Claudiu chuckled. "Don't worry about me. You should be worried about yourself and the little one you're carrying. Just breathe and peace will flow into you."

At that moment, I couldn't think of anything else to do but panic. I didn't want to leave but I didn't want to stay. I just wanted to be back in Damir's arms and have my baby Devraj close to me. I wanted to forget the rest of this trip ever happened and the death I witnessed. I wanted to start the day over and choose not to leave the haven I barely tolerated in Makaar.

But at that moment, Claudiu didn't give me much of a choice. "If you follow me, I have a cart. I can take you to camp. It's very safe and friendly to all."

You must live to be a mother, came Neha's final wish in my mind. I wanted to be alive to raise Devraj and Sanjana who still struggled and fought within me. I began breathing as Claudiu instructed, but it felt like my lungs were lodged just behind my tongue. It felt too heavy and difficult to breathe. I still felt panicky and distraught.

Warriors heal to fight another battle. I needed to heal. It felt like taking a huge continental step away from my husband and son, but I knew that when I was strong enough, I could come home. I wouldn't be gone for long. As soon as I could, I would inspect the bodies, give my loyal handmaidens a proper cremation, ensure that this assassin was hung for their crimes, and never let my family out of my sight again.

I extended a hand and Claudiu took it. As he pulled me closer to him, all I could remember was whispering with the last of my strength, "I am Queen Anjali and I need your help."

At that realization, I shot up from my bed. As I held my hand to my heart and my belly, I realized that I wasn't pregnant. I was just reliving that moment again. This time, I saw everything with such clarity and detail.

I remembered my parents' counsel to truly interpret every detail of that moment to learn more about my assassin. The black arrows stuck out to me, and so I lit a candle and began recording—both in words and hastily drawn scribbles—what I both saw and heard. When I was done, I prayed and thanked Ishka for opening my eyes and giving me the courage to relive that day without breaking down again.

Damir rolled over and murmured something I couldn't hear. I touched his shoulder gently and he turned again comfortably.

I knew there was still so much to decipher and pick apart, but this was a good amount of work today. After a bit more sleep and a better sketch, I could ask Damir, Ray, and Claudiu what they knew about these black arrows.

CHAPTER
TWENTY-THREE

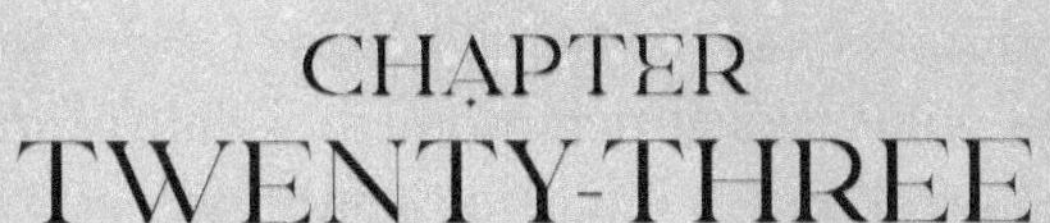

After a week of watching the Eyes and finding nothing helpful, I started my new day with a challenging workout. I used to do my training for fun—to keep up my skills. I even thought it would impress my future husband long before I met Damir. Training helped me concentrate, give thanks for my body, and center my peace.

Now, I train to protect or kill without hesitation. It has been a while since I've trained and felt happy once I've finished. Now I just feel angry—wondering who I should be suspicious of and what I would do if I turned a corner and suddenly fell under attack. What would be the quickest way to get my children out of the castle if our rooms were under attack?

I looked at the scar on my left calf. I tried to redirect my thinking towards gratitude. There was a time when I could barely walk because of this wound.

It was this line of conflicting feelings that took control of my waking thought. And it was in this stupor that I accidentally bumped into Benedikt.

"Ah, Anjali. You're up with the sun, per usual," he said with a tight, cold smile.

"I normally don't run into you in the light. What a surprise," I said, composing myself. I was still wearing my training trousers and blouse, so I knew I didn't look regal or refined in his eyes at that moment. I didn't care.

"Will we receive a report on your findings today? Or sometime within the calendar year?" he said, raising an eyebrow. I rolled my eyes slightly. I could remember a time when it took them months to finally decide that it was acceptable for me to wear royal outfits with trousers around the castle grounds.

"Perhaps I'll wait until I catch the killer myself. Or maybe I'll take the same amount of time it took for you to find Damir a new wife."

"Ah, touchy this morning, aren't we?" Benedikt chuckled lightly. "My wife was also sensitive to every word she heard when she was mothering our children. I'm sure it's something every good woman gets control of eventually."

My eye twinged. I pitied his wife. "Don't you have someone else to sneer at in your schedule for today?"

Benedikt kept his hands behind his back and laughed.

"I know your people encourage bold and honest talk but when will you learn that it has no place here? Here,

we keep our tempers in control and speak with respect to those who deserve it."

"When you can maintain a household that doesn't murder their queens and unborn princesses for being brown, then I will evoke all the respect my spirit can give." I could hardly keep my spit in my mouth. "Until then, I will solve my own mystery at my own pace."

I didn't nod or bow at him, but rather, I walked past him so I could return to my rooms before saying anything I might regret. My muscles tightened as if I was about to dive into another training hour.

These people and their respect are the reason why I can't get anything done around here. Damir has to tip-toe around everyone's wants and wishes until I have to practically arm wrestle for mine. I knew what Benedikt wanted: he wanted me to give up on Damir and give up being queen. He probably preferred a quiet Makaarian as my replacement.

"Not so fast, princess," Benedikt said quietly. "What are you even going to do once this killer is known? How will you prove their guilt?"

"I won't have to prove anything," I said defiantly over my shoulder. "I will kill them where they stand. Don't pretend like I don't have the strength to do so."

"Stop this impulsive and ridiculous display of womanly vigor," he scoffed. I was still walking, which meant there was quite a distance between us. He had to raise his voice to insult me. "Our court will not sustain your word when the alleged guilty cannot speak for themselves. They will execute you for murder. And with no one on your side, who will advocate for you? Who will believe you?"

I finally stopped in my tracks and turned around.

"You speak as though you know something that I don't know—and something you shouldn't," I said coldly. "Are you admitting that you know who the assassin is?"

"You are testing me," Benedikt warned. "I do my job. It's time you did yours."

"I am doing my job—I'm researching what you chose to ignore. You buried me and embraced your new white queen. I know what you did. You never looked for the assassin. Care to tell me why? Don't insult me."

"How dare you—"

"And why do you talk to me like I'm some child? Do you talk to your sovereign king in such a way?" I took a few steps closer to him. "And if I find out that you treat Einora or Devraj or Sanjana similarly—"

Benedikt raised a brow in surprise and grinned. The whole courtyard was silent—stale enough that I could hear horses neighing in the stables across the courtyard and beyond.

"Answer me, you slimy coward," I said. I knew how to tense my body to express every curve and muscle of my body.

"As I mentioned," he said quietly, still smiling. "I do my job."

"Don't you ever refer to me as 'princess.' I am your queen. Your job is to remember that."

Benedikt scoffed and gave me a pointed look before continuing on his way. "Enjoy the rest of your day, Your Highness."

I stood there for a few moments and watched him calmly walk away like he was floating just off the ground.

I knew I could punch him down and he would sleep. In fact, I envisioned that idea multiple times before scowling and returning to my rooms.

I had to admit—he was right. I would need evidence to support my claims if I wanted to keep Damir's loyalty and get the justice I and Sanjana and my maidens deserved. Damir can't stand with me if I started killing people I didn't like.

I scowled again. Benedikt. His demeanor made it hard to pierce him with anything. He acted so uncaringly and unfeeling. I could insult every flaw in his body, and he would still sip his tea like he was paid to be insulted. For years, he treated me like filth. No matter what I say, Damir never really seems to see what I see.

As I walked, I squared my shoulders and refocused myself. I could find the killer. I had the passion and the power. And then I'll be queen again.

After a few angry steps, I turned. What if Benedikt was the one who sent someone to do his dirty work? He and the rest of the council have been a thorn in my side and have always pushed against my goals to unite our two countries. Were they tired of answering to an Ushallavi woman?

I've always been suspicious of Benedikt but now...I have my Eyes on him.

CHAPTER
TWENTY-FOUR

My dearest sister,

I received your inquiry and the account of your dream. My heart breaks to think that we were so close to losing two bright stars without reason. The gods—all of them—were truly guiding you when we couldn't.

But there's only so many tears we can shed when there's something we can do to seek out the villain of you and my country.

I am relieved to hear that you have access to the Eyes. Again, Ishka sees our family and knows what we need to rule and bring the truth to light. I urge you to remain diligent. Your people are with you. The moment you discover the threads, I and my advisers will come and ensure this murderer stands for their crimes. I understand you must keep your husband (ex-husband?) involved in this matter but do not forget me and your family.

Enclosed are historical documents that my scribes have copied for your convenience. There is a copy translated in Makaarian as well. Here, we lay out the events that occurred before, during, and after your designated trip to Ushallav. While I cannot fathom who would dare call themselves my subject and yet attempt to murder you and our beloved Sanjana, I understand that these are sensitive matters. I choose my words carefully when I say that I suspect that you must explain very obvious details to those who work for Damir. I still trust Damir, but I question his associates.

I also had our palace craftsmen and historians research the black arrows you described. We don't know of any past or present groups that use this style of weapon. They hypothesize that your attacker had something to hide. Perhaps they didn't want to put the blame on their country, or they wanted the living to bicker over who is responsible. It's clear that your killer underestimated your power to survive.

I caution you, dear sister. Your enemy smiles sweetly while they plunge the knife into your gut. I agree with your theory: this person knew your travel plans and therefore is closer to you than you know.

Surely, this is a heavy burden. I, our parents, and our siblings hope you will consider our invitation to return to us. We've missed you. We also worry about Devraj and Sanjana. They are also close to danger. We can protect you while you put the pieces together. We wonder whether the Makaarians' protection is conditional. In the meantime, I will send out hunters *and skilled trackers to examine your travel path for more clues. As you will see in our historical documents, we were able to recover the fallen Ushallavi who died nobly. But if Ishka is giving you dreams and urging you to return to that spot, perhaps that is a message for me, too.*

I look forward to good news any day. I believe in you, little sister.

Your brother,
Ray

I leaned back in my chair. Ray clearly did not trust Damir as much as he conveyed in this letter. The ink blotted by my husband's name as if my brother pondered long and hard before communicating his thoughts. Perhaps he imagined that his letter would serve as evidence. Beyond the blots, Ray gave me the historical documents among the personal correspondence I received from my family. This meant that he wanted me to read it first before any Makaarian had the opportunity. Perhaps he was worried that these documents would never cross my path had he delivered them to Damir's office.

I was in the middle of a severely delicate political mess. I wasn't sure which was worse—being murdered by an obscured coward or being spared as part of their plan so I could watch my marriage and political power unravel.

That last paragraph encouraged a long sigh. This had mother and father written all over it. Ray was protective in some ways but not like this. He protected me by sending handmaidens and ensuring they arrived safely. They help me *here*. I'm sure it's the royal grandparents who are the ones sick with worry.

Damir's parents didn't live to see or meet Sanjana. The queen fell to illness and the king followed suit in grief. I let myself stand in Damir's shoes and wear his crown—burying his parents and then "burying" me. Perhaps this was why he remarried—to avoid repeating history. Maybe I was being too harsh on him. Of course, now I wonder if all this death is connected. I shook my head. One mystery at a time.

I read over the historical papers for any new clues. There was a neatly recorded list of people who knew I was coming—my family and any employed handmaidens and midwives. We specifically planned a late spring journey, so I'd arrive and be ready for a summer birth. It looks like they sent out a messenger a day or so after no one arrived. It meant that a week went by and Damir was completely unaware of the situation.

Ray copied any and all correspondence between the two nations about the situation. Just like that moment of solitude with the Eyes, I felt like a vengeful spirit as I read Ray's and Damir's letters—the emotions held back on behalf of civility and fragile trust. It was clear that both of them were waiting for the other to reveal the truth.

There was a sketch of a map—a simple bird's eye view of the two bordering kingdoms and the designated route that tethered them. Little Xs dotted along the path and into the nearby mountains to declare what they found and where. Lots of arrows. Blood and footprints. Neither side had any idea who would do this.

Many funeral records. I wanted to vomit.

Records of what the Ushallavi palace Eyes saw. Nothing amiss except the moment Leela arrived, bloodied and alone. I wasn't sure what they expected their Eyes to show but they see it as proof that this problem didn't stem from Ushallav. There's a description here of Leela's side of the story. It checks out with what she told us at Einora's party. I still remember Claudiu's wary expression.

A headache bloomed just behind my eyes, and I put everything down on my desk. I'd seen enough for one day. Perhaps there was more to divine from these records but I felt like they confirmed what I already knew. Someone close. Someone personal. And at that moment, I was willing to give up everything except Ray's letter to Damir's council.

As if sensing my troubles, I heard someone approach.

"My queen, is everything okay?"

I turned and it was Ziya. She's the quiet one of my new entourage but she's tough in the training ring. She tended to be more comfortable and open with me once we were stretching and cooling down.

Sometimes I forget that I don't have to do everything. I smiled wearily.

"Everything's fine. My brother just sent me some information about my…well, about the…"

"The ambush?"

"Yes. Thank you. But the royal family is in good health. I think I even have some personal letters for you here that belong to you and the others. Please sort through and give the rest to Damir in his office. I think I need to lie down."

Ziya's brow furrowed as she nodded. "I understand. We'll be happy to take care of this. We'll wake you if the children need you."

I waved my thanks before kissing my babies on their cheeks and finding my bed. I needed a moment to shut out the noise and the light before I took another step.

CHAPTER
TWENTY-FIVE

I just thought that you might understand Damir's demeanor a bit more. Is he always this distant?"

I chewed a bit on my lip.

Einora glanced at me nervously while she drank her tea. She just described to me how Damir had hardly been speaking to her that week. I tried to explain to her that my parents had put a lot of pressure on him and the rest of the council to help me find the assassin. While I reviewed years of memories within the castle, Damir had been meeting with citizens all week for more intel about that day. I tried not to feel guilty about how much I relied on my new team of handmaidens to take care of my children.

I also didn't mention the many nights Damir and I found each other and relished private moments.

At that moment, I knew she was asking for personal advice. I could feel it tapping against my personal boundaries. Her relationship with Damir was none of my business.

"I can tell he's stressed. But it's not fair to you. I'm sorry that it's affecting you. What are you going to do?"

Einora blinked in surprise and then straightened her posture.

"I definitely don't know what I can do. You know, besides tending Gregori and ensuring you can use your special room."

Her eyes darted to the wall where the entry remained invisible and closed. She helped in other ways. There were some "well-meaning" nobles or council members who would reach out to her to ensure she was "well." I knew that old tensions were opening again. People were thinking about the old war and what we all lost and gossiped about all sorts of things I could be doing to make my replacement miserable.

I wrote down those names. I paid attention to whether the Eyes would show me their true characters.

"Are your concerns about Damir coming from your own mind or someone else?" I asked. This was something I had to ask myself regularly. I wasn't going to be tricked by people like Benedikt again.

She slumped her shoulders and put her face in her hands.

"They are so insufferable," she croaked. Her chest was heaving in excitement and mild rage. "The court. My family members. They tell me that you're taking advantage of me and I'll be left alone. I tried to tell them about what you've been through, but they never seem to understand."

I put my hand over her hand and wrist.

"You once told me that your feelings are your power. Do you ever show compassion for yourself? Do you take care of yourself the way you care for Gregori?"

Einora made noises of protest but just sighed.

"I don't want to say that my life here was anything like yours, but I wonder if the loneliness just comes with the crown," she mused. "I just don't know how Damir manages to deal with it all the time. I can't stand it. I can't even count on my family to help me. But when I've been left alone so much—and especially during this stressful time—I can't help but wonder if all the talk is remotely true."

I raised my teacup like a toast and put it back on the low table. "Speak on about the Makaarian nobles. You'll feel better, trust me."

Einora laughed and dabbed the corner of her eyes and her nose.

"The nobles. I'm so sick of them. Why do we need them around? All they do is make me sad and lonely. I feel like all I'm supposed to do is make them happy. Well, how can I do that when they make it such a challenge and a chore? I have a baby to take care of now. I can't go on caring for these grown adults like babies, too. How did you do it? How did you keep strong?"

Before I could say anything, Einora took my hands in hers. "I know it's so much to ask of you, but I should really ask you everything there is to know about being a queen. Is that too much to ask? I feel so foolish sometimes like

I'm forgetting how painful this must be for you. I want to do my best with whatever time I have left."

For a moment, there weren't any words. I could tell Einora was filling the air with words because she couldn't stand the awkwardness. She couldn't stand the truth that was painful to say and to hear.

"I'm sure things will become much easier for you once the assassin is caught…and I move on with my children," I finally mustered.

"Move on? What do you mean by move on?" Einora questioned. Her bottom lip trembled.

"I…I'm not sure yet." I wanted to continue but went in another direction. "Look. All I know is that people are obsessed with the drama—one king, two queens. The gossip will move on once justice is served. These people who are talking to you probably care about you, but you know what's best for yourself. I'm not going to tell you how to be a queen or a mother. You're already *doing* it."

Instead of sharing my real feelings, I chose to comfort Einora. It's still too painful to be with Damir and see him with my replacement but even I couldn't bear to say that out loud. She couldn't see his love for her, but I could— like a tree reaching for sunlight.

I wiped my eyes before the tears could really come. How can I feel strong when I wasn't powerful enough to keep my marriage intact? I don't know who to blame. I disappeared. They pushed him to consider remarriage. He chose Einora as Devraj's second mother and Damir's second chance at being a happy father and husband.

The more I thought, the more I wondered where I

fitted in the frame. And I wondered if I needed to be in the frame in the first place.

I looked up into Einora's face and she was freely weeping, two rivers of tears dribbled down her face.

"I think you're disguising your true feelings. I know I'm *me*, but you can tell me the truth. You don't need to protect me."

She was right. I had a soft spot for her, but I didn't need to sacrifice any part of myself to play nice.

I took in a breath. "You know, I'm strong and I'm this and that. But I sometimes wish I never came back. I wish I could leave Damir and his kingdom alone. At least I would always preserve that feeling that Damir was waiting for me to come home. Maybe I should just move on."

Einora, still grasping me by the wrists, enveloped me in a hug.

CHAPTER
TWENTY-SIX

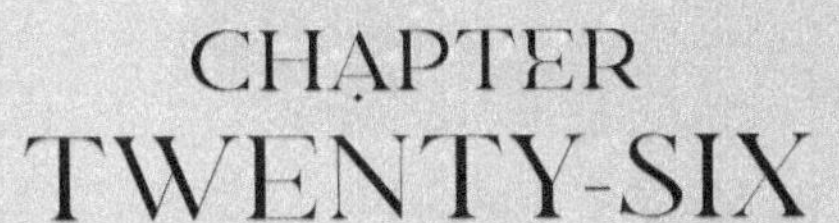

Instead of watching the walls crumble around me, Einora ordered more tea and cakes. It gave me time to compose myself. I couldn't believe that I just told Einora that I remotely considered stepping down and stepping away. But it didn't feel completely horrible. It felt like an option.

Einora poured me another cup of tea—the blue-purple fruit and flower mix swirled calmly within. After I took a calming sip, I gave Einora somewhat of a shy smile.

"Forgive me," I interrupted. "You initially asked about Damir. Let's figure out what to do—together."

"Oh, yes." Einora looked pained, as though she knew how she sounded. Defeated. "First of all, I had no idea you…felt that way. About moving on."

I looked at my drink. "Honestly, I didn't know, either. I haven't let myself go that deep—with anyone."

"Not like you have to listen to anything I say but no matter what, I hope you feel comfortable here. You deserve it. Your children deserve it, too. You're a good queen. Maybe I'm selfish but I'm fond of having you around. You're my closest friend," Einora insisted. She looked at me and sighed.

"One big problem at a time. I'm not going anywhere. I'm looking for the assassin. Let's just talk about Damir and putting these pithy rumors to rest."

I earned a chuckle from Einora. "Ah, Damir. Well, I should start by saying that I received some training from Wendi and Marita about my new role after I married Damir. But I feel like lately, my brain isn't what it used to be. Sometimes the answers are so obvious and other times…"

I nodded. I recognized that feeling—that haze that clouds my mind. No matter how many handmaidens were at my side, I still forgot things or didn't feel as quick as usual. That feeling was worse when I was alone in a wagon with little Sanjana.

I knew where to go with this.

"You have a mother's gut. It's hard to explain but you still know what to do even when you feel forgetful or scattered. When I had questions about Damir, I just asked him. Maybe I broke some rules, but I didn't care. My time as queen involved showing up to meetings and doing things my way until someone stopped me. Being married and being royalty is so different from any other relationship."

"You're so right," Einora nodded. "I didn't think about that. Well, I *did* but I didn't think there was ever a good time."

"You should do what you feel is best. Go talk to Damir instead of letting the talk get to you."

"I'll consider it. I would like to spend the evenings with him. Hear about his day. I'll ask him if it's okay that the baby sleeps with us."

"The worst he could say is no," I shrugged, trying not to choke on my tea. I didn't like hearing the word *sleep*. Sure, I know how Gregori entered the world, but I did not want to come across as recommending her to sleep with *my* husband. "At least you will hear from him directly."

Einora looked at me, reading the situation.

"Have you asked him how he feels about you, now that you've returned?" Einora blurted. She gasped at her question, and it caused me to blink for a few moments and return my hands to my lap.

"I can't seem to get a straight answer out of him. I keep making the mistake of blaming him for things that frustrate me about his council, so I haven't given him a fair chance."

"He would take you back in a heartbeat," Einora returned. "I can tell. Compared to you, I feel so young, like I shouldn't be here—"

She trailed off as I stood up. Einora must've felt just as stuck as I did—the future felt so muddy because we didn't know who would stay and who would step down.

I bowed my head. "Even if you stepped down as queen—even if someone forced you—we can't erase what happened. It's not so simple. We couldn't be a normal family anymore. We *aren't* a normal family and that is okay."

Einora sat there with her hands over her face, forgoing all attempts to preserve her makeup.

"I don't know why I'm crying," she huffed. Tear drTeardropskeup dusted her lap. "I just feel awful. I don't know how we can all just be happy."

"Hey, cheer up," I said softly, crouching before her. I grabbed her handkerchief and dabbed the tears away from her face. "We're facing a problem that neither of us created or started. But we still have to see it through. Luckily, we don't have to face it alone or as enemies."

Einora looked into my eyes and smiled. "That ought to show those nobles a thing or two. I will talk to Damir first thing about my concerns. If he'll have me."

"Good for you," I smiled sadly. I mentally waved goodbye at my nights with Damir.

"And if that goes to plan, you get to move in here," Einora said. She opened her arms and gestured to the walls around us. "It's only fair. You need that secret room, after all."

I shook my head slightly and guffawed. "What? Are you serious?"

"Of course, I am!" Einora said, clasping her hands together. "Why should you stay in that smaller, simpler room when you've got two children? Not to mention you were queen first."

I stood and looked around as though trying to imagine the rooms as they used to be with all my things arranged how I wanted them. I definitely didn't sleep in here, but it

was a haven that I sorely needed during our first year of marriage.

"I-I don't know what to say. Thank you." The wheels were already turning in my head. "

Her eyes shone brightly as she nodded enthusiastically.

CHAPTER
TWENTY-SEVEN

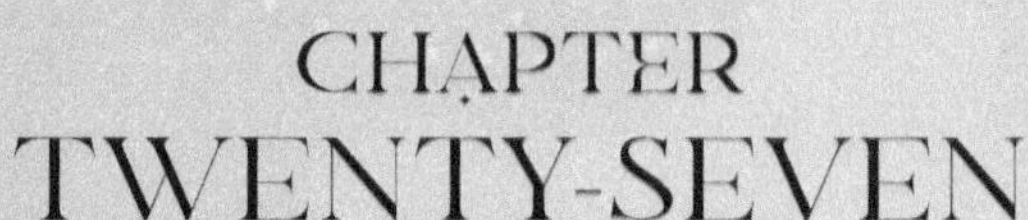

The servants neatly stacked my things on the corners of the rooms—just as I requested. I wanted time to myself to handle my own things. Besides, I missed my usual training session for the day, so lifting heavy furniture seemed like a fair replacement. The children played with their new toys on the bed since that was already in place and I didn't want them roaming around while I was carrying heavy things.

I never expected to set my roots in this deep when I approached the castle a month ago. I definitely didn't expect to get my private rooms back so soon. With the time I spent with Damir and training with my handmaidens, it almost—*almost*—felt like my life wasn't turned upside down three years ago.

As I was working, I heard a knock at the door. The guard at my door announced that Damir was here.

"Come in," I said. I looked up and saw him enter. He wore his velvet robes and tunic—his typical garb for a day of boring business. He smiled softly and I gave a polite smile as he entered.

"Don't worry, just stay here," he told a guard before they nodded and closed the door.

"Your timing is impeccable," I said. I pointed to our kids snoring on my bed. "The children just barely wore themselves out."

"Yes, I know. This is about the time they take their naps."

I chuckled in surprise.

"I poke my head in from time to time when the children are playing with Marita. I know how much your research in your room means to you and I don't want to disturb you."

Why should I have expected any less? Of course, he cares enough about his children. Of course, he's trying to set things right and be a good father. I was honestly touched.

My throat tightened. "Sometimes, when it seems like I'm seeing nothing through the Eyes, it feels like it would hurt less if I never returned."

"I'm glad you did," Damir replied. He reached out but withdrew his hand. "How else would I get to meet our daughter? And how else will we get real justice for you and your maidens?"

"You would've found the killer and their band because

I know you would do it to honor my death. At least, I would hope so."

Damir watched me as I placed some decorations on my bed's side tables. He tugged a blanket up and over the kids.

"You're so carefree and delightful when you're around Einora," Damir said, ruffling his hair. "What can I do to put you at ease around me again?"

"I know where I stand with Einora. I'm not sure I can say the same for you." When he didn't say anything, I wiped a hand on my sweaty brow. "If you had to tell your council right now, who would you pick—me or Einora?"

Damir gasped and froze. I could tell he had a moment of panic. I let him flounder for a second or two and then gestured to his posture.

"See? You either don't know or don't want to say. Einora and I can be honest with each other. She thinks you're going to divorce her, and I think your council is urging you to divorce me and send me back to Ushallav."

"That's not—" Damir lowered his voice as Sanjana stirred. "That's not fair."

"We both know that things are hardly fair for kings and queens. I know this is hard for you but deep down, I'm still hurt."

"Why are you still giving me hell for all of this? You were the one that put it in Einora's mind to move rooms. Maybe I'm not so sure about you, either. What am I missing?"

"I know how your court can be. Out of everyone, she came to *me* for advice. She felt ignored and lonely, so I

gave her my advice. If anything, I just let her talk. None of this is fair to her and I'm…I don't know what I'm doing. I don't want to be anyone's enemy and look what that got me."

We weren't exactly answering each other's probing questions. I could tell that we were pissing each other off. I looked down at the floor and folded my arms.

"I suppose I never asked you why you came," I said. "Just passing through or do you need something?"

Damir just grunted like he was fighting off a throbbing headache. "I just want things to be better. The council is pushing me to make decisions and it's clear that you and Einora are avoiding the inevitable like I am. I just wanted to tell you that the council genuinely wants to keep Devraj in line for the throne. They love him, Anjali. I knew you were worried about him. The problem is that if they're willing to accept his birthright as future king, it means they would have to accept—"

"—that I'm the queen and your wife."

"Something like that, yes," Damir said. "This is a unique situation but no matter what we adults do, Devraj will one day be king."

I sighed a thousand relieved sighs. I could finally believe that I or Damir wouldn't have to be the only ones willing to protect the beautiful, blended family that we've created together. It does mean that if the attempt on my life was motivated by my nationality, my children still needed extra protection.

"There can still only be one queen. The law forbids polyamory, and I don't want a mistress—"

I almost laughed.

"And while I don't want to look down on people who do that, I need a partner to call my own. I wasn't raised to share, you know. And never mention the word 'mistress' around me again."

Damir chuckled and nodded. "Yes, you deserve the kind of marriage you want and not to settle for less. Things would be much easier if you were the king, not me."

"What is with you and Einora debasing yourselves to make me feel better?" I countered. "I hear it all the time from her and now from you. Just do your damn jobs and I'll do mine."

Damir blinked and gasped.

"I don't think I ever got used to that."

"Damir, just be straight with me," I said, pointing at his chest. "That's what Einora does, and that is why I call her my friend. Just…take off that crown every once and a while and be Damir instead of the king."

He pulled my accusing finger and hand over his heart. "I still have strong feelings for you. I refuse to forget how I felt about you—how I still feel about you. I'm doing what I can to respect you but give you space to discover the truth."

"Oh, Damir," I said wearily. I sat in the nearest chair and collapsed. "It's just like Einora tells me. This would be so much easier if we all hated each other."

Damir smiled softly. "Perhaps. But our kingdoms really benefit from the kindness and friendship between the three of us. Maybe they'll understand that one day."

I put my hands on my hips and looked up at him with genuine respect.

"Well," he said, breaking the spell, "I just wanted to tell you about Devraj's status. It won't change regardless of what you choose to do. I wish you luck with your re-decorating project. Also, may I…accompany you in your morning training sessions?"

"For old time's sake?"

"We did it while we were engaged—why not train to catch a killer together?"

I chuckled. "You can come if you wake up early enough."

As I rose to lead him towards the door, Damir suddenly placed his hands on my shoulders like he wanted to pull me in for an embrace. He faltered and pulled away.

"Hugs aren't forbidden, are they?" I whispered. I lowered my voice like we had broken a sacred oath. He rolled his eyes at my dramatics and pulled me into a warm hug. I gave him an extra squeeze before we parted. His hands instinctively went to cup my face but quickly pulled away when we heard a bold knock on the door behind us.

"Milady, it's me, Leela," came a voice from the other side.

"Come right in," I called, wiping my sweaty hands on my trousers. Damir saw his opportunity and gave me a quick bow before going towards the doorway and seeing himself out. Leela came in and noticed the children were moving slightly but still asleep.

"The king paid you a visit?" Leela asked, lowering her voice. She was clearly mimicking the Makaarian court gossipers. I grinned.

"He saw the work leftover and decided he'd come help later."

"Lifting things is what we do best. What shall I move for you, my lady?"

"If you could take down the existing curtains and replace them with mine, that would be wonderful," I instructed. She was here earlier helping me repaint the walls. The flowers were replaced by a hazy blue that gradually turned into a shade of pearl.

Leela gave me a look. I knew that look. I could count on her to always be on my side and let me be honest.

"Has he made up his mind?"

"I honestly don't know. But he did say that no matter what happens, Devraj is still considered his heir."

She nodded and smiled at her prince before hoisting the curtain rods over our shoulders.

CHAPTER
TWENTY-EIGHT

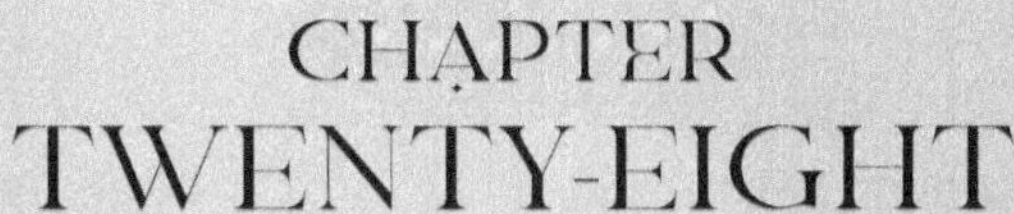

Marita and my maidens went out for a walk. Without having to explain it, they knew I needed a moment to myself in my room. It was warm and overwhelming to see everything where I like it. My initial design was meant to bring a piece of home with me. I wrapped my arms around myself like a hug as I paced around my space and blinked away a few tears.

By the time we were finished, the sun was setting, so rays of orange and red streamed through the breezy curtains. It's too cold to have a balcony but I have a pretty big window to brighten my mood. My tall, skinny cupboards were full of clothing and linens. Each drawer was shorter than the next—creating the appearance of stairs. Devraj loved crawling up and down.

We unfurled all my carpets, stacked my multi-colored pillows, dusted off my writing desk, reinstalled my low-hanging lanterns (more for decoration than for lighting the space), and draped thick downy blankets on my bed. It was still weird seeing my own bed. I already planned on encouraging the children to fill the empty space during bedtime.

As I paced, I noticed a few ways to really root myself in this place.

"But why?" I asked myself out loud. "Am I really going to stay in this room for long?"

I'm either going to take my rightful place and keep my marriage or I won't. And if I don't, I don't think I can stay much longer. I never wanted to live in a shadow—no matter how beautiful.

It hurt to think about the future. I glanced over to where the secret door awaited me. It also hurt to think about the past.

When I shook my head, I noticed a stack of parchment on my desk. A lot of my things were already organized but there were a few clusters strewn across the dark wood. I sifted through and reorganized what I saw. A lot of it was letters—read, freshly delivered, and half-written (by me).

There were a few, neatly folded pieces that were unfamiliar to me. They smelled like floral perfume.

"What?"

They weren't addressed to me. Why were they on my desk? Were they Einora's? Perhaps we didn't move everything out of the room.

The seals were already broken—many were a deep

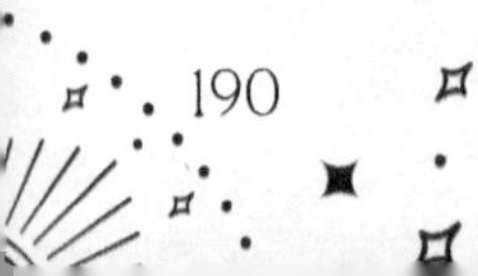

blue-purple. I was curious. I unfolded the first one and began to read. I felt lightheaded.

I opened another. And another. Nausea was taking over.

Makaar deserves a strong heir. How can the heir have a mother who may come and go with the seasons?

She's alive—how is this real?

I want to tell you more about her secret room. I know where it is.

Thank you for getting back to me about the previous queen's belongings. I don't care if we keep those gaudy pillows—I just want them gone.

How many of those eye paintings can you blot out? We really must move on and begin a new reign.

**All I need to do is wring my hands and widen my eyes—Damir will dismiss her.*

I tore through a damning pile of letters—most of them a year or so old. Some fresh. All of them featured delicate Makaarian handwriting and Einora's letterhead and seal.

Einora. Einora. Einora. I clutched the letters and reread them—it's possible I misunderstood. But these letters were real and in my room.

I turned around. In a panicked sweat, I considered using the Eyes to confirm my suspicions. Biting my lip, I shook my head.

Damir needed to see this immediately.

* * *

Soon enough, I was just outside his office. I imagined he had yet another late evening of work; the guards outside the door confirmed my suspicions.

"Please, I need to see him."

When I was met with dubious stares, I spoke up again.

"I have important information that is for his eyes only. Do not make me ask again."

They glanced at each other quickly before one knocked on the door and opened it. I took my chance and slipped through the doorway.

Damir looked up from his work, taking his spectacles off his nose.

"Since when did you wear reading spectacles?" I couldn't help but grin. He rubbed his eyes and stifled a yawn.

"I use them on long and dark hours. I'm not getting too old yet."

Well, the letters I held behind my back might age him a year or two.

"So, everything's in order," I smiled. "You should stop by and see my room sometime."

I wasn't sure how to read his face. He looked equally sad and proud. I needed to stop stalling.

"I noticed some things that were left in my rooms. I wanted you to see this."

Before I regretted it, I handed the bundle of incriminating parchment over. He took it in both hands, clocking the deep lavender seals.

"The seals were already broken when I found them."

Damir frowned and began to read.

"This is Einora's handwriting."

"I…yeah, I guessed."

"This is her perfume."

I shook my head. Damir didn't speak.

"Where is Einora? I think she needs to see these."

I didn't look away. In my heart, I knew I unabashedly trusted Einora. I wanted her to explain this. She's allowed to have her own private thoughts and she's allowed to hate my guts. Gods know I felt the same before I met her. What I needed to know was whether she knew something or was involved in the assassination attempt.

Damir acted like he didn't quite hear me. "It's her handwriting but this isn't her. And who is she talking to? She doesn't address anyone. Did she write them and never send them?"

"Maybe we could order a few stiff drinks," I shrugged. Damir snorted. He leaned over to the side and opened a small drawer. He pulled out a dainty piece of parchment with a matching seal. He held it up against one of the damning letters. His eyes darted back and forth.

"I could be tired from a busy day, but this really looks like her writing. But it doesn't sound like her."

"What's in your left hand?" I gestured to the document he pulled from his desk.

"It's a personal letter to me," Damir replied. "It's something she slipped under the door when we were engaged." I couldn't ignore the slight blush to his cheeks as he diligently compared the two sets of handwriting.

He got up from his chair and excused himself. He quietly talked with the guards outside and then came back inside.

"They're going to bring us drinks and send Einora in."

After an uncomfortable handful of minutes, Einora poked her head in.

"Oh! Damir and Anjali. So good to see you."

She looked pleasantly surprised. I tried to soak in her demeanor—whether this was her or a ruse. I cleared my throat and gathered my senses.

"I found these letters on my desk once everyone left."

I handed them over and watched her inspect them. Damir and I watched as the glimmer and sparkle in her eyes dulled. She looked up, stunned.

"I...I didn't write all of these. Some are fake."

"But that's your handwriting, correct?" I sounded a lot calmer than I felt.

Einora blanched at the pages. She shifted through them all again like she could hardly believe her eyes. She put a hand to her head.

"The perfume is so strong," she murmured. "I promise—a lot of these are fake. Anjali, I don't feel this way."

She looked up at me.

"You're the kindest person I've ever met. Part of the reason why I wanted you to have your room back was so you'd feel comfortable and stay as long as you wanted. We haven't even discussed why *I* am still here—"

I shook my head while Damir groaned.

"This is not a conversation I want to have right now. I just want to know why I found these letters and what they mean. If you can prove that they're fake, then who would go through all this trouble? What is going on?"

Einora found the nearest seat and sat down. She had a hand to her head like she was nursing a headache.

"I don't…I don't wear this perfume. I've always had it but it's too much."

"She hasn't worn it much since the pregnancy," Damir explained quietly.

Einora's pale skin was void of color. I wondered if she was going to faint.

"Show us the real ones, dear," I whispered.

Einora shakily nodded and began dividing the letters into piles. According to her, the real pile included a letter reaching out to my brother—thanking him for the good wishes he sent when he heard about her upcoming pregnancy. A letter asking Marita for help—she struggled to relate with my son…

"I know it's silly but ever since Damir began courting me, I've been practicing—writing letters, I mean. I wanted to sound like…y'know, like a queen. These are drafts. I wrote this one to King Ray and I eventually just spoke to Marita in person. She's very lovely and understanding.

"The point is someone must know about my writing. I should've burned them. It's stupid—I know. But someone knows where I keep my things—my perfume. The bottle is so pretty so I never got rid of it."

I realized she was looking at me. She wanted me to believe her.

I picked up the fake letters. "These don't sound like you. You're better than this. What concerns me is that someone in the castle knows that we are friends, and they want us to distrust each other."

I looked to Damir for support. He agrees with me, but my conclusion is still pretty bleak.

"Someone put in a lot of work to frame you, Einora," Damir murmured. "We are running out of time. We need to find the culprit before real harm is done. I'm adding extra guards and I don't want you to be alone."

"Gregori," Einora breathed. Distraught tears rolled down her face.

"You can protect him. I can protect him," Damir urged.

"I need to go to him. Now."

Einora stood, expecting resistance. I had a sudden urge to find my children, too. These letters effectively put us all on edge.

"Anjali, if you have found any information from the Eyes, you need to tell us." Damir made a point of looking at me straight on.

"I'm not holding back," I insisted. I gestured to the fake letters. "Someone put these on my desk, and I brought them right away. Someone wanted me to see these letters. If you trust me, I can confirm this with the Eyes. It's what they're here for."

"We'll interview everyone who helped move your furniture," Damir decided. "They didn't just magically show up."

I sighed, exhausted. I'm already trying to research who tried to assassinate me and now we need to unravel this new detail. While I'm tempted to delegate this to Damir,

I honestly don't trust the council to handle this quickly or efficiently. These interviews would drag everything.

However, working with minimal Eyes means that I can see who was in my rooms but not who snuck through Einora's private things. And like reading a book, I don't have the luxury of keeping my place in multiple times in history. If I revert to the present-day image, it could take me hours or days to return to my initial research progress.

"I don't like this," Einora shuddered. "I just won't be alone, okay? Someone is trying to scare me. Someone's trying to get Anjali to think that I don't like her. That's not true!"

"Look, we are winning this battle by being honest with each other. We're on the same side and we're working together—our enemy knows this and is trying to separate us. But they didn't succeed because it didn't work. We'll continue to move forward together." Damir and Einora looked at me with mixed emotions. "We love our kids and we'll protect them. We also love this country and we'll protect it. My question is should we trust anyone else with this? Should we pretend that this ruse worked? What are we going to do so things don't become worse?"

Einora, still standing, was inches away from the doorway. She hugged herself and stepped toward this conversation.

"I trust you two. I don't really trust anyone else outside this room. And I don't want to hear gossip about me and these letters. Damir, I trust you, but I don't know if the council needs to deliberate on this incident." Her voice wavered a bit, but she stood her ground. I couldn't help but agree with and admire her.

I spoke up, "I have a feeling that our enemy will only become bolder. Perhaps we should meet together first and then share something with the council. Damir, I know you're just trying to be just and measured. But if I find the person and they threaten any of us, I won't wait for any approval to take them down."

Einora blushed and nodded. She looked like she didn't need my training to transform into a mama bear.

"Let's be safe. But I think this is our best move forward." Damir looked at me and murmured in accented Ushallavi, "Anjali, I still care for you."

I tried to nod as if he said literally anything else. Einora looked between the two of us expectantly.

"He thinks that you should train with me if that would set you at ease," I lied. I smirked at Damir's reaction.

"You mean it?" Einora began. "I've honestly been very curious but too shy to ask. Will you come get me in the morning? That's when you train, right?"

After nodding, I said, "I hope you're an early riser. Gregori can come, too."

After hours of undoing my work, I reviewed the Eye's images—hoping to find a quick answer about the fake letters. I put my face in my hands. The mastermind behind this chaos had time on their side. After reviewing what I could, it was clear that they meshed themselves in the moving process. All I can see is that they came in, left the letters, and smoothly moved on.

I had nothing. No answers.

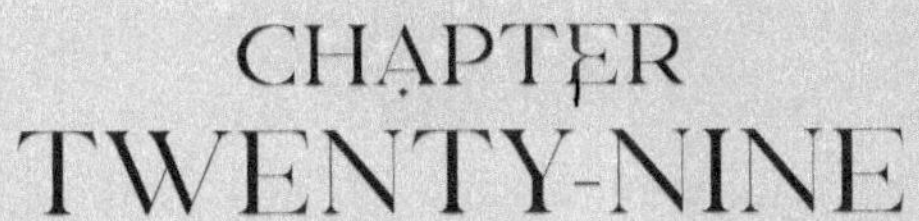

CHAPTER
TWENTY-NINE

I had a good morning of training and couldn't wait to return to my children and snuggle with them before breakfast.

As I approached my room, I thought I could smell something odd. I wrinkled my nose but figured the odd smell came from me.

After taking a while to wash my hair and perfume myself just the way I like it, I put on a simple kameez churidar—a pair of relaxed trousers and a long tunic. I dressed for a relaxing morning that involved breakfast with Damir, Einora, and the children, some light reading, a meeting with Claudiu to compare notes, then hours of research with my Eyes.

"All right, breakfast time," I called. The children were already dressed and playing on the floor. They scrambled to their feet and took my hands. As we approached the door, I could smell that awful odor again. I ruled out myself as the source. I had also changed the children's underpants, so I knew it wasn't them.

I shook my head and sighed.

I let go of Sanjana's hand and opened the door. We took a left towards the main eating hall when I saw it. And the smell was awful.

"Oh, Mama, that stinks!" Devraj exclaimed. He let go of my hand to cover his nose and mouth with his hands. "Stinky bird!"

He saw it before I did. There was a dead crow in the middle of the hallway. I only approached it to confirm my worst suspicions and I practically hissed as I recoiled. I looked up and saw a Watchful Eye looking over us. The message was clear. And I was terrified.

I screamed. I didn't mean to, but I held my children closer until Claudiu came running up the way.

"My lady, what troubles you?" He looked bewildered as he tried to reach out to me but also determine the problem. He looked down and answered his own question with,

"Oh, a dead bird. Would you like for someone to... dispose of it? Queen Anjali, talk to me."

"It's an omen. An evil omen," I said. The children were starting to cry over seeing my discomfort. I felt hot and embarrassed.

"An omen of what exactly?"

I collected my wits and my breath. I took a few steps away from the scene and assured the children that everything was okay. As I knelt to Devraj's eye level, I said to Claudiu,

"In the past, people would pierce the eyes of a creature and lay it before the Watchful Eyes. They beseech Ishka to intervene when the royal family shirks their duties."

I looked up at the Watchful Eye above us in the corner of the wall and ceiling and Claudiu narrowed his eyes to better focus.

"Is this a death threat? And one that the king can easily handle?"

"Yes," I replied, trying to calm my breathing. "Usually, people know we can See them, but they do it anyway. That's how serious they are."

Claudiu held out his arms and I gladly wept and sniffled into his shoulder, and my children took part in that embrace. He's a stoic man but his hugs aren't half bad.

"Perhaps your assassin is here and wants you to know it."

I heard a shriek behind me, and I realized that Leela and the other maidens were behind us.

"My lady, it's—" she began. "How horrible. Oh, how horrible."

"Go fetch Damir, if you can," Claudiu said to my handmaidens. "The queen is deeply troubled."

I looked up at Leela, who paused at the request. She really only took orders from me.

"Damir needs to see this," I said in my brave queen voice. She didn't move until I nodded. She grimly nodded in return before turning around. I completely lost my appetite.

"I can't believe I unhinged so quickly," I murmured shakily once she was gone. Claudiu patted me on the back and helped me up.

"What's important is that everyone is safe. And, you are still capable," Claudiu continued. "You're also surrounded by people who can protect you."

"I'm not always sure about that," I said. "No one could protect me that day. It was run or die. If you and your people weren't passing through…by the gods—"

"Remember to breathe."

"Mama, I'm so hungry," Sanjana insisted. I nodded and hoisted her on my hip. They didn't understand any of this. And may the gods grant that they will never see such an omen on their doorstep.

Meanwhile, I knew I would have to watch this scene again through the Watchful Eyes later today; I needed to know who placed the bird with pierced eyes.

In a few moments, Damir came to understand the situation. Einora and the baby were not too far behind.

"We hear there was trouble, Anjali," Einora said. She held the baby close to her chest and shoulder. I could tell that Dipa and Pari were unfamiliar with such informality, but I didn't care about protocol much. Protocol never seemed to help me.

"I think I feel better now," I said. I stepped back and let the royal couple see the dead bird.

"I will take the children to eat," Leela said. She looked past us and gestured for the rest of the handmaidens to approach. Dipa and Ziya joined the group heading to

breakfast and Pari stayed with me. She rubbed my back for a moment before giving me space.

"Yes, thank you for thinking one step ahead," I said and gestured to the children to go. They looked warily at me but let my handmaidens take their hands.

"My lady, if I may add," Pari began. "Whoever this killer is, they understand our way of life too deeply."

"Well spoken," I replied. She was right. Whoever left this bird knew it would upset me—and I would see them later through the Eyes. I always had a hunch that some Makaarian disapproved of my rule and wanted me gone. This incident created a wrinkle in my theory. Was this caused by an Ushallavi citizen who had a problem with me or was this just a cruel, well-researched Makaarian?

"We'll get to the bottom of this," Damir said. "I'll round up my guards and ask for witnesses to come forward."

"This bird troubles you?" Einora said. "I admit I don't understand. I didn't think *you* would be so disturbed by this dead thing."

Pari spoke up. "Your Highness, it's a cultural taboo. The Watchful Eyes represent the eyes of the royal family or the eyes of Ishka. If someone wants to defy the gods and their moral rulers, they protest by…harming a bird the way you see here before you. This is a promise of future harm."

"This sounds serious. We must find the guilty person at once," Einora said. Her already pale skin was almost void of color. We didn't say anything, but we were thinking about the letters. Both incidents felt very violating and deeply personal.

"But who would do this?" Claudiu asked. "If I may speak, Your Highness." He bowed slightly to Damir and didn't make eye contact.

"Of course, you may speak," Damir replied. He turned to me, concern piercing his gaze. It almost took my breath away.

Claudiu turned to me. "Do you think your assassin is trying to scare you? Or finish the job?"

"Frighten me, yes," I replied. "Again, all signs point to someone close. A person who smiles to my face but wants to stab me in the back."

"We can double the guards patrolling these wings until they're caught. I will arrange a cup bearer," Damir said.

He was serious; it was clear that he was tempering his anger a lot better than I was. I stayed silent and nodded.

"This is dreadful," Einora sighed. "I know I'm not much help but let me stay by your side during these troubling times."

I gestured for everyone to quietly follow me. I wasn't about to continue to have this conversation out in the open. The six of us filed into my room since it was the closest.

"A wise move," Damir said calmly. It sounded like he addressed the whole group, but he looked directly at me. "This person is getting too bold. But I refuse to let this person disrupt my court more than they have. They have done enough to shake up our lives. We can show that we're not afraid by continuing to live our lives and enjoy the good, beautiful moments. We will not let them thieve away our joy."

I nodded. But I could hardly think about joy. I was just *mad*. The sooner this nightmare was over, the sooner I could even define what joy could look like for me. Whoever tried to take my life would regret it. I silently swore on the life of my parents and my babies—I would never let down my guard again until my revenge was secured.

Einora grasped my forearm as I clenched my fists, seething.

"The letters and now this." I shook my head. I realized that Pari and Claudiu didn't know what I meant but it didn't matter. "We need to start listing all reasonable suspects and start narrowing them down. I can search the Eyes for weeks and it won't be fast enough. I wanted justice *years* ago."

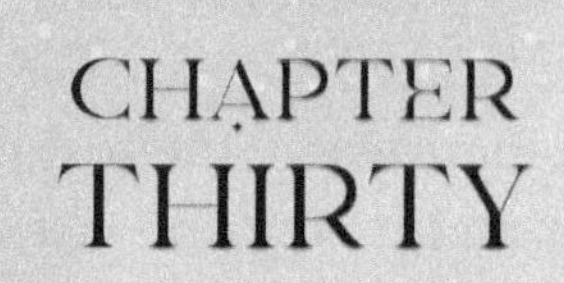

CHAPTER
THIRTY

After a quiet and stale breakfast mood, I decided the reading could wait. I wouldn't feel at ease until I talked to Claudiu. He said he wanted to tell me something that was only for my ears. Pari understood and accompanied us and guarded my door.

Claudiu looked noticeably calmer once we were finally alone. I knew that look in his eyes—he was prepared to be unbelieved.

"I don't quite trust Leela—or any of your handmaidens. I know my Makaarian and Ushallavi are not good, but I trust my eyes. I do not trust Leela."

I didn't want to immediately blow him off, but my half-filled stomach flipped at the thought. I tried to sound reasonable and calm.

"She's been here for roughly two weeks. How could you come to such a conclusion?"

"Who else would know about the damn bird? Who else has access to this part of the castle and the royal family? Before and after you left," he hissed. He didn't want Pari to hear. Claudiu gripped my arm, which he hadn't done since we returned to the castle. He pulled me a bit closer to whisper but maintained his firm but concerned pull.

"I know you want to do what's best for your children, but that servant girl is not good for Devraj and Sanjana."

My heart thumped in my chest as I recalled all the moments—daily moments—where she specifically answered the call to watch the children. She made them happy. She was teaching them our ways of life and our language. Their Ushallavi vocabulary blossomed after my brother brought me new handmaidens.

But something in the back of my mind wouldn't let me completely relax.

"You can let go of my arm." I gave him a determined look before he loosened his grip. "Tell me what you know."

He sighed in quick relief and nodded before continuing.

"I think she intends on harming the current queen."

"You mean Queen Einora?"

"Yes, whatever her name is," he said, rolling his eyes. "Her story hasn't added up and it still doesn't."

"You mean how she came back?"

"I mean how she survived. You said so yourself. Everyone was on the ground, bleeding. Whoever attacked you was supposed to take everyone out."

"But they didn't. I survived," I stammered, my heart thumping more. "What makes it impossible for her to survive? They are trained for this and handpicked for the job."

"I understand. But we would have found her in the woods with you if she was truly trained to protect you and badly injured. And she didn't report back to either kingdom about what happened. You had to tell your own story. They didn't know you were alive until a month or so ago."

"Listen, I value your insight, I do. But…" I stopped myself as the violent memory unfolded itself again. How many bodies did I see? Do I know for sure? I shook my head. I lowered my voice. "This is just bringing all of that back, and I need time to think. I'll talk to you about it later, promise."

Claudiu ran a hand through his hair and grunted.

"Get your mind cleared soon, my queen, because I have a feeling that something bad will happen. There is so much to regret in life, but this includes your children now. Heed my warning."

"I need Leela's help to find the assassin—"

"No, you don't. You can trust literally anyone else to watch your babies. You almost lost them once—"

"Enough," I said, and pointed towards the door. I knew Claudiu was trying to help but he was pushing past the boundaries of queen and citizen. My shoulders slumped, recognizing that he was not my subject and yet sought to protect me. "I will consider your warning, Claudiu. I've just had an eventful morning. For now, it's enough."

Claudiu grunted his goodbyes and excused himself. I tried to calm my heart. Breathe, as Claudiu likes to say.

I…believed him. He had no reason to lie; he was clearly sincere. But if he was correct, then I was wrong about Leela and potentially the other handmaidens.

It meant that if my kids ever get hurt, it's all my fault. Whether or not that's true, it's what I felt.

When he was truly gone, Pari came into the room and joined me. She looked between me and the doorway where Claudiu was moments ago.

"My queen, are you all right?"

"I'm still grumpy. It's been a rotten day and I wish I could start it over." I wanted to read for enjoyment but now I was too upset. I might as well toss the whole idea. If anything, I was too spooked. I'll feel better if I spend more time with my kids and devote an hour or two to the Eyes.

"If I may?" Pari spoke up.

"Of course." She would eventually accept the fact that my handmaidens could tell me anything. They were more like sisters than subjects.

"That man seems to care a lot about you and the kids. He doesn't seem keen on any reward."

"I've wondered the same thing. He is very thoughtful."

"Let's relax for a bit. You deserve it after the day you've had thus far."

I nodded and sighed. I extended my arm so we could hook arms and we left to find the others. I could use a decent snack.

<hr>

When I was finally alone (and ensured Marita had eyes on my children), I locked myself into the room of Watchful Eyes to have my own quiet space to think. I've never revved up the dials and spindles quite as fast as I did at that moment. *Who could be so stupid as to frighten me? Who will be executed before the day is done?*

I must've watched the tapes a few times over before reaching further back. What I saw was confusing: nothing. One moment the hallway is clear, except for the staff going about their business. There are a few moments where the scene is still. Then, the dead bird appears. There's no proof of who put the bird there. Impossible.

The images are there, so I knew the Eye wasn't busted or covered. I turned away the moment I heard my son point out the bird in the recording. I knew what happened next.

I turned a dial, and the image shows everyone walking backward. I replay the image again. I repeated this a few more times until I notice someone in plain robes walk past. The bird falls dully from a long sleeve; I can't see the shape or color of the hand. The person does not slow their pace; they simply move with the bustle of the staff. Long, messy brown hair covers their head so it's unclear whether the person is a woman or young man.

I could see that they moved like a shadow and took advantage of a busy moment of the day—the staff worked their magic and the Ushallavi women were away training.

I didn't know who to blame. My eyes glistened as my dark thoughts betrayed me. This sudden revelation—or lack thereof—felt like an omen that I and my family were doomed. Something awful would happen if I didn't act. I was ready to break something.

I didn't know if I could trust Leela—or anyone—at the moment, so I burst out of the room of Watchful Eyes and sealed it shut. I shoved a chaise close enough to the door to take the temptation away to look through the images again. I knew checking a second time wouldn't change what I didn't see. I changed my clothes and that felt better. I also drank some water, realizing that a headache was blooming between my eyes.

As I approached the door to leave the room, I rolled my shoulders and took a deep breath. With or without the Eyes, I knew I had what it took to find my killer and beat them at their own game.

After asking a few members of the staff, I found out that my kids were still with Marita in their playroom. I sighed with relief.

"Marita, it's so good to see you," I said quietly, trying to smile. She waved from her chair where she watched Sanjana and Devraj play.

"Leela taught me a game!" Devraj declared. He explained it and pantomimed it for me, and I could tell it was a common game that Ushallavi children enjoyed playing.

"That was kind of her to teach you a delightful game," I smiled. I sat next to Marita and asked her, "Where is she, exactly?"

"Oh, she's preparing to return to Ushallav. It's kind of you to let her travel home so often. I assume she's packing up her things in her private quarters or she might have already left."

I looked up at no one in particular but tried not to look too upset. This information, paired with Claudiu's warning, made me uneasy. Her timing was suspicious. But I remembered giving her permission during the party. Should I force her to stay?

As if sensing my disappointment, Marita added, "I'm sure she will bid you farewell before she leaves."

"You're right," I said. Marita handed me a plate of food—some goodies from breakfast that I passed over hours earlier. I smiled with gratitude and started to eat. In no time, my children noticed and begged for a bite. Marita was wise enough to anticipate their interest.

"I heard about the bird. How dreadful."

I chewed silently and sighed.

"I asked the Eyes to reveal the person who put it there, but I couldn't see anyone. It's a mystery."

Marita gave me a concerned look. She didn't know much about the Eyes—she never pressed me for information—but she knew this wasn't normal.

"Pari told me this is a significant, evil thing. How can I help?"

"Reminding me to eat is helpful as always." I gestured to the fruits and breads on my plate. I turned to Devraj. "Chew with your mouth closed, Dev." I gently moved his chin up to clamp his mouth shut. He giggled as I ruffled his hair. Sanjana was faring no better, leaning over my plate and nearly brushing her hair into my food.

"This is not how Ushallavi children eat," I scolded. Sanjana laughed and ran towards her toys before I could wipe her cheeks. I could tell by her movements and volume that she was reaching her highest energy levels and she was fighting off the urge to nap. It would be a matter of time before she started to fuss or collapse on the nearest pillow.

"Knowing I have you to watch these two helps me focus on my research. Without you, I think I would forget my head on my pillow some days."

I earned a smile from Marita. "You are sacrificing a lot of your time and energy to learn the truth. I trust that one day, you will find what you're looking for. I am still grateful that you're here after all that time. You have unfinished business and I know you'll have the strength to see it through."

I wasn't sure what she meant with her encouragement. It was as if she wanted to say something deeper but wanted to still respect the boundary between us—my status. Still, it felt like she could see my heart. I gripped her hand and gave it a squeeze. She gestured to my food with her other hand. I understood the message. I chuckled and obediently ate.

CHAPTER
THIRTY-ONE

This day wasn't going to get much better, so I decided to take care of some business before I went to bed and prayed for a better tomorrow. I shared some documents with Damir that Ray gave to me. Surely, there were some updates on that? I was prepared for all answers under the sun.

Ziya came with me as I went to see Damir and his council. They squeezed some time in for me—how kind. I chose to bring Ziya with me since she seems like the bolder of my handmaidens. She told me in private that she's not quite the one who loves to tend children and would rather help me with the physical and political aspects of my responsibilities. I felt better knowing that I count on her wisdom and strength.

We took our seats. I kept a few documents hidden on my person, like Ray's letter in Ushallavi, just in case I wanted to refer to it.

After a few stale greetings, I tried to get right to the point so we could be on our way and I could tuck Devraj and Sanjana in bed.

"I don't want to take up too much of your valuable time. I'm just checking in about some historical documents that I delivered to you recently. Have you gleaned anything from them?"

They were *so* curious about the Eyes and expected me to find clues within hours instead of weeks, so I half-expected that they would prioritize quick work. I rolled my eyes at the perceived double standard.

"We heard that we were going to see these documents but haven't had an opportunity to inspect them ourselves. Is that why you're here—to drop them off?"

I wanted to scream and break this table in half. Ziya smoothly joined the conversation.

"We delivered the documents per Queen Anjali's request," she explained. "We went straight to King Damir's office."

Damir nodded.

"No one stopped us, and we didn't delay in this task. So, these documents are out of Anjali's hands and in yours."

"Your Highness, where are these documents now?" Benedikt spoke up. His voice vexes me.

"That is a good question. Ziya and the others delivered the documents. I meant to bring them to the attention of this council, but I haven't seen them recently." Damir motioned to the servant standing at the door. "Could you check my office for documents with the Ushallavi seal and bring them here?"

The servant nodded hesitantly and left—probably out of temporary relief. I spoke once the door clicked shut.

"King Ray sent them to us in good faith. He wants to work together to solve this problem. And their research is…*missing?*" I seethed inside.

"No need to be so emotional about the turn of events," a council member tutted. "If they're so important, they will show up in the servant's hands."

I stood and slammed the table. "What do you sit around and discuss all day that is so much more important than my safety? We've endured political stunt after political stunt, and you can't manage a stack of documents from our allies?"

"We can't analyze what we don't have, my lady. Are you suggesting that King Damir is responsible for the missing documents?" Benedikt shot back. "Who is more trustworthy—our king or your new handmaidens?"

Ziya remained motionless but I could tell she wanted to hold him in a headlock.

"This is unnecessary." Damir held up his hands at either side of the table. It was enough for Benedikt to sit back and exhale. "With everything going on, my memory isn't up to par as it should be. The servant will arrive, and we can then continue the discussion."

"Perhaps the next time the Ushallavi king sends vital information, he ought to send it to King Damir directly. Isn't that more prudent?"

"I'm still the queen, so King Ray acted appropriately." I arched my eyebrow in defiance.

"If the servant comes empty-handed, we will search my office to find the map and other remnants that might still be there. I must assume that if anything is gone, it is lost to us. Perhaps, we can discuss what Queen Anjali learned from the documents at another time. In the meantime…"

There was an uncomfortable pause as Damir looked at Benedikt and the other council members.

"Over the past few days, there have been handfuls of citizens who are speaking up about the…current situation. For now, it's just a few loud people being loud but it's possible to expect more physical altercations and mobs," Benedikt explained.

"What are they upset about?" I dared to ask. This wasn't uncommon in either country, but this sounded serious.

"Makaarians know that you're back home. And with that news, it means they have their own opinions about what we should do—who should be the one and only queen. There's also confusion and arguments over which child will be Damir's first heir. Rumors and misinformation have made things worse. And things will likely get worse. We're considering another few weeks or months of limiting travel in and out of the castle."

We all collectively sighed.

"This is what we've been discussing recently," Benedikt murmured. I tried to ignore the nerve. "If you have time, you can stay to discuss—"

"It sounds like my job is to find this assassin."

I didn't want to stay much longer. The council always upsets me in a way I can't always fully define. Here I was trying to be involved and help. And it all continues to backfire. I can't tell who's at fault or who's wrong. What felt wrong was that there was nothing I could do to earn the respect of Damir's council.

"Let's pick up this conversation later. It has been a particularly trying day." Damir stood and the rest of us gladly pushed away from the table and filed out of the room. Ziya helped us make our escape as quickly and smoothly as possible.

"Are all meetings like this, my queen?" Ziya whispered.

"That was a fairly mild one," I groaned.

"Those men are either terrified of you or don't respect you. I don't know how you do it. But we're here to support you. We trust you and love you—no matter where you go or what you choose."

I made an appreciative and tender click with my tongue; I don't hear that sentiment nearly enough. In a rare moment of exhaustion, I pulled Ziya in for a side hug as we walked back to the playroom.

CHAPTER
THIRTY-TWO

Weeks later, Einora started to have reoccurring nightmares. She described someone coming for her and her baby. And normally that wouldn't concern me, except I was told through Damir that in these dreams, she sees me. She sees my face on a stranger's body. I wished she would've told me to my face, but things were not quite the same after the fake letters incident. I would have nightmares, too, if I knew a murderer wanted to prove they had access to my personal space.

Still. It felt like the dreams were my fault.

After Damir found them too difficult to ignore, he summoned me to meet with him and his council. Dipa interrupted my morning training and let me know what was coming. I had a brief amount of time to stretch and cool down before I faced them. I let Marita, Dipa, and Ziya be with the kids when they woke up. Pari accompanied me.

When I entered the room, Pari was behind my left shoulder. She wouldn't leave until forced.

"Good morning, gentlemen."

"Good morning, my queen," Damir answered. "Hello, Pari." He stood to acknowledge me. Pari and I nodded in return and took our places. The only two seats left for us were several spots away from my husband. I didn't like the mood of this room and we barely began. My muscles tensed under my training clothes.

"We will get right into the discussion," Damir said, getting himself comfortable while organizing his papers. The guards closed the door from their post outside the room.

"We will begin with the dreams our queen has been experiencing," Damir said with a pinched frown. He didn't look at me even though I dared him to.

"I don't understand why Einora's dreams call for a meeting," I said, trying my best to be patient. Benedikt sighed and folded his hands on the table before looking at me.

"It's not just the dreams, Queen Anjali," he explained. "Numerous sources have focused our attention on several complicated events. We didn't bring you here to punish you. We need to work with you."

I raised a brow and avoided rolling my eyes. "So, you need my help with something else entirely."

"There have been numerous accounts of mild poisonings among the staff," Damir explained. "And Einora's cup bearer has fallen ill as well. She won't say it, but I think the

nightmares are getting worse because of the real-world threats. The ongoing uprisings and protests haven't helped. We must take this seriously."

"I agree," I said as the heat rose in my chest. "Please tell me what you need, Your Majesty."

Damir pointed his gaze down at me, begging for patience with his eyes. I met his gaze with a smoldering glare. I never used that title—in public or private.

"Our medicine women and men say that the main herb used for this poison only grows in Ushallav."

He produced a small stone bowl—something I imagine an apothecary uses—and inside was a fistful of thin, long herbs. I recognized them instantly and groaned.

I picked one up and held it up for Pari to see. "This looks like Death's Needle. Yes, they speak the truth. The name comes from its needle-shaped appearance." The flower at the very top was dark red and the shape of a needle's head or the shape of a corn kernel.

"If I may," Pari added. "This herb is often used for poisons. You have to amass a field's worth of these herbs to make just one draught. As you can imagine, it's illegal to plant or harvest these plants in Ushallav. After the war, the king ordered that all remaining crops be burned."

I did my best to keep eye contact. "Ultimately, this also means that whoever is poisoning the staff must've put in a few seasons' worth of effort to create these small doses. Meaning, someone planted these illegally long before the carriage ambush. Are the victims recovering?"

The council looked at each other and then back to me. I handed the dry Death's Needles to the nearest council member.

"They're managing the best they can, but the doctors are working on the antidote. They'll need this little batch back—depending on how many more victims they must tend to."

"How very fortunate," I said, still not sure why they needed me. "Were they not able to tell you the basic information about Death's Needle or—?"

"We're facing rumors that you and your handmaidens are responsible for these actions. We have to put them to rest."

It felt like I could see red in the back of my mind. They were blaming me.

"And what does this illustrious counsel think?" was all I could manage. "We are trying to find a killer—not emulate one. We already told you that it is illegal to grow the stuff in our country and we have no reason to harm Queen Einora and the other Makaarians. What have you done to set the record straight?"

No one bothered to inform me of what was going on. I had no proof this was even a problem. Why hasn't Einora told me anything? I thought she trusted me. Was this a test?

"Queen Anjali, we don't have any intention of bringing you to trial until sufficient evidence is raised—"

You all must be heartbroken, I thought to myself.

"—but we are putting an immediate lockdown in the castle until further notice," Damir finished. "No one can enter or leave. In the meantime, we will sort out who is behind all this."

So far, this didn't sound awful, but I waited for more details.

"Who is 'we' in that statement?"

"The council has hired investigators to do a sweep of the castle and arrest anyone who seems suspicious. We don't want any innocent people getting into harm's way. They'll make the arrests, the council will question them, and we'll have our justice."

"So, you're certain the murderer is here and is willing to risk staying here and getting caught?" I asked.

"Once the royal family, the nobility, and the staff are properly secured in secret locations, the real murderer will squirm in the open."

Oh, so this meant I'm being forced to sit in an unfamiliar room while some idiots with half my handmaidens' training will try their hand at saving the day. None of my concerns spurred such action. Now that Einora was clearly in danger, they wanted to pull all the stops.

I slammed both my hands on the table and sat up straight.

"What about my investigation?" I demanded. "Why would you stand in my way—in my own castle? Will I have to sit around while you find this assassin? How will locking the royal family up resolve anything? Do you know what this looks like?"

"No progress has been made for the past few weeks, so forgive us when we say it is our turn to look into these matters in our *own* way," Benedikt cut in.

He'd been asking about the Eyes room for days. I bet he would lose his mind at how simple and boring it is—or that I've shown Einora how to use them. It was only a matter of time before he and the rest of the council pressured Damir for access.

"I still don't understand how the lockdown would benefit the rest of the household. Quite frankly, it's not worth putting us through this over a rumor you refuse to settle properly. Damir, it appears that we're skipping over several options and going for the most dire one."

With the bird omen and this sudden rumor problem, I was really starting to hate mornings.

Damir let out a huge exhale and read from his paper.

"The council hopes to catch the person before things worsen," he said. "We imagine that you would only need to sacrifice a week of your time."

I didn't like this "we" he was using. It didn't sound like him at all. It felt like Pari was the only present advocate. I sat back down and folded my arms.

"I hear what you're saying but I fail to see the logic. We already have someone with free access to the castle who is using my customs to torment me. Now you want to punish me and my family? I haven't even heard about these rumors. Where is your proof that we have cause for concern?"

"Would you like to be escorted to the infirmary? Would you like to see Queen Einora's cup bearer?"

"As a matter of fact, I would." If I was going to be barred from my training or access to the Eyes. They wanted me to go without my queenly privileges and be grateful. I wasn't going to agree with anything unless I heard some sense. I looked at my husband while he studied the parchment before him. "And what will you do? What will happen to Queen Einora and Gregori?"

"I as the king will be summoned when necessary to

keep things going smoothly in the castle, or to help apprehend the assassin," he answered. "Einora and Gregori will be fine with Wendi's assistance."

"So, this is for my protection and to prove I didn't do this? For someone who wants to protect me, you don't seem to like or trust me," I huffed. Benedikt betrayed no emotions, but the other five council members looked unhappy. "I am disappointed that this council has already decided what I should do without informing me. Does Einora even know? I did not poison anyone—nor would I want or need to. And I disagree that being sequestered in some random corner of my own home will help this esteemed council find the guilty member with any amount of extra efficiency. I officially declare this to be a mistake and a miscalculation."

A council member nodded and scribbled down my words. "Duly noted in the official records," he said. "May we also gather a statement from your handmaidens?"

Damir sighed and put his head in his hands.

"You may gather statements from my handmaidens. They are all available except Leela. She recently took personal leave to visit her husband in Ushallav. If you find it absolutely necessary, you can seek her out in Ushallav for a statement. My parents can assist in the matter."

"We will notify you if that is necessary," the council member said to his paper as he wrote additional words.

Benedikt cleared his throat. "We suspect that a traitor is in our midst that wishes to stir up war between our countries. We only wish to keep everyone safe and guarded until the person is found and imprisoned."

"As I've mentioned, this is the first I've heard of it," I said, looking to Damir for his explanation. He winced slightly and sighed.

"It's no secret that there has been unrest since your disappearance. Rumors never cease. Perhaps our people wish to fight each other—even if their royal families do not," Damir said.

"It would serve you well to not keep me in the dark. I could've done more to communicate to my countrymen of my safety, goodwill, trust in you—"

"Yes, a letter would've done something," Benedikt rudely cut in, "but for now we will have someone escort you to your rooms and ensure your children are safe. As appropriate, we will also send someone for you for further meetings and we will send you updates."

"I don't even know these so-called investigators. Damir, have you even vetted them? Does this not seem too rushed? We can do things correctly and without rashness."

I was at such a loss for words. This was an actual nightmare. They either couldn't understand me or willfully ignored my voice. I wanted to return to my training quarters and punch something.

Before I could argue any further, Damir looked at me and gave me a brief glance. It was the first time he offered a smile during the meeting. I knew he wanted to squeeze my hand, to tell me that things were okay and that he believed me.

But by the way he stepped aside and let someone else wear his crown, I knew I couldn't trust that. He didn't really stick up for me. I did not return his smile.

"Your willingness to comply will serve as an example to everyone else. We only ask for your cooperation."

I looked down at the table. My cooperation would hopefully prove that their methods were inferior to mine. But I won't be entirely passive and submissive.

"I will do my part to speed up this process—even though I still disagree that this is the best course of action."

"Duly noted in the official records," came the reply.

CHAPTER
THIRTY-THREE

After a week of complying with the counsel's wishes, I held a stack of letters for Damir. At this point, I don't know if it was even worth it. I just wanted to know what was going on. And I wanted to vent.

We felt quite literally left in the dark. I was convinced that everyone else was living their lives while I was barricaded in this room with my children. Perhaps this was some way to play a joke on the Ushallavi queen. I know Marita insisted that only a week has passed, but I was still losing my mind.

I was keen to hear what these inquisitors, investigators—whatever—found or discovered. I half hoped they found something. I'd rather swallow my pride and resume my normal schedule than stay trapped here in this one room.

Instead of delivering these mostly angry letters to Damir, I started writing a quick letter to Einora. I wondered if she knew more than me. I needed to know that I still had allies even though it seemed like I was all alone.

I love my children very much, but no one was getting sleep. I've already apologized a few times for swearing in Ushallav. I had to admit, Devraj's accent sounded amazing when he gleefully repeated me. The other handmaidens stifled their laughter.

Still, this was no laughing matter.

* * *

After everyone took an afternoon nap, we finally got our first visitor. Our guard opened the door and in strode Damir. I immediately stood up and the children rushed towards him. He stood with his hands outstretched to collect his children. He knelt so they could hug his neck. He chuckled at their voracity.

"Please! Take us for a walk," Devraj spoke for all of us. I just stood there, holding my arms by the elbows.

"Well, do they get to go on that walk?" I asked. "And can the adults get to tag along?"

"I'm afraid not," Damir said. He stood straight again and surveyed the room. "Have you been comfortable?"

I glared at him and gestured around the whole room. It was covered in small beds and littered with children's toys. If it wasn't clear enough, we didn't get much alone time.

"We could all use more than just a walk, Damir. It would be more helpful if we could hear any news. Have the investigators found anything?"

Damir nodded at the guard and the guard returned the gesture. He pulled the door closed from the outside and left Damir inside with us. "The antidote is working well and there haven't been any more attacks. Well, one or two but they were very mild. Perhaps this assassin is running out of poisonous materials. In the meantime, there's been a few arrests."

"So, what does that all mean? Are we still suspect?"

"No, because you have been in here the whole time, correct?"

"Of course!" I protested. "Don't test me."

"Then there's no problem. Remember, this is for your safety. No one in the castle except your guards knows your location. You and the children are safe."

"Damir, the children need to move around. They're too little to understand what's going on. And we need to live like normal people. This is madness. We can't even have personal space to think."

Damir opened his mouth to answer but I held up a finger to stop him so I could continue.

"I am not finished. We have no idea what's going on. It feels like we're the only ones in the dark. It's maddening and you're doing nothing about this!"

"I am doing absolutely *everything* in my power to help. It took enough negotiating to set up this visit," Damir said.

"How is that supposed to comfort me? Should I send your council a basket of fruit? It must be nice to have a week's holiday from taking care of your children. Even with my handmaidens and governess, I wasn't cut out for single parenting."

I didn't care if he or his counsel thought they were doing us any favors—I wanted to use my time to really let him know how angry I was. The others did their best to give me and Damir any semblance of privacy but judging how my voice carried, it hardly mattered.

"Your Majesty," Marita piped up. "If the staff is recovering, does this mean that we have a handle on the situation and we can resume our regular duties?"

Damir's jaw set and I knew I wasn't going to like his answer. "The council needs more time to interrogate the arrested individuals."

"But if you have proof that it wasn't us, why are we locked away?" Pari asked.

"It's not just you. Einora, Gregori, I, and our personal attendants are in similar situations. I get letters and updates from Benedikt. It's for our safety."

I was getting very tired of that excuse.

"You can't leave without telling us when we'll be free," I said before taking a step toward him. "The council promised a week and mustn't go back on their word. Can you at least tell me if Einora and Gregori are doing well?"

Damir paused at my question but finally answered.

"Einora and the baby are doing well. Einora passes her well wishes in return. She misses you and has gotten your letter," Damir said, putting his hands in his trouser pockets. "As for your first question, I can't say for sure when you can return to your quarters. I apologize. I wish I had better news. I just wish I could do everything for you, but I can't."

He turned away and I questioned, "Damir?"

Maybe his solitary confinement was getting to him too. The bags under his eyes said as much.

He whispered, "Would it help if I spent time with Sanjana and Devraj? I admit I haven't had much time with Sanjana. I don't want her to feel like I'm more of a king than a father."

"What are you suggesting? There is no more space in here."

I appreciated Pari's slight snort in the corner. Damir smiled, off guard.

"I mean that they could spend a few days with me. You deserve a break, and they could benefit from a change in scenery. I could take them now, maybe?"

I looked at the other adults in the room. Their tired faces told me they'd be extremely grateful if I accepted that offer.

"Give me a second to think, Damir."

The offer was music to my ears but immediately spiked my anxiety. Just like that? I can just send my two babies to another undisclosed area of the castle? A moment of peace to think or exercise would be swell, but I wasn't sure I could just be without my kids. It wasn't like I didn't trust Damir. I just didn't trust anyone. He took my hands in his.

"I promise I know how to take care of these two. Are you okay? You don't look so good."

Ziya approached us, her arms folded. "With all due respect, Your Highness, but we've been in this room for a week with barely any breaks to relieve ourselves or bathe.

Queen Anjali's killer is still unknown, and someone left an ill omen for her—and we're supposed to wait in here because we're Ushallavi. Have I left anything out?" She looked around at the other women. Marita bowed her head while the other handmaidens gritted their teeth.

The king looked at me. I could tell by the pleading in his eyes that he was just trying to help. He just wanted to be a father and a husband. I sighed and looked down at Devraj and Sanjana. They clung to my clothes and waited for my answer.

"Damir, we just need information. If we have to stay here longer, you can at least tell us what the council knows." I looked at Devraj. "Would you like to stay with Papa for a few days?"

"Can we? Will Sanjana come, too?"

"If she wants to."

"Yes, Mama!"

"Okay, gather your toys. We'll stay here. You'll have lots of fun with Papa."

"I can accompany them, my queen," Marita offered. I sighed with relief and nodded. Marita was a saint among gods. Damir also looked grateful.

"Well, then it's settled. You'll take them for two nights and then I'll take them for another couple of nights. Hopefully, this will all be over soon."

The kids gathered toys in their arms while Marita helped. The room seemed to grow larger the tidier it became. Before long, Damir had his arms around each child and kissed me on the cheek.

"You're a good mother. I just want to be a good father. I'm trying to be the man you need me to be."

I didn't have an answer for him. The exhaustion over-whelmed me. Maybe I could fight or strategize with a bit more sleep. I just kissed him back and kissed Devraj and Sanjana before they eagerly went out of the room and shut the door behind them. Marita gave me one last look before following them.

Dipa, Pari, and Ziya all but forced me into my bed. Like sisters, they pushed the beds together to create one large bed. I wasn't wearing any makeup, but they helped to wash my face, comb my hair, and massage my shoulders. Like a stubborn toddler, I didn't want to rest.

"My queen, we will protect you. Sleep well."

I obeyed and laid down in one of the middle beds. Ziya pulled a blanket over me. She then laid next to me and covered herself in blankets. Pari joined me on my left. Dipa sat in a chair.

"I'll keep watch. You'll feel better in a few hours."

I nodded before laying my head down and closing my eyes. As I was sinking into sleep, I could hear shifting. I think Ziya or Pari sat up.

"I think she's asleep. She deserves it."

"I wonder what has her so worried. We can trust the king, right?"

"I would be upset if someone tried to kill me and is waiting around to finish the job."

"Once this is all over…do you think Queen Anjali would choose to stay here?"

I heard a snort.

"I certainly wouldn't. At the first possible moment, I would seek a divorce and go right back home. To Ushallav."

"But the children?"

A sigh.

"The children."

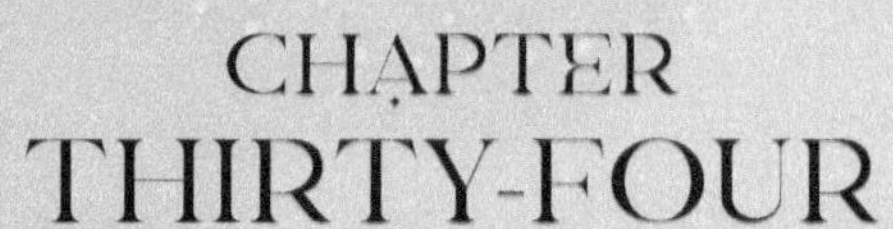

I wasn't sure how long I slept but I dreamed about vital moments that occurred two years ago.

Sanjana was born a week before she was predicted to be due, two weeks after my entourage was attacked in the woods. I kept her safe inside as long as I could. I tried to understand as the Gavril women insisted in broken Makaarian that the stress we endured was all it took for Sanjana to arrive a bit early. They gave me what I needed and let me cry and scream in Ushallavi.

I soon held little Sanjana in my arms. Just like Devraj, she had so much of me and Damir in her features. While her dark brown hair matched mine, the new strands fell into little ringlets. They would one day curl like Damir's once they were long enough. There would be no question that she's a princess and she belongs to me and Damir.

Looking into her face made this whole set of new circumstances that much easier.

"We will soon be with your father again and all will be well," I whispered to her in her native tongue, and I kissed her forehead. "You will be raised in a world where you belong, my little Sanjana."

She snuffled in reply as she tried to find a comfortable position to sleep. I adjusted her as carefully as I could so she could sleep undisturbed in the crook of my arm.

The women gave me a head shawl to wrap around my hair and cover my features. I used it to create a cover for Sanjana's pinched face. She continued to fuss and stir, but with the adequate darkness and a short lullaby, she was comfortable and content. At that moment, I wished I had Devraj at my side. I missed his little face and his already-feisty personality. Having him near meant that he was safe and I could ensure that safety.

"Anjali? Your Majesty," I heard outside Claudiu's covered wagon.

"What is it?" I hissed back. I didn't want to be rude, but his timing was awful.

"Oh, forgive me," Claudiu said, once he saw Sanjana asleep in my arms. "You must come see this. It's dire."

"But—?" I managed, holding up my arms a bit as if ensuring he could truly see why I couldn't leave.

"Bring her with you. Yandra will tend to her." Yandra was just one of many midwives; his suggestion was good enough for now, but it caused my stomach to tighten. What was so dire? What news did they glean?

It took me a few minutes to properly stand after using a free hand to grapple with Claudiu's pillows and hanging pots and pans to fully stand up. He repositioned the little step ladder so I could carefully step out of the wagon and into the afternoon sunshine filtering through the trees and foliage.

As if on cue, Yandra came and said soothing things in Makaarian to me and gracefully took Sanjana out of my arms. I kissed my baby's brow twice before following Claudiu. His face suggested that I wouldn't be trekking back to Makaar any time soon. My shoulders slumped at the thought.

"Our scouts recently found this while surveying the area," Claudiu said. As he finished, he led me to a small pile of arrows. Those black arrows. As if opening a third eye, I imagined the arrows piercing through my coach and killing my beloved handmaidens. I clutched my chest as though I was pierced myself. My leg ached.

"They are familiar," I said hoarsely. "My killer used these arrows."

Claudiu nodded gravely. "We're heading up north and west around the Makaarian border. We want to keep you somewhat close to your kingdom but keep on the move. These arrows were used for hunting a mile or so away from the site where your people were shot down. We suspect that it means the assassin is still looking for you as you predicted."

"Once I am strong enough, you can just take me to the palace," I protested. "You and your people have already done enough for us." What I really wanted was an excuse to finally leave and return to my family.

Claudiu revealed a folded piece of parchment from one of the men standing around the bundle of arrows. He handed the parchment to me and said, "Our scouts found this letter. It's for you."

I looked up in shock, holding the paper in my hands. The scouts didn't lock eyes with me, but they nodded their heads in respect. So now they knew I was Makaar's queen. I wondered if that would help me or not.

"Where was this letter, exactly?" I asked, my voice shaking. I almost didn't dare unfold and open the letter. It felt heavy in my hands.

"They just came back from scouting the area to see what became of your people—just as you asked," Claudiu began. "It seems like the letter was left for you, but the whole place was deserted. Since the letter is from His Majesty—"

"Damir wrote this?" I cried, almost as if the paper were aflame.

"Yes. The letter was there but the bodies were gone. Perhaps your kingdom found them and took care of them?"

I knew we were already at least twenty miles away from that incident, but it burned in me—the idea of running back to the destroyed carriage in hopes of finding Damir's search party. They wouldn't have to mourn me any longer. I could return triumphant with my baby girl. I would come home and never leave Damir's side again.

"We'll give you some privacy," Claudiu nodded towards the parchment in my hands and walked a few paces away to continue chatting with his people. He was just close enough that we could see each other.

"Well, let's see what this says," I said to myself and unfolded the parchment. In Damir's simple hand, the letter read as follows:

My Dearest Anjali,

I have sent my soldiers out to find you and your party. We heard from your parents that you never made it to Ushallav. We are doing everything we can to find you and bring you and our precious daughter back home.

If you receive this letter, know that I came as quickly as I could to find you. My heart feels like it's torn in two without you near me. Gods forbid anything has happened to you. I didn't find you here with your entourage and I assume the worst. I now look to my council to determine who did this and how to bring you home. I have a feeling in my heart that you are still out there—alive.

As much as I want you to return straightway, I must beg for you to stay hidden and wait for further letters and contact. We will send messengers in all directions to find you once we've learned more. I promise you that I will find you, even though it seems like I'm telling you to stay away. For now, it is safer for you to hide until we find them and bring them swift judgment only my gods and your gods can provide.

My darling wife, be safe and be wise. We will bring you home safely within the month. You have my word.

Your husband now and forever,
Damir

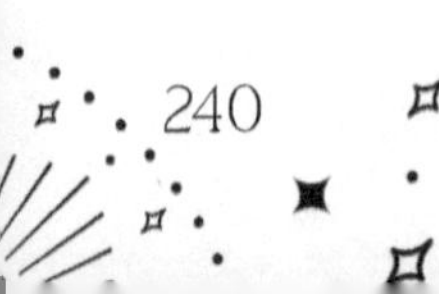

I looked up from the letter, feeling confused, elated, and every other imaginable emotion. Damir was so close. I could ride out to meet him, but he insisted that I stay. Although tears threatened to fall, I decided to respect his plans. I didn't have much of a choice, anyway. It still hurt to walk; I was far more emotional after Sanjana's birth than I ever imagined.

When I showed Claudiu the letter and explained the situation, he put a comforting hand on my shoulder.

"I'm sorry we can't take you back to Makaar," Claudiu then said. "But your enemy is dangerous. A few of our men and women have already been seriously wounded or killed just by searching the perimeter. It's too risky for us. We are not great fighters."

"You don't have to explain, Claudiu," I said, looking him in the eye. "You and your people are wise. I couldn't ask for more. The king promised to handle this."

"I know it's still not ideal for you, Your Majesty," he replied. "But we would take you in—whether or not you're the queen."

"That's reassuring," I said, trying to smile. "Thank you."

I looked down at myself, dressed in donated clothes from the other women. I was starting to blend in—to my benefit. Even though our facial features and skin tones were not identical, I clung to my anonymity gratefully. I didn't want to get caught by any persistent enemies and I didn't want these people to take the fall for our politics. In the meantime, I picked up some of their language (easy to pick up if you know Makaarian) and found comfort in their customs.

I sighed and said, "Sometimes I think I wouldn't cry so much if I could punch something."

"Punch something?" Claudiu repeated. "Oh yeah, I heard something about Ushallavi women loving combat."

"Our training is tradition," I smiled sweetly. "The entire royal family is expected to train their bodies hard to protect themselves. It shows that they are strong enough to take care of their own family and the rest of their kingdom."

"Is that right?" Claudiu mused. "Well, you tell me when you're fit for exercise, and I'll help you find something to punch."

He nodded at me slightly and left me inside his wagon once more. I had a little grin on my face at his suggestion. Yandra and the others said that I would need time to recover. I prayed to Abhijita that my body would be whole once again so I could retain my previous training. I could be strong for Damir until the good news came.

Once I woke up, I sifted through the dream-memory for clues. The black arrows are ever-present. I remembered how frustrating it felt to know that the assassins were combing the area and prevented me from going home. They were ruthless and restless. I thought more about the letter. Considering that someone already tried to copy Einora's handwriting, I pondered whether Damir's letter was real. It hurt—that letter kept me going for a long time. I thought it was proof that I could come home when I was safe—when my intuition told me it was okay to take my daughter home.

My stomach soured. I searched for the worn letter where I kept my private things. I pulled it out of a carved box and read the real letter again. Damir asked me to stay hidden in the letter and then asked me what took so long in the flesh. Maybe I held another forgery; maybe my killer wanted to corner me in the mountains until they found me. Regardless of its legitimacy, I held a brittle wish.

CHAPTER
THIRTY-FIVE

The adults-only days went by too quickly despite our cramped quarters. Soon enough, the children were back. Safe and sound. Later that evening, something woke me up.

"Mama! I had another bad dream," Devraj whined. He kept repeating himself until I woke up completely.

"Where is Marita?" I asked, rubbing my eyes. I had an eyelash in my eye, so I tried to un-blind myself while Devraj woke up his sister with his whimpering. She also insisted that she was having nightmares. I noticed that everyone else was still, so I sat on my bed with my children in my lap. I held them in my arms and rocked them until their breathing calmed down.

It felt unsettling once I noticed that none of the four other grown women stirred from their sleep after hearing my kids cry. I fumbled in the dark and lit a candle. I didn't want to spoil their sleep, but it had me worried.

Marita, Pari, Dipa, and Ziya were missing. I rubbed my eyes with my free hand; surely, this was an actual nightmare.

"Devraj, did you see the others leave?"

"I don't know, Mama! I haven't played with Marita for hours and hours! I was asleep."

I furrowed my brows and sighed. Looking down at my children, all I could do was squeeze them a little tighter into my hug. They gripped my night clothing.

"Did everyone go pee?" Sanjana questioned. Part of why our situation was so unpleasant was that we were only allowed to leave for periodic baths—we used chamber pots in this room and took turns giving each other some semblance of privacy. That's something I'd like to see the council pull off during the next crisis.

No, something was wrong, and I wouldn't be able to fall asleep any time soon.

Thinking about my dream—about that letter wishing me to stay and hide—I decided half-sleepily that we deserved a small walk around the halls. We were strong enough to move and act. My handmaidens help me—I feared that now they needed me.

I took Sanjana in my arms and hoisted her on my back; she gripped my neck gleefully. I took Devraj's hand and told them we would go look for Marita and the handmaidens. We could at least ask the guard if they knew anything.

Together, we padded out of the room and out into the castle gloom. When I opened the door, I could tell we were awake before dawn; the halls were still dark and still. That should've made me nervous. It meant that my sisters had been gone for a long time.

I expected a guard to flinch and turn toward us the moment we appeared, but we were met without any resistance. I ventured forward with my candle to look for a guard. Devraj gasped and clutched my leg.

"Something touched me!" he cried in a harsh whisper.

"What?" I returned. I crouched to his level and my eyes were adjusted enough that I could see a heap of armor. A guard. I tested his pulse and the moist results told me everything I needed to know.

Our guard was dead. But why stop with the guard and not come into the room? I didn't share my thoughts with Devraj or Sanjana. My heart thundered in my chest. My muscles begged to move, and my instincts cried out for vengeance. No one comes this close to murdering me or my children *twice* and gets away with it.

"The guard can't help us find the ladies. Come with Mama," I told Devraj, yanking him sweetly but swiftly away from the dead body. I directed him back into our room and I closed the door right behind us.

The side of my body became flush with the door as I tried to collect my thoughts. Devraj was whimpering a bit and I walked back from the door, sure that if the killer was close, they would potentially destroy the door.

"Come here, sweet boy," I soothed, crouching down. Devraj came to my chest and Sanjana climbed down my back and I arched my back so she could land safely on the floor.

"I want Papa," Devraj sniffed, on the verge of crying.

"Father makes you brave, huh?" I said, also fighting the tears. "Let's be brave for your papa until he comes to us, okay?"

I knew I needed to leave this room, confront my attacker, and put all of this to rest. I felt a surge of energy through my limbs—even in my teeth—that I needed to do something now. I was done recovering. I was done waiting. I was done doing things someone else's way. But the children. I couldn't leave the two here in this room alone.

While I was still crouched, I took my children's hands in mine, and I kissed them both on their cheeks.

"It's time to be brave, my littles," I said to them, wondering if they truly understood.

Devraj returned my kiss and proudly responded, "A prince must be brave. And princesses, too."

"Brave princess! Brave princess!" Sanjana chanted. She kept chanting that while I grabbed my long shoulder sash and used it to strap my brave princess to my back. I also tied and wrapped my nightgown around my waist and put on trousers—just like my warrior handmaidens are trained to do.

"We are going to walk through the halls and find Papa. If you hear anything, tug on my hand, Devraj. You need to be sneaky and quiet."

"Sneaky and quiet?"

"Yes, just like a warrior prince. Sanjana, hold onto Mama tight."

I felt Sanjana nod her head in my hair.

After dressing my boy and kissing his forehead again, I lit a sconce, blew out my candle, and thundered down the hall.

My first instinct was to head to my room of Watchful Eyes. Perhaps, we could catch the attacker and pray that their work wasn't completely done in darkness. I tried not to panic as I slowly made my way through the halls. It took three wrong turns to figure out where we were and re-orient ourselves.

No one crossed our paths. My children were surprisingly quiet despite their labored breathing. With a few cues from Devraj, we righted ourselves and soon found ourselves in the royal wings of the castle.

Again, I saw no guards. I was starting to worry. I didn't even see any victims slumped on the ground like my guard outside our door. My children were blessedly quiet throughout the ordeal.

After I fiddled with the door, we finally burst in. The whole room was a mess, and my heart sank. Most of my heavier decorations were left undisturbed, but whatever could be toppled over was splayed all over the carpet. I gasped and immediately rushed into my room of Watchful Eyes.

Each eye fizzed and popped as I entered. With a bit of light, I could tell every last one was smashed. I was blind. Even the pillows and curtains were ripped to shreds One of my relics from home was carelessly tossed aside, so I understood quickly what my attacker used to destroy all my evidence.

I seethed with anger, frustration, and fear. Someone close to me was capable of this. The bird, the herbs, and now this.

"What are you trying to do?" I murmured aloud. "What do you not want me to see?"

I studied the room to look for any more clues. I noticed that the most ornate Eyes were the most abused. I remembered which rooms they oversaw, and I knew where I needed to go. The smear of blood trailing from the room toward the hall gave me grim assurance that I was on the right trail.

I collected my children and we dashed out back into the darkness. I hoped I wouldn't be too late.

CHAPTER
THIRTY-SIX

Devraj practically sailed behind me as I held his hand and padded quickly through the castle. Sanjana nearly choked me with her grip. Our next destination wasn't too far away. Surely, we would see some guards. But alas, no one heard us.

Based on the clues left behind in my destroyed Room of Eyes, there was one last room left to check. I threw open the door to Gregori's nursery without knocking or listening. I gasped; my children were gulping for air, too. My sconce and the open windows revealed a sight I didn't wish to see.

Leela stood very close to the open window with Einora's baby in her arms. With a quick glance around the room, I could see that there was some sort of struggle in here. Again, pillows, curtains, and furniture were torn and discarded. My stomach tightened and squeezed at the sight of my other handmaidens strewn around the room, unmoving.

I ushered Devraj behind my legs.

"You've been busy, Leela. You never had a partner, did you?"

"No. I wasn't much of the marrying type," Leela replied coolly. She wore an odd version of her handmaiden uniform. Seeing her in a different color—a dark maroon—was a bit unsettling. "After watching you struggle despite all your privileges, I knew there was no hope for a handmaiden like me. No community—no help. No real love."

Gregori snuffled and squirmed in her grip. She bobbed him in her arms—much like she used to do for young Devraj.

"I saw your work—you destroyed the Eyes. Why would you do such a thing? You know how long I've been searching for answers about the past. Am I to believe that you're responsible for all this? Everything?"

She tried to look demure and sorry but we both knew the truth.

"You tried to kill me in the forest that day. You're the assassin." I murmured between breaths, "You were trained for better things, Leela."

"You shouldn't have come." Leela dared to look me in the eye for just a moment before looking at the carpet.

"I order you to calmly hand over Gregori. Right now."

She recoiled and my heart crammed into my throat. She was so close to that open window, and she knew it.

"You would be the queen we deserve if you would just let me help."

"He's just an infant. Give him to me. Now." She wasn't making any sense. Her "help" killed my handmaidens years ago—nearly killed me and my daughter.

Leela turned her body, so Gregori was facing the window. She looked at me, daring me to come any closer. I held up my hands and clenched them into fists before lowering my arms.

"We watched and watched, and you did nothing. You had this chance to do something and Damir and his fucking, bloated council just walked all over you. You got soft. You left your Ushallavi side at home and you…you changed."

"So, you decided to *kill* me?" My pulse boiled. "I wasn't good enough for *you*, so you decided to take me out right then and there?"

Leela looked defensive but I kept going.

"Instead of using your voice as my handmaiden, you decided to murder me. Instead of talking to me, sharing your feelings, or doing anything reasonable, you set all of this up to hurt me. Why punish me for all of this? Out of anyone you could have punished, you targeted me?"

"I am still willing to do what you won't do, my queen," she countered. "I wasn't trying to kill you—I was trying to start a war. Zayant closed his eyes too soon. Everyone moved on too quickly after the fighting stopped. You actually trusted Damir that he would just make all the slurs and animosity go away. They treated you like filth here. We *tried* to tell you what was going on. You let us down—your vision of the future means nothing because it didn't work. You say I did nothing reasonable? *I'm* the only one with the guts to act and do what was necessary. I dared to tell the truth and move us forward to action."

Leela wasn't making sense. She was unhappy with court life and thought that her ambush would alleviate our tense relationships—or send us backward and back to the battlefield? And then when I returned, she created more chaos and unrest—for what? What good I could perform was halted before I could begin. Her unraveling logic concerned me even more. This unwell woman was holding a baby.

"Look how quickly Damir replaced you with a Makaarian lady. Does that not boil your blood? I orchestrated an attack to show how weak the Makaarians are. I knew you would live. But if you perished, then perhaps it was Abhijita's will. You are not strong enough to emulate her."

"You are one to talk about strength and emulation—you murdered innocent women out of your impatience for change! Tell me—why did you betray your sisters? Your sisters died for you to make this dream a reality."

"Don't! Don't you dare call them my sisters."

"You were all sisters to me," I nearly shouted. "I was all alone in this castle, and I knew you would catch me if I fell. I trusted you with my babies, Leela. I trusted you with my life and my sanity when I felt broken. Yes, they were your sisters, and you were theirs. And you killed them!"

"No!" Leela shuddered. "I chose to step up and do the difficult thing. I told the others that Damir wasn't good enough for you. He let you fight for your seat at his table alone. We shielded you from many harmful things that his people said about you, Devraj, our practices—everything. I was tired of keeping quiet and waiting for Damir or anyone else to give you a fighting chance. The handmaidens didn't listen to reason, so they died doing their jobs. If I must die to do my job, so be it."

Leela looked over her shoulder and out the window for a brief moment, but it was all I needed. I took Sanjana's nuzzling blanket and suddenly threw it at Leela, covering her face momentarily, which allowed me to snatch Gregori, free my right arm, and jab her in the throat. She knelt on one knee to recover and take in huge gulps of breath.

I dashed past Gregori's cradle, looking for cover. I could see Wendi crumpled by the foot of the cradle—her eyes glazed and dead. I pulled at the cradle and placed Gregori inside and whispered to Devraj to stay behind the cradle and watch over his half-brother. I wasn't sure if I wanted him close to me or the baby, but I didn't have much time to decide.

Leela glared at me and unsheathed a sword—one she was required to conceal and wear at all times. She was still breathing irregularly, and her throat matched her maroon clothing.

"I don't want to use this against you, Your Highness."

"Ziya, Pari, and Dipa—did you kill them, too?"

She gripped her weapon tighter.

"They put up a fair fight. Much more than the pithy investigators. Your hubby trusted these men to do a woman's work, huh?"

"Your use of Abhijita's blessings is a waste. We fight to preserve life. We strengthen ourselves and our community.

You've torn everything down—and for what? You attend a few meetings with me during my first few years as queen and you think you're a political expert?"

Left, right, duck, uppercut, knee.

Leela went right, left, block, block, dodge, swipe with the sword.

"All I know is that the people responsible for the abuse and injustice we Ushallavi women faced were sitting at that table and ignoring us. I refused to be ignorable."

"I still don't understand why you would plan to kill me and threaten my children and yet you didn't lay a finger on the Makaarians. You know that out of all your victims, I'm the only one who can fight you now."

Leela's face quaked like her emotions were pressing against her skull and eyes, begging to burst.

"Damir wasn't supposed to remarry. His Majesty wasn't supposed to sympathize with a Makaarian. These kings should've taken their grief to the battlefield where it belongs."

Sharp exhales shoot out from me as I bend my knees to get in her pocket, leave some bruises, and step out. She's turning purple and my nightgown is becoming crimson. I dodge her blade as it slashes through a curtain and drags down the fabric.

She let out a roar. I tore my bedclothes to create new hand wraps.

"Your plan failed at every turn, Leela. And you're going to tell me if it was your sole legacy or whether you have help."

Leela flashes a sneer. Her lip quirks on her right side and her teeth glint.

"Shut up and forget it. Forget everything—like the bird and the letters and the arrows," Leela murmured as she lunged forward.

I could tell she had nothing to lose, and I was the opposite. I realized I was defending three young children and my honor against a woman I trained myself.

Sanjana was continually weighing me down. She seemed to get that because she tried to wriggle free. I ducked out of Leela's way and untied the wrapping around my shoulders and chest so Sanjana could spring free; she hung onto my neck until I leaned backward, and she hopped down. My baby ran from the fight; I watched her lay next to a motionless Pari in fright. I bent my knees deeply and leaned forward as Leela swung. She nicked my cheek, and I felt the sting.

Leela readied herself again. She jabbed quickly and harshly. I dodged as best as I could. I knew what to do to protect myself from a sword while unarmed. As long as she didn't come near the children, I could control the situation.

This came to me in a flash, and I surged with hope. Even though I felt my blood trickle and dry against my cheek and neck, I knew I could do this. I had to. A mother's will flowed through me—something Leela could never understand.

She began swiping at me again with the sword and I ducked or darted away in time. She was losing her control and giving into anger. I had to slap the blade on the broad side a few times in defense, but I timed it as best as I could.

She began backing me into the same corner where I moved the cradle. The baby also started crying and fussing. Gods, I hoped there was at least *someone* Leela hadn't killed that would soon hear the cry and come. Someone who wouldn't make things worse.

I wanted to block and evade until I could inch near something to hit her with but there aren't very many weapons in a nursery. When I had the chance, I threw whatever was on the floor to distract Leela. Toys, blankets, rags, and clothing flew into her face, and she ripped them away—just as I taught her. She knew I was stalling.

"Are you going to fight me or what? Fight me!"

"You know the consequences of testing me. You threaten my family? Only one of us will live and leave this room."

She left just enough of an opening for me to plant a firm kick into her chest. I took my moment and slammed my other foot into her stomach. It sent her back a few steps—enough for me to side-step into a safer position. She still gripped her sword and kept her eye on me.

"I caught that white bitch using the Eyes. You showed her how to use them, didn't you? If I'm your sister, why did you never teach me?"

I ducked and swung my fist into her side. "You clearly didn't deserve to ever see what the Eyes could show you. She was worthy."

Leela growled at this.

"You were going to let her be queen, weren't you? You were meant to bring our people joy and advantage! You embarrassed us with your consent to her power!"

"Killing does not help!" I struggled. "And her name is Einora!" She swung close and I darted to the side to snatch her wrist. The blade quivered close to my breast and shoulder. I held her steady, but I couldn't hold her off for too long.

CHAPTER
THIRTY-SEVEN

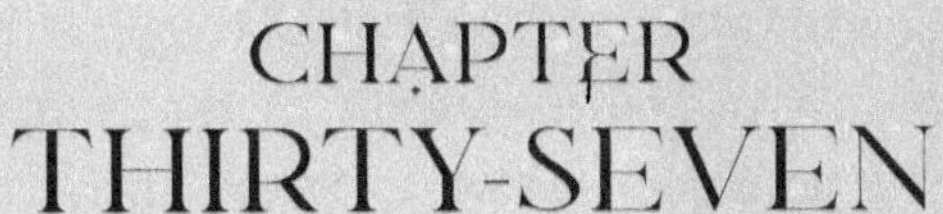

A chamber pot suddenly tore through our space and hit Leela in the arm. It was enough distraction for me to lunge away and disarm Leela.

I looked for the source and saw none other than Einora on the floor. She had a host of scratches and cuts up along her arms and legs. Torture lines. She had dragged herself towards the cradle, leaving a trail of her own blood, and sobbed at the sight of her son.

My children sobbed to my right. So much sobbing. I needed help—Leela's job was to help me. And here she was, sticking her thumb in my metaphorical wounds.

I was so, so tired of everyone taking their frustrations out on me.

With tears in my eyes, I flew into a rage. I didn't care that Leela was close to picking up her weapon. I landed blow after blow to her already wounded arm and pushed her into the soiled carpet. I certainly wanted to kill her.

She's the reason for my suffering.

She's the cause of so much death and she dared to stop Sanjana from coming to this world.

She's the reason I missed two years of Devraj's life.

She dared hurt my family.

She left me and her black arrows in the dirt.

Soon, it became punch, punch, hook, dodge, duck, punch. Everything was a blur, but at one point, I yanked her arm up and away—hard enough that I finally broke her arm. She screamed, slowed down, and yielded. She bowed her head and with a half snob, half snarl, she conceded:

"Spare me, Anjali, I beg you. I yield."

I held her wrist until I heard the tell-tale pop and crack and I stared at her.

"That is Queen Anjali to you," I murmured, watching her clutch her broken arm and bite her lip. I knew she was in considerable pain and by her training, she showed little weakness in her face. "I regret the day I thought you were fit to watch over my children—your prince and princess."

"They would be so much more if you killed this false queen and took back what's rightfully yours," Leela said between gulps of breath.

"Don't you even dare pretend you know what is rightfully mine. Don't you dare act like you know what my life has been—privileges and all. I fought in the woods—I know what's rightfully mine."

As if all at once, I felt the weight of my age and fatigue fall on me all at once. My fighting spirit left as quickly as it came and I panted, putting my hands on my waist.

Before thinking further, I remembered Einora, and I rushed to her side.

"Einora!" I cried, kneeling next to her. Einora leaned heavily into the cradle and stroked Gregori's cheek, trying not to get her blood on his skin. Einora shrieked a bit, likely in fear. Her shriek morphed into a sob, trying to communicate her pain and anguish.

"I know it hurts, Einora. I do," I hushed.

"Everyone is dead," she stammered. "Marita was running through the hall, but she was cut down, and Wendi lies dead across the room. I couldn't call for help—"

"Yes, I know what she did." I tried to slow my breathing—her blubbering was making me anxious. I tried counting heads to make sure everyone was still okay.

Sanjana must've been hiding because I couldn't see her head of curly hair.

"How could you let this monster in the castle? The children—"

"Sanjana?" I choked, ignoring Einora.

"Mama!" Devraj screamed. I turned and saw Leela looming over Einora, the crib, and me—the sword held high in her good arm.

"No!" I cried, crossing my arms over my head in a foolish but sudden defensive pose.

I only felt the sting and slice on my arms, and I'm shocked. My stupid decision should've cost me my arms. They began to bleed, and I began to scream but nothing more.

The sword fell clumsily from Leela's grasp as she slumped to the side, moaning and gurgling in pain. Einora and Devraj screamed. I took hold of the hilt to toss it across the room and away from us. Devraj clung to me and wouldn't stop screaming.

"It's okay, baby." My blood was everywhere. He clutched at my clothes while I held my injured arms close to me.

With all my remaining strength, I shoved Leela away with my shoulder and she rolled, hissing in pain and grappling at the carpet. Footsteps entered the room, and someone took the sword from where it lay on the floor. Three more guards grabbed Leela and propped her up to her knees. At that, she used her remaining strength to roar and scream in Ushallavi. All at once, I realized she had an arrow in the back of her thigh and neck. Served her right.

I breathed heavily—who shot her? As my vision swam and refocused, I saw Damir and Sanjana in the doorway. He dropped his bow and arrows to pick up Sanjana. She bawled and clung to him.

"Sanjana brought me here! Everything is going to be okay!" he cried, coming near us. My daughter spilled out of his arms and rushed into mine. I had streaks of my blood on my forearms, but I didn't care. I held my brave princess and rocked her.

The tears finally came. My mind was scrambling to make sense of everything that just happened. I felt more strong hands around my neck; Devraj was near and crying into my shoulder.

"It's over. Mama's okay. We're all safe now." I continued to soothe them in Ushallavi and dried their tears with the wrap I use to carry them.

"You have to take Einora to the nurse," I said, looking up at Damir. "She was badly tortured and needs attention. Now."

Damir nodded. He tenderly kissed my forehead and soon ordered his bodyguard into the room. "Help me carry her."

"Your Grace, we'll have to do this carefully," the guard nodded. He snatched a blanket in the cradle and tried to wrap a frantic Einora with it.

"My son!" she cried, resisting. "I have to take my son!"

"You're badly hurt, Einora!" I protested, though fully understanding her demeanor.

"Watch him, Anjali! Please!" She locked eyes with me. She was scared but I could see that she still trusted me. To show good faith, I went to his cradle and stood watch. He was crying in his crib and there was nothing I could do except let him grip my red, red finger. My arms were too injured to carry anyone.

"Gregori," Einora called out. The guard and Damir quickly lifted her and carried her out. She sobbed at the pain and was soon gone down the hallway. The open windows assured us that the sun was finally ready to rise.

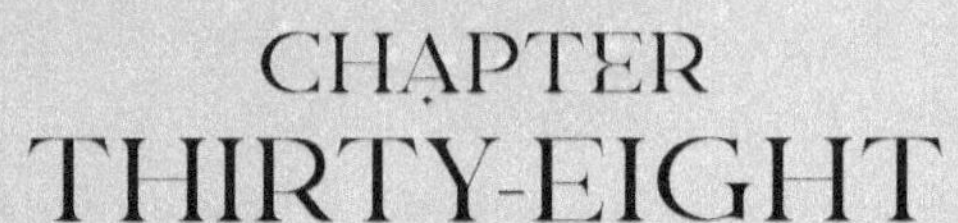

CHAPTER
THIRTY-EIGHT

Even though Claudiu wasn't with me, I could hear his words in my mind.

"Breathe in until your lungs and belly cannot bear it any longer. Then release it all. Release until you have no more breath to give. Think on your breath until you feel a little better."

While I was alone with Gregori, I breathed and held my bloody arms close to my body. With time, I can see that Leela cut skin and muscle. Thanks to Damir's timing and good shot, that was the extent of my injuries.

"Dev, come with me and Sanjana. It's okay." Damir returned to the room and tried to patiently guide our son out of the room—likely to get him somewhere calmer and safer. Who is still here to watch him besides his parents?

Devraj clutched my clothes and sniffled. He cried so

hard that he hiccupped. Terrified, he looked at me and I weakly encouraged them to go.

"I'm right behind you, baby. Papa will protect you. He's very strong. I need to watch Gregori for a minute."

"Mama," he whined, nearly ready to unleash another cry. I wanted to cry, too.

"I love you, Devraj. I love you, Sanjana. Papa will get you cleaned up and get you some breakfast."

Devraj looked between me and Leela's body and rushed towards his father.

"We won't be long," Damir called to me. He picked them up and rushed down the hallway.

Soon after, a few guards filed into the nursery. Before they could approach me and the crib, I pointed to Leela's body.

"The baby still lives. This woman is responsible. Take her away. I'll be right here. Take care of her first."

Leela groaned as the guards obediently picked her up by the arms and carried her away. Her eyes looked half-dead as she disappeared from view.

I didn't know how long I was alone with Gregori, but it couldn't have been too long. Maybe a few minutes. I heard an uproar going on in the hallways and I hoped someone would eventually come for me. I waited patiently, wrapping whatever linens were nearby around my wounded arms. All I could see was red splattered everywhere except for Gregori and his swaddle.

He whimpered and snorted. The baby needed to be held and comforted. My arms ached like nothing else, and I couldn't help but cry. *You can't even pick up Damir's second son.*

"It's all right, little one," I cried softly. I wasn't sure if I was soothing the baby or myself. I tried to sing Sanjana's favorite lullaby and it helped somewhat. Gregori didn't cry, but he still kicked and tried to swing his head. He was reaching for comfort. He looked at me with Damir's eyes and whimpered.

"It's going to be all right," I heard from behind me.

I turned and let out a cry and a sob. Damir rushed to my side and tried to pick me up. I tried to tell him to take his baby, but an older woman—possibly Einora's mother? I couldn't tell—rushed in and comforted Gregori. She scooped him up and sailed out of the room.

Damir couldn't lift me. He panted and let his shoulders sag. He just held me by my shoulders and pressed my face into his chest. I could feel his voice hum through his chest as he called for medical aid and someone to come help him lift me.

He turned and rocked me slightly, kissing the top of my head.

"It's going to be all right," he repeated. "I won't lose you again."

When I woke up, I didn't think I had fallen asleep. I was pretty sure I was still spending a moment of peace with Damir.

I wanted to move my neck but found that painful and futile. My arms were also not moving, and I feared the worst. After trying to wiggle and wake up, I realized I was tended to by nurses—I was one of a handful of people in a row of sufferers. Pari was right there and patted my leg. She had bandages wrapped around her neck and chest, but she was otherwise sitting upright and watching over me.

"My queen," she breathed. The other handmaidens gathered around me.

"My sisters." My voice didn't sound right. I sounded so weak and small.

"The nurses were able to heal the wounds in your arms. You'll need to be careful and let the salves and stitches help."

"I'm so relieved you're alive." I cracked a broken smile over the surviving maidens. "I thought—"

Dipa frowned. "Leela almost killed us, but we prevailed. But we'll need our own time to recover."

"We just wish we were there with you, *truly*. We protected Einora and Gregori as best as we could before she left us on the ground." Ziya's voice sounded sharp and bitter.

"We will help you find a suitable replacement for Leela. We will soon have happier days." Dipa's voice quivered with emotion. "Or perhaps you do not want us as your handmaidens anymore?"

I shook my head even though it hurt.

"I need you," I whispered earnestly. "Leela dishonored herself and our people. She could never tarnish our bond. Seriously, who will watch the kids so I can nap or listen to Devraj tell the same joke a hundred times?"

The three laughed quietly, trying to respect the other injured people.

"Wherever you go, we will be there to protect you. And carry snacks." Pari smiled. She stood up and placed my hand near my side. "We'll give you some space."

Before I could ask her anything, I heard tiny footfalls.

"Mama!" I heard. Tears stung my eyes. I smiled and slowly moved my neck as Sanjana and Devraj bounded into the room and next to my cot.

"I'm here, yes," I croaked, wanting to reach for Sanjana's curls. "Look at my two brave warriors. I'm so proud of you."

"Be gentle, children. She's still hurting," came a calmer voice. "Softly, Sanjana."

The room hushed as Damir caught up with the kids and approached my cot. Everyone huddled where I could see them, and I was at a loss for words. He's here; where is Einora? Did she not make it? My handmaidens all but glided out of the room and left me with my family.

"You know I hate being seen like this," I moaned, earning an expected chuckle from Damir.

"That's what happens when you show your strength," Damir answered. "Sometimes the weakness comes out, too."

"What happened? What did I miss?" was all I could really ask. I had a bad taste in my mouth, and I imagined it was from doses of medicine.

"Well, Leela is currently detained. We treated her wounds to the point we could question her. She confessed to everything and will be executed for her crimes. Well, you and Einora can add your witness accounts before that happens," Damir said, bouncing Sanjana on his lap. Devraj was holding one of my fingers and tracing something on them absentmindedly.

"Einora's okay? Is Gregori with her?"

Damir put his hand over mine but didn't dare squeeze or apply pressure.

"You saved their lives, Anjali. She came in to treat the cuts a few days ago but preferred to be alone with Gregori and her mother."

A few days ago? I've been here for a while.

"What about Leela's accomplices? Do we know who helped her? Did your investigators arrest them?" I tried not to tense up.

Damir sighed; he probably didn't want to discuss this matter in front of other people. I gave him a warning look and he continued.

"Leela told us she hired a mix of people—some Makaarian and some Ushallavi. According to her, she betrayed them and killed them so they couldn't reveal the truth. We are confirming that before fully putting this behind us."

"Thank you," I whispered.

"Mama tired?" Sanjana probed. I smiled drowsily and stroked her cheek.

"I am. But I'll feel better after I take my medicine and take a nap."

"I'm-*I'm* not tired. We get to play outside today!" Devraj proclaimed excitedly.

"Oh," I tried to sound extra impressed. "That sounds fantastic. You were so good when we had our big sleepover. Remember that?"

"Yeah, that was boring." Devraj scrunched his face. That earned a laugh from his parents.

"Do you want to tell Mama what you heard from the cook this morning?" Damir prompted.

"The cook said—he said you're a hero, Mama!" Devraj cheered. He chopped the air and kicked to mimic me.

"Woah, woah! Careful, Dev," my husband blocked a little foot from bumping my elbow. "But that's correct. Word has spread far and wide of the Ushallavi queen battling a terrorist."

My eyelids fluttered shut in frustration. Of course. Politics. Court gossip. I still tried to brave a smile for my children.

"Leela chose to harm Einora and baby Gregori. I couldn't let them get hurt. Remember that we only fight to protect ourselves and others."

I looked over at my husband.

"How is she *really* doing?" I pressed.

"She's fine and constantly asks about you. She'll likely come visit sometime today. I think she really wants that training. Actually, a lot of the staff is interested."

I sighed deeply.

"They already knew I could fight. People always give me a look—you know the one. And now they want to sample Ushallavi culture?" I murmured.

Damir's face scrunched in pain. This happened anytime he thought things were finally harmonious in his court and I point out how things are hardly so. My passion butted against his patience.

"I wish these people saw me for who I am as their queen. They probably only want to associate with me because I rescued a Makaarian. The friction is so palpable and Leela only opened it for the world to see…"

"Anjali," Damir groaned. "Just—forget them already. You have the cunning and resources you need to be whoever you want to be. You just have to be that woman I love and forget the ignorance of my people."

I shook my head. I know he was trying to comfort someone, but it wasn't me.

"Can I *really* be whoever I want to be? After everything I've been through?"

Damir thought about his answer. "Even as your king and your husband, I don't think I can tell you who you are or who to be. And that's honestly what brought me joy and hope when we got married. But I sense something has changed, and I want to honor that. I love all the versions of you."

"Our children deserve a home where they don't have to ignore the staring, the ignorance, or the comments. People watch how you react—I know what that pressure is like. But instead of working together, I had to deal with most of this on my own. I can only shield them from this behavior for so long—they will soon notice and wonder what they did to deserve the behavior. Could we make things better for our children and the other children in both countries? *Really* put this war behind us?"

We tried to reduce the political or work talk around the children, but I had to speak my mind on this. Damir kissed my forehead gingerly and gripped my hand to assure me. We were born to dream big dreams. The gods—someone—put something in our hearts so we wouldn't give up. As long as my children did not inherit the animosity of their grandparents, we all have a chance at peace.

I silently cried; the pain fresh again. Here I was again thinking about everyone but myself. I remembered that he was still married to someone else. I'm the hero but I'm also the replaced.

Sanjana put her little hands over Damir's—both of them were holding my hand.

"Mama." She cried with me and petted my hair sadly.

Despite the pain and disappointment, something in my gut told me it felt right—for now. It only felt right because I still had choices and I still trusted myself. I had my children, and they have everything.

All I needed to do was decide my own future—knowing deep down that it wouldn't be with Damir.

I'm not going to live here and teach classes for the staff. I'm not going to hold everyone's hands and encourage people to play nice. I've got so much to learn about myself, and I want to see who my children will become.

"Don't cry, Mama," Devraj said, shoving his fingers towards my eyes. I could tell he wanted to wipe away the tears but instead, he accidentally poked my eyes. I had no choice but to laugh. This was going in the journal.

"Don't blind me, Devraj!" I laughed in the middle of my tears. He giggled at his own mistake and pressed his face against mine in embarrassment. I struggled again, realizing my arms felt heavy and dull.

"I will likely need help from Marita—I mean, my handmaidens—to carry the children until I'm strong again." I suddenly remembered that Marita was gone.

She died protecting us. Leela worked with her and still murdered her. I just shook my head and looked away from Damir at the realization.

"We'll figure it out as things unfold," Damir smiled. He then gently took my hand and looked me in the eyes. I looked away briefly. I felt so dull and sad.

"What are you thinking about?"

I rolled my eyes and smirked at his tell-tale sign that he was concerned. "It's a lot to take in. And I feel terrible that I believed Leela's good intentions and let her almost hurt everyone."

Damir shook his head. He wanted to grip my hand, but I was tender.

"Leela's testimony convinced everyone that she acted alone. You still have everyone's trust. And I'm responsible, too. We will soon have a huge meeting with your parents to discuss what happened and how we can move forward but peace is still assured. We should hear from them soon."

I wanted to cry out for my parents. I wanted my mother to come and comfort me.

"When will they come?" I asked.

"Well," he began, placing my hand at my side and pulled the kids closer, "We will travel together to Ushallav to meet them there."

I craned my head as much as I could. Did I hear him properly?

"You miss it, don't you? You miss your home." Damir said, his eyes glassy.

"Yes," I sighed sadly. "This is all for me, isn't it?"

"A major part, yes," Damir said. "Einora also insisted that many of us could use a break from the castle and what happened. I don't know if she'll ever go in that nursery room again."

"I don't blame her."

"We'll talk more about it later. I'll update you with any other news, I promise," Damir said. He stroked my cheek before gathering Sanjana in his arms.

"I love you, Anjali," he whispered. "I always will."

"Me too," was all I could say.

"Give Mama kisses. She needs to sleep," Damir encouraged. He held Sanjana over my head, and she smacked her lips on my forehead. Devraj just put his arm over my lap and rested his head on my stomach.

"I love you both so much," I said in Ushallav before they waved and left me alone.

CHAPTER
THIRTY-NINE

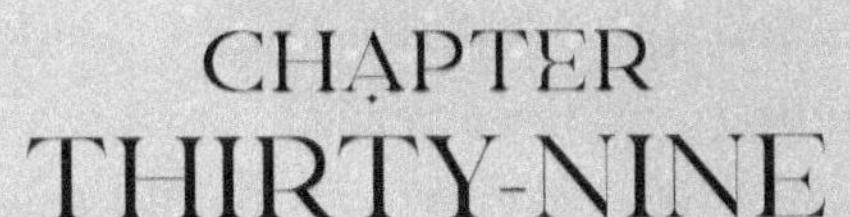

Once the nurses said I was free to move, I wanted to *move*. Einora walked with me around the palace grounds—my handmaidens and palace guards not too far behind. It felt good to stretch my legs and take tentative steps towards normal life—whatever that may be.

I already told her in private of my decision to, well, divorce Damir. It's still so hard to say. But after everything that had happened, I decided that it was time to carve a path for myself. Damir needed to figure out his relationship between his marriage and his crown; I needed someone who trusted me completely.

There must be someone or something that felt better suited for me. Perhaps, there is another way to advocate for lasting peace and yet be the mother and wife I want to be. I ultimately couldn't stand the thought of including Damir's council in any further decisions.

I don't have to be everyone's queen. I don't have to be the one holding everything together. It might sound laughable but it's true. I just want to be a mother, warrior, and partner. I didn't want to waste my time being anything different.

Einora was naturally happy and sad about the idea. It meant that we wouldn't see each other as often. I knew I would miss our time together, but I would feel much happier spending our time raising our children without worrying about our safety or who would stay married to Damir. A normal friendship.

She said something that made me laugh. It garnished the attention of a few ladies making their tour around the gardens a few paces to our left. They looked at us and had no other words but walked at a slightly quicker pace. I quite enjoyed the effect our friendship had on others. We confused the court.

"You were brave that night," I reassured, tipping my head so it touched hers. "Courage flows in your veins."

"After seeing the things you would do for the children, it wasn't a hard choice to make."

Einora was still witty and charming, but I could tell the sparkle in her eye dulled after that day. She still wouldn't show me the parchment-thin lines that laced up and down her arms, legs, and neck.

"Queen Anjali!" I heard from across the way. I turned, and as I did so, my arms pinched a bit. I hissed in pain and Einora quickly let me go. My discomfort soon turned into relief when I saw Claudiu crossing the gardens to greet me. A few guards flinched but they kept to their posts. Claudiu went unimpeded.

"I heard the craziest story about you," Claudiu said. "And knowing you, I believe it."

I smiled widely. I kept my arms stiff—the bandages were still firm and laced up and down my arms.

"Your arms—are they all right?" Claudiu said, noticing the bandages, too.

"They will be someday. Soon."

"This is Claudiu, right?" Einora said. "We met at Anjali's party. It's a pleasure to spend time with you again."

"I heard about your bravery. I feel safer being near you two queens."

"Oh, you jest!" Einora blushed. She gave me a look—a raised eyebrow and an intrigued grin.

"Well, as soon as I was allowed back out, I had to make sure you were all right," Claudiu said. He was still out of breath from trotting up to greet us. "You may have heard—"

"Yes, you were arrested for a brief time," I replied tersely. "I'm so sorry you were stuck there. I've yet to let the council hear the end of it. I should've listened closely to your council. You saw something that I wasn't ready to see. But your foresight still likely saved lives."

The man shook his head like he wouldn't accept a mote of praise. Einora beamed.

"Why would she betray you, my queen?"

"She claims she did what she did for the sake of our country and my happiness. She didn't think Damir or this country were good for me."

I wasn't sure how to translate such complicated and confusing logic to Claudiu. I also didn't know how much I wanted to dwell on Leela's words while others were likely listening in on our conversation.

"She's got some funny ideas about happiness," Queen Einora retorted, folding her arms.

"Chin up, my queen. We can all rest now. I wasn't sure I had enough evidence, and I wasn't sure if you would believe me. I'm just happy to see you on your feet."

Claudiu put a friendly hand on my shoulder before remembering who I was and where we stood. He straightened his tunic before asking,

"So now that Leela is gone, what will you do now?" He locked eyes with me and glanced over at Einora. I could see the question forming in his mind. *Which one of you is leaving?* He wasn't the only curious one.

"Ah, quite the cluster of people we have here," another voice called from several yards away. I wasn't sure how to react to the sound of Benedikt's voice, but I assumed vomiting was not the appropriate first option.

"Good afternoon, Duke Benedikt," Einora said before offering a smooth curtsy. Claudiu and I followed suit and Benedikt accepted the formal gesture.

"Don't allow me to sour this joyous occasion," Benedikt said with a thin smile. "I just came to personally let the two queens know that I'm grateful for their health and safety. I'm also quite relieved that the royal children were safe during such a chaotic time. We would also like to invite you to a small private meeting to discuss important matters."

That was his way of describing "ironing out my future." He gave a polite handshake to Claudiu.

"Master Claudiu, you are the gentleman that saw that Anjali here was kept safe during her pregnancy," Benedikt smiled politely.

"My people and I would help anyone whether they be rich or poor," was all he could muster.

Before I could stop her, Einora took the words right out of my mouth: "Duke Benedikt, are you feeling well?"

I laughed, unable to hold it in. He was acting *way* too nice to me.

"I see that Anjali's bright demeanor is rubbing off on you," Benedikt answered, allowing his smile to widen a centimeter. "But yes, I am well."

My eyes widened as he abruptly bowed again at me specifically.

"I look forward to your swift return to Makaar. We will miss the children especially. Try not to have any detours en route."

He was referring to my plans to visit home—for real this time.

I was touched, shocked—amused? I wished he didn't mention my travel plans at the moment. Leaking my travel plans to the wrong people changed the course of my life, after all. I did my best to form a tight smile.

"I shall do my best, thank you," I murmured. He gave us a bow before turning on his heels and continuing on his way. We all stared at the thin, upright man until we were certain he was out of earshot. I turned to Einora and said,

"You dare call out the duke on his change of heart?" We each giggled and Einora wiped a single tear from her eye.

"Oh, that was worth it. All of your faces. Priceless!" Einora replied happily, pointing at both of us. Claudiu held his hands up in protest.

"I'm confused by everything right now," he said. His face pinched with worry. "You're heading back to Ushallav?"

"Only for half the year," I answered. "Damir, Einora, and I will discuss further relations between our countries in hopes to smooth out any ruffles made with Leela's rebellion. I will stay with the children for a well-deserved holiday."

"I can't wait to truly see Ushallav," Einora said. "I'm ashamed to say that I haven't been outside of Makaar, and I don't know much about your country besides what you've explained."

"I felt that way when I first visited Makaar. You'll be fine," I winked. I turned to Claudiu and asked with a bit of seriousness, "You're probably heading back on your travel routes again, aren't you?"

"Yes. Everyone would love to see you smile once more before we leave town."

"That would be lovely," I smiled.

"Right." Claudiu cleared his throat. "Well, like the dusty man that just passed by, I must also be on my way. I'll find a moment of your time to greet the Gavril people. I don't know when we'll meet again."

"I am looking forward to it," I answered. Claudiu turned as if to leave. I pulled him in for a weak-armed

hug. He understood what I was trying to do and pulled me in for a friendly embrace.

"Thank you for everything," I whispered before we parted.

"Long live the queen," Claudiu said, giving a two-fingered salute from his forehead. "Well, long live *both* of them."

CHAPTER FORTY

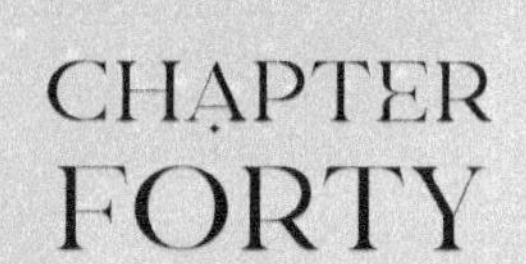

We did our best to explain our new future to the children. They were invited to the big fancy meeting. I don't think they'll understand just how much Einora, Damir, and I love them or how difficult it was to be the one to move on.

The kids seemed happy to know that Damir was still their father, I was still their mother, and Gregori was still their brother. What they don't grasp is that many onlookers might not see this as a boon or a blessing. In time, they'll have to learn when to listen to their guts—even when their subjects disapprove.

I know the children don't care but I was relieved that Damir chose Devraj as his heir—even though I'm no longer the ruling queen.

I actually felt sad during the meeting. As much as I didn't feel extremely welcomed in Makaar, it wasn't all bad all the time. That is sort of how I feel about Damir. I will miss him, but I still felt good about my decision. I had visible and unseen scars to heal.

Once I and Damir signed the papers, I was drained of emotion. Everyone quietly filed out; I asked Pari and Ziya to take the kids while I stayed behind. As if understanding my needs, Damir stayed behind. It was a rare moment for just the two of us. Einora nodded with trust.

I looked dully at him from across the table. He returned my gaze. For a moment, I wanted to say something, but the words left me. I didn't know what I wanted to leave with him. Or maybe I just felt too heavy to move.

"Anjali?" Damir called softly. His voice echoed. "I will always love you. It…means a lot to me that you care about Einora and Gregori. Thank you for letting me love them."

I swallowed. "Thank you for letting me be free. For once, there is no next step except raising the children. I look forward to it. And I know you're ready to stop living in the past, too."

His eyes welled with tears. I wished we lived in another lifetime where love didn't feel this painful. I wished Leela never put herself between me and Damir's marriage. But here we are. For what it's worth—my whole world was in his arms. I wondered what existed beyond our two kingdoms. Soon, I wouldn't have to wonder much longer.

"I just have one request." I rose from my seat. "Don't let Einora believe that your council shares your bed. They are wise in their own way, but you didn't make a marital vow with them—you made those promises to Einora."

Damir looked like he wanted to correct me somehow but just closed his eyes and sighed.

"If I can't be the man you always dreamed of, I won't miss my chance with Einora."

"Good." I smiled through my tears. We had one last embrace before I exited. I looked back and noticed Damir back in his chair. Pondering.

Never in my life did I ever envision myself seeking out Benedikt's attention. But something was tickling my mind that needed to be said.

Duke Benedikt was in his office doing whatever his job entailed. I honestly didn't care. He kindly gestured me to an empty chair and closed the door.

"My lady, this is honestly the first and potentially the last time I expect to see you here. What can I do for you?"

I clenched my fists in my lap, which caused my arms to ache. I strained under the slight pain I caused and shook my head.

"I wanted to talk about some things that have bothered me."

Benedikt honestly didn't deserve to know my thoughts, but I deserved to have the last word.

I took a sigh before continuing.

"I can one day forgive you for the way you looked down on me, belittled me, and essentially proved I didn't belong here. But I will never forgive you if you treat Einora

similarly. She's too good for you. Arguably too good for Damir."

"My queen, you astound me. And believe me, I'm not used to anyone astounding me." He leaned back in his chair. For once, he didn't interrupt me.

"You know what you did to me when I was engaged to Damir. And you know what you've done since. You decided to challenge me instead of respecting me. I have already made myself clear in countless meetings. I won't waste my breath defending myself any longer."

Benedikt sighed in frustration that told me he knew what I was talking about. Nor did he move his lips to construct a denial.

"I have spent nearly my whole life serving as Damir's confidant and protector. He's always been a kind, gentle person. He never let his privilege distract him from his duties. And then you waltzed in. This wild warrior girl who wants to change so much, right away. Even in your supposed death, you changed our way of thinking. It was perhaps foolish of me to think I could do anything about that."

I rolled my eyes. I changed their way of thinking? I nearly snorted. Wasn't that the whole point of my marriage to Damir?

"My so-called 'wildness' does not excuse lying. Look at what you did. I'm going home soon. If I didn't know any better, I'd assume that this was your plan all along."

"That line of thinking is inappropriate and incorrect. I never told you or Damir to separate. I never encouraged Einora to sever your bond."

"Benedikt, there are no Eyes in here. You don't have to kiss anyone's ass. Instead, you ought to take responsibility for the space you take. Damir has always respected you and your insight. If I didn't know better…"

For a moment, I wondered if their trust ran deeper than friendship. I wondered if Benedikt wanted to rule with Damir rather than watch from afar.

Benedikt sighed and looked at something off to his left. He thought. And for a moment, I knew that was all I would really get from him. No confirmation but no rebuttal. I wanted Benedikt to take responsibility for misleading and disrespecting me during the past five years, but he wasn't my problem anymore.

Finally, my shoulders and chest relaxed. I couldn't change much but I felt heard.

I chuckled. "You know, I want to hate you. Especially after you voted to lock me in a room with my children for weeks."

"You barely made it to five days."

"I'd like to see you have to share a chamber pot with a 5-year-old. *And* I managed to still save the day without a babysitter."

Benedikt actually laughed.

"I will miss these little chats, too. I wish you safe travels, Your Highness. Makaar will miss you and remember you."

He rose from his chair—I rose to meet him. I reached out my hand to shake his. He held my hand firm and kissed it before ushering me out of his office.

CHAPTER
FORTY-ONE

The carriage moved along through the brush and onto the road to Ushallav. Summer was coming to an end and the winds were ushering the sun and the warmth away. I looked out of the little window to watch the leaves dance along the forest ground and animals scurry away from our party.

It was easier on my heart to look out the window than to see Einora holding Gregori while leaning against Damir. Mother and son napped—a miracle despite the wind and the bumbling terrain. Sanjana stroked the hairs of her little doll—a mini version of herself. Devraj sat on my lap and looked out the window with me.

I couldn't sleep. We were getting close. I had a feeling that we would soon approach *the spot*.

I sat back in my seat and tried to close my eyes.

"Breathe in until your lungs and belly cannot bear it any longer. Then release it all. Release until you have no more breath to give. Think on your breath until you feel a little better."

Claudiu's words came back to me, and I began my breathing practice. I felt anxious and shaky at first, but I could eventually feel my heart start to calm down.

"Everything will be all right," Damir murmured. I looked up and saw that he was watching me.

"I can feel that we're getting close."

"And that's why Einora and I are right here with you," Damir said. "Along with nearly fifty guards."

I chuckled softly and nodded. They were marching dutifully around the outside of our carriage. I knew my handmaidens were in the carriage in front of us—poised and ready.

When bravery touched me again, I peeked out the window. I felt anxious; when I shifted in my seat, I could feel the three concealed knives rub against me. I wouldn't even get in the carriage without them. As I looked, I suddenly heard a faint, little noise. It sounded like a little plucking sound—a stringed instrument.

I strained my neck to hear. The plucking sound soon smoothed itself into a slow and steady lullaby. I started to hum along. As I peered into the trees, there stood Claudiu with his fiddle under his chin. He didn't look at me but instead closed his eyes to feel his music more deeply.

He was playing my lullaby—the song I sang for San-jana. Her ears perked at the song and looked up at me, wondering what I would do and say.

"It's your friend, Claudiu," I whispered excitedly. "He's watching over us."

"Claw!" she said—her version of Claudiu's name. She clambered to get a better look until I had two children on my lap. Claudiu was soon flanked on both sides by men and women forming a line like a wall of protection. Many of them had slingshots or bows and arrows, but they held them lax and pointed toward the ground.

They remembered the spot. And they were here with me a second time. I smiled and waved. I wasn't sure if they could see me and the children, but I still waved. I blinked away tears.

"Claudiu! It's us!" Devraj cheered. I immediately shushed him before he startled the baby. The baby was fine, but Einora inhaled sharply and woke up. Damir comforted her by patting her head and encouraged her to lean back against his shoulder.

I peered back outside the carriage and Claudiu was still playing his fiddle. He kept playing until I couldn't hear any more. We didn't stop or slow down. We merely passed through.

It almost felt like none of this ever happened. No signs of struggle—the horrors were swept away and gone. Only Damir's second wife and second son served as a reminder of how things would never be the same.

"I wish you didn't have to go through all of that without me," Damir murmured. I looked back at him, and I could see his sad smile.

"The past is finally in the past. We did that together."

Damir smiled as Sanjana scurried up into his lap and curled up next to him.

"I hope you know that I'm happy for you. Einora is a treasure."

"It means a lot to me that you two are friends," Damir said.

"Me too," I answered. "I think Leela would have truly won if Einora remained my enemy."

"I hope you know...letting you go will be the hardest decision of my life," he said, his eyes glossy and shining. "May the Father and Mother never make me choose against you ever again."

My eyes were glossy, too. I hated seeing him so emotional. I felt his pain and I wanted to take both our pain away. But we chose this harder, better path.

"Now you're free," Damir said. "You can go anywhere and be with whoever you want to be with—" He tilted his head out of the carriage and towards the Gavril people we passed by.

"I'm not in love with Claudiu," I interrupted. "Einora won't stop going on about it. She is a hopeless romantic."

He smiled as I grinned and rolled my eyes. I looked out the window to see the sun setting early. The sky was a soft pink, orange and purple.

"We'll be taking a rest in about two or three hours. Once we get to the border, we can stretch our legs and check in to that one inn you like on the border."

"Perfect," I murmured. "I think I can finally sleep peacefully tonight."

"Everything will be all right," Damir said, reaching over to squeeze my hand.

"Just one step at a time." I nodded.

THE END

Reader

Thank you so much for reading *The Throwaway Queen*. This story is near and dear to my heart. But don't worry! We will check in again with Queen Anjali and her family in an upcoming sequel.

If you have any thoughts about this book, please write an honest review on Amazon, Goodreads, Storygraph, Readerly, or wherever else you chat about or buy books.

To learn more about me, future books, or my book editing services, please visit:

WITANDTRAVESTY.COM

Instagram: @whit2ney

Facebook: Wit & Travesty

Twitter: @whit2ney

ACKNOWLEDGMENTS

I'm honestly floored that I'm here—a three-time published author. While I was the one in charge of all the writing and rewrites, many people helped me get to this point.

First, a thousand hugs and kisses go to Travis McGruder—husband and editor extraordinaire. You were there to celebrate with me when I reconstructed my whole work schedule to give myself more author time. You also served as an honest and encouraging soundboard and supported me while I participated in my fair share of retail therapy and real therapy.

I'd like to thank my parents, siblings, friends, and author friends who supported me while I wrote this dang thing. It didn't take a decade to finish but it did involve a few years' worth of NaNoWriMo to get this out. Someone's gotta encourage me to push through my self-inflicted deadlines. Basically, if you've ever told me that you were excited for this book to come out, know that I absolutely needed that form of support. This encouragement helped me believe that this story had some spunk for a very under-represented audience—parents.

At the time of writing, I am not yet a parent. So, I must thank Ari Velez, Adrienne Biehl, and Lorraine Hayashi for finding time in their busy schedules to be early readers and offer feedback about parenting. Other parents told me to include "a lot of picking up and putting down."

Thank you, Karen Dunstan, for consistently serving as the president of my fan club. You provided excellent feedback as a major "who done it" fan but you also talked me through the ups and downs of the drafting process. You're the best hype woman a gal could ask for.

Haley Gibson, you've kept me smiling and optimistic through everything—I know I can reach out and feel so much better about my book and all the other life things that still go on. Thank you for being an empathetic listener, for being on board with what I'm trying to achieve, and for being a grown-ass lady boss example to me.

I must also thank Zarmina Rafi, Neha Patel (Salt & Sage Books), Ramya Hasini Penugula, and Sana Khatri for serving as sensitivity readers for this book. While I created fictitious cultures for this book, much of Ushallav is inspired by Indian/South Asian culture. Thank you so much for providing honest feedback so I could confidently share a diverse cast that speaks to many non-fiction experiences.

If you're in love with the cover and the book layout like I am, please join me in thanking Naimly A. who brought Anjali to life, and Enchanted Ink who transformed my manuscript into a beautiful book. Thank you for helping me create a work of art.

And of course, many thanks to the readers who have supported me from the beginning or very recently. I appreciate that you've bought/borrowed this book and shared it with others. It's your encouragement that inspires me to write and share stories.

WHITNEY MCGRUDER

is an author, editor, cosplayer, and self-proclaimed selfie queen. She can't help but emulate strong female leads. While she's a bit too obsessed with books, she puts her knowledge and experience to good use. McGruder strives to write, edit, spotlight, and indulge in inclusive stories.

Besides spending all her money on her fandoms, Mc-Gruder enjoys cross-stitching, drawing, dancing, D&D, MMA practice, watching funny videos, hosting get-to-gethers, and making her husband laugh.

McGruder believes that book publishing should be about community—not competition. You can find her advice, books, and editing services over at witandtravesty. com. You can also be friends over on Instagram at @whit2ney.